TONI ANDREWS

CRY MERCY

MIRA®

MIRA®

Recycling programs for this product may not exist in your area.

ISBN-13: 978-0-7783-2648-9

CRY MERCY

www.MIRABooks.com

Printed in U.S.A.

It's said that writing a novel is a solitary activity. While it's true that at some point the writer must slink off to his or her cave and commit words to paper, sometimes the greatest joy in the writing process comes when words are shared with other writers.

I dedicate this book to Corrina Lavitt and Olivia Lawrence, my wonderful critique partners. Their humor, honesty and creativity continue to turn what can be work into play. I might have been able to do it without them but, boy oh boy, am I glad I didn't have to!

1

I've always thought I'd die by drowning.

I don't remember exactly when I started to believe this. I didn't grow up near the water, and my early swimming experiences were mostly in public pools. My foster- and group-home years had seldom included even this questionable luxury.

But from the first moment I saw the ocean, I knew I would never again live farther from the shore than the sound of crashing waves could travel. Air without the tang of salt and sea feels wrong to me, as if my lungs cannot truly extract what they need to nourish my bloodstream. And I don't actually *fear* drowning. I just have this odd certainty that it's somehow inevitable that, someday, the Pacific Ocean will claim me.

"Hey, Mercy. Penny for your thoughts." Sukey knelt on the blanket next to me, her red hair made even more brilliant by the reflection of the sun setting over Catalina Island. Salt air had caused her curls to coil into tight springs, and her freckled cheeks were pink from exertion—she'd taken Cupcake for a run along the firmer sand left by the waning tide. The one-hundred-and-thirty-five-pound rottweiler flopped on the sand in front of us, tongue lolling. He panted loudly enough to be heard over the waves.

"Just thinking how close the island looks." Although Catalina Island is only about forty-five nautical miles from the Balboa, California, shore, it's often invisible, hidden by the ubiquitous coastal haze. Then the prevailing winds change, and you wake up one morning able to make out the details of the cliffs and even see the tiny dot on the shore that is Avalon Harbor. Tonight, it looked like an easy swim.

"Wasn't a bonfire the *best* idea?" Sukey nodded over to a few figures standing near a concrete ring that designated where the city of Newport Beach allowed open fires. "I got Grant and Skip to make s'mores. I think there's still a couple left. Want one?"

I shook my head. "No, thanks." I turned to face her. "Sukey, before I forget, I need you to rearrange the office schedule next weekend to give me an extra day off. I…I'm going to Tucson."

Her eyes widened. "Really? You decided to see them?"

Them.

"Yeah. It's not like I'll ever be more ready than I am now." I got to my feet, brushing some of the sand that had crept over the edge of the blanket from my knees. "I don't know whether a weekday or a weekend is better, so I figure if I go on Saturday and Sunday, and they're not home, I can try again on Monday before I head back."

"You haven't called? Was the phone number I found not working?" Sukey had just finished reading a book on private investigation, and she'd used a skip-tracing exercise to locate the unlisted number of Thomas and Roberta Hollings, the couple who had given me up to the tender mercies of the state of New Jersey. I refused to call them my parents, even mentally.

"I haven't tried it."

Sukey nodded. She knew me well enough to understand that my first conversation in over eighteen years with Tom and Bobbie wasn't going to take place over the telephone.

The Hollings weren't my birth parents. They had adopted me when I was only weeks old. They may not have been Ozzie and Harriet, but my life had been stable enough until late adolescence, when strange things had started to happen around me.

Very strange things.

Sukey got to her feet and shivered just as the last sliver of the sun dropped behind the island's central peaks. When the sun goes down in Southern California in November, it doesn't take long for the air temperature to drop. "I'm going to take Cupcake back to my apartment, then go to the bar. Do you want to get a beer?"

"Maybe in a while." I picked up the end of the leash from where it rested in the sand. "You go ahead. I'll take this stuff home first. Cupcake can stay at my house tonight."

"Are you sure?" On paper, Cupcake belonged to

Sukey, but she didn't really have room for the pony-sized dog in her apartment, and he stayed with me at least half the time. My cat, Fred, was even starting to get used to the idea. On most days, anyway.

"You two packing it in?" Grant walked over from the fire, wiping his hands on a handkerchief that he stuffed back into his pocket. I wondered briefly if any men under the age of sixty still carried handkerchiefs. Could you still even buy them?

"I'm going to Jimbo's," Sukey told him unnecessarily. She probably hadn't missed a Friday night at the local dive bar in three years. Well, other than the time a few months before, when she'd been recuperating from a heroin overdose in my guest room. She hadn't taken the drug on purpose—it had been given to her by an ex-boyfriend. Rocko wasn't likely to show up in Balboa again any time soon. I'd seen to that.

"I'll probably head over there myself." Grant reached over to scratch Cupcake's big head. "I'm hoping Tino will show up. He was supposed to come by my house today, but I didn't hear from him, and his cell phone is off."

The friendship that had sprung up between Grant, a retired millionaire, and Tino, a Chicano street gang leader, still seemed strange to me.

"Did you try Hilda's?" asked Sukey. It was no secret that the wealthy widow sometimes shared her bed with the much younger Tino. For some reason, this felt less odd to me than the Grant/Tino connection. Maybe because Hilda, perpetually in search of her lost youth, had always enjoyed the company of younger men.

"She's not answering the phone, either," said Grant.

Sukey shrugged. "Maybe they took off somewhere together."

Grant shook his head. "He would have told me. He's taking the real estate exam in less than a week, and we still have a lot of material to cover."

"Tino's getting his real estate license?" I don't know why I was surprised. Tino was about as predictable as an earthquake. And as hard to ignore. Just because he had a violent criminal record and had never finished high school, it didn't mean he wouldn't be running the planet next month.

"Yeah, it's the next step in his plan to go legit." Grant made a mock bow toward Sukey. "May I escort you to the bar? I like being seen in the company of sexy young redheads. Good for my image."

Sukey giggled and took the proffered arm. "Are you kidding? With all the women after you, I'll be the one getting a boost to *my* reputation." As they ambled off in the direction of the parking lot next to the Balboa Pier, Sukey turned to glance back over her shoulder.

See you later, then? She didn't have to shout over the sound of the surf. I could hear her voice as loud and clear as if she had spoken in my ear.

Maybe. I didn't really like telepathic conversations, even with my best friend. They made me feel too exposed. I watched Sukey nod ever so slightly and turn her attention to Grant.

I released Cupcake long enough to fold up the blanket, then retrieved the leash and waded through the softer sand, crossed the boardwalk and stepped onto the patio of my apartment. I lived in one of the upstairs/downstairs duplexes that lined the wide pedestrian-and-bike path running along most of the Balboa peninsula's length. I knew my landlords were undercharging me for the rent, but I wasn't going to argue. The monthly lease payments for my hypnotherapy office were bad enough, even though business had been good in the months since I'd started my practice. Between Sukey's natural ability to make friends with everyone she met and my special…talents, my success should have been guaranteed.

Except that I wasn't sure I knew what I was doing anymore.

It was less chilly on the sheltered patio than on the beach, and I sat down in the decaying lounge chair rather than enter the dark apartment. Cupcake nosed his way through the sliding glass doors, shouldering a panel aside easily, and I heard the slurping sounds that told me I would have to refill Fred's water dish. I wasn't ready to go inside. The boardwalk was postseason quiet, the hushed sounds of passing joggers, cyclists and dog-walkers a pleasant contrast to the cacophony of drunken summer revelers.

I loved this time of year in Southern California, especially when the days stayed warm, as they had this season. I knew many local business owners lamented the departure of tourists and day-trippers, but the rest of us were always happy to get our town back. I looked over to where the last remnants of the fire still winked and saw that all but a couple of the silhouetted figures were gone. Probably to Jimbo's, like Sukey and Grant.

I'd once heard one of the uninitiated question Sukey about spending so much time in a bar. She had replied, "I don't really think of Jimbo's as a *bar*. For locals, it's more like our living room annex." I'd laughed at the time, but it was a pretty good description.

Balboa is technically part of Newport Beach, but a narrow stretch of water separates the peninsula from the higher-priced environs of Corona del Mar and, farther south, the new and glittering Newport Coast. While there are plenty of multimillion-dollar homes, especially near the surfing Mecca known as the Wedge, there are still seedy apartment buildings and crumbling seasonal cottages interspersed with the mansions.

In an alley that I sometimes used as a shortcut on the way to the post office, I pass two often-open garages that sit no more than twelve feet apart. One holds a brand-new Rolls-Royce Phantom and the other a mostly paintless 1962 Ford Falcon. I've seen the respective owners sharing a pitcher of beer at Jimbo's bar, dressed in similar outfits: khaki pants, deck shoes and T-shirts advertising something to do with salt-water fishing or marine fuel. Hilda, always on the lookout for her next conquest, says the only way you can tell the rich men from the welfare recipients in Balboa is by their watches. And, according to her, the fakes are getting harder to spot. I'm not sure if she's talking about the watches or the men.

A random gust of wind swirled dust devils in the thin

coating of sand on the boardwalk, and I decided I would join Sukey and Grant after all. It didn't have anything to do with reluctance to enter the empty apartment. Well, empty except for Cupcake and Fred. I was used to solitude and, in fact, preferred it. That's what I'd gotten used to believing, anyway. But, loner or not, I often found myself on the path that took me down a side street and through the alley that led to Jimbo's tiny parking lot, then through the back door into the dark, stale-beer-scented room with its single pool table.

I didn't bring Cupcake, although he would have sat placidly by the back door, accepting greetings from the regulars. Probably. His previous owner had trained him to attack, hold and, presumably, kill based on voice commands. The problem was, we didn't know all of the commands. As I entered the room, returning nods from a few familiar faces, I looked around for Sukey. I wanted to remind her that she was supposed to be re-searching canine obedience schools, to see if it was possible to *un*-train a dog. I spotted her at the opposite end of the bar, where she was perched on a stool, talking animatedly with a local real estate agent.

When she saw me, she stopped speaking abruptly and made what looked like a shushing gesture before smiling hugely—and falsely—at me. Spots of color appeared on her cheeks.

I don't consider myself paranoid, but it was obvious that she had been talking about me, and also that she didn't want me to know it. As I pushed my way through the patrons along the bar, realization hit me.

"Hi, Mercy," she said brightly. "Maureen was just telling me about her daughter's wedding."

I nodded in Maureen's direction but didn't break eye contact with Sukey. I knew exactly what she had been talking about, and it wasn't a wedding.

"Sukey, I want you to look me in the eye and tell me you haven't planned a surprise birthday party. I mean it. Don't make me—" I didn't finish the sentence, but I didn't have to. Sukey knew I could compel her to tell me the truth, even against her will. But she also knew that to do so would be against my principles. Which I almost never violated.

"Why are you so dead set against having a party, anyway? You were at *my* thirtieth. And you had a blast."

"*You* had a blast. I spent the night hiding in the corner."

This wasn't strictly true, either. While large drunken celebrations weren't my style, it had been fun to watch Sukey's unadulterated delight at the decorations, the presents and the stripper.

God, I hoped she hadn't hired a stripper for my birthday.

"I repeat—there will be no birthday party. *No fucking birthday party.* Am I making myself clear? Is any of this getting through?"

"Sure, Mercy." Sukey smiled even more brilliantly and took a sip of her margarita, leaving salt on her lip. "Whatever you say."

I looked at her critically. She was the picture of innocence—red curls, cherub's mouth, gold-dust freckles. I didn't trust her as far as I could throw her.

No, that wasn't true. I trusted Sukey more than anyone in the world. Including myself. I just didn't think she believed me when I said that I had no intention of celebrating my thirtieth birthday.

She sighed, a tad theatrically. "Okay, you win. No party. But can we at least go out to dinner or something? I'll take you to the Villa Nova."

"You can't afford the Villa Nova." I knew what she earned, because I signed the paychecks.

"I can once a year," she replied. "And if we invite Hilda, you know she'll insist on paying."

"If we invite Hilda, we'll have to invite Tino and Grant, and we're right back to having a party."

"Fine," she said, in a tone that told me it wasn't. She got down from her bar stool and stalked ostentatiously to the chalkboard next to the pool table, then wrote her name on the list. She didn't ask me if I wanted to play.

I'd only been there about three minutes, and I was already regretting my decision to come. Would it be rude if I stepped out the back door and walked the three blocks home? Probably. But none of my friends would really be surprised if I left without saying goodbye.

My friends. It was still an unfamiliar phrase. I'd spent my entire life keeping people at a distance. For their own safety, or at least that was what I'd always told myself. Then, one by one, they'd started to breach my carefully constructed walls. First Sukey, who'd done so with all the subtlety of a battering ram. She'd punched a big hole in my defenses, and before I knew it, people were pouring in like a flood.

Grant, who I realized was sitting at the bar right next to me, spoke up. "Why no party? You don't seem like the type to be worried about the big three-oh."

"I'm not. I don't especially like parties, and, anyway, I may be out of town."

"Where you going?"

"Tucson," I told him.

His Andy Rooney eyebrows rose. "You're going to go see your parents?"

"They're not my parents. They adopted me, then changed their minds." *Eleven years later.*

Grant nodded. He knew the basics of the story, and why I'd been considering the trip. "You think they'll know anything about your birth parents?"

I shrugged. "I don't think so. I'm hoping they at least still have the adoption records. I'm not even sure what state it took place in. We always moved around a lot. But I think it was probably the same state where the adoption was dissolved."

"Makes sense. Where was that?"

"New Jersey."

Grant squirmed on his stool, a behavior not typical for him. He took a sip of his drink, then put it down with an audible click.

"Mercy, I'm just going to say this once, and then I won't bug you about it anymore."

I was surprised. Grant never got personal with me. "What is it?"

"These people in Arizona. They treated you like

crap." His face held a searching expression, and I wondered what he was getting at. I waited.

"Adoption can be tough. I can almost understand someone giving up after a few months. But from what little you've told me, it was years for these people."

I nodded but still didn't speak.

"That's really shitty. After all that time…they were your parents, Mercy. And parents don't walk away from their kid."

They do if that kid turns out not to be human.

"What's your point, Grant?" It came out sharper than I intended, but Grant was a pretty tough old bird. He paused, but it wasn't because I'd hurt his feelings. He took a sip of his drink, and I could tell he was formulating his words carefully. Not to spare my feelings, but to make sure he was being accurate. Once an engineer, always an engineer.

"You say you're going to see them to find out if they have your adoption records. Hell, Mercy, you could do that over the phone."

He was right. I'd considered and abandoned the idea. It felt like something I should do in person.

"Again, Grant, what's your point?" This time I didn't sound as bitchy. Or at least I didn't think so.

He gave me a direct look. "There's something you do to people, Mercy. I don't know what it is, but I've always thought you could be…dangerous if you wanted to be. I wonder if you've thought about why you have to see these people face-to-face. Whether you're going to do anything other than ask about your adoption records."

Holy shit. I'd had no idea Grant had any inkling of my special abilities. Hell, I'd used them on him the first time we'd met, and he'd seemed oblivious. If he'd noticed, who else had? A sour taste filled my mouth, and I became aware that I was gripping the edge of the bar to the point of white knuckles. I relaxed my hand and turned to Grant, who was watching me carefully. He'd noticed my near-panic attack, there was no doubt about it.

Suddenly he chuckled. "You get uptight when someone picks up on your secrets, don't you, kid? Relax. You know I never miss anything. I'd bet a million bucks no one else has a clue. Other than Sukey, of course."

I did relax—a bit. Grant's powers of observation were one of the first things I'd noticed about him. Also, I realized what he was doing with his last comment.

"You're fishing, Grant. Pretending to know something already, so I'll open up." I smiled so he'd know I wasn't angry with him, but I still felt tense.

He guffawed. "You? Open up? That's a good one, kid." Then, still smiling, he said, "I'll tell you what I know. I know that there's something I *don't* know."

I shrugged as if to say "maybe." Grant was too smart to buy complete denial.

He went on.

"Think about what I said, Mercy. You might be tempted to do something to these assholes, and they probably deserve it. But you'd regret it."

Oh yeah. Regret I understand.

"Grant, Mercy, thank God you're here. Don't either of you ever answer your cell phone?" Hilda plopped down on the bar stool that Sukey had abandoned. She looked as flustered as I'd ever seen her, although her shining hair—blond this week, I noticed—was in perfect order, as was her makeup. Right down to the Tammy Faye Bakker false eyelashes. But both her voice and her tiny bejeweled hands shook.

"What's the matter, Hilda?" Grant and I said simultaneously.

"Tino's in *jail*." She blinked up at us, and I realized she'd been crying. Not something tough-as-nails Hilda did very often.

Jimbo, who had been passing by us on the other side of the bar as she spoke, stopped.

"Who's in jail? Casanova?" He filled a glass with ice and added club soda to it before sliding it in front of Hilda. "Don't get so bent out of shape, Hildie. I'm sure it ain't the first time."

"Well, it's the first time since *I've* known him," she snapped, picking up the club soda and drinking as if it were something stronger that would steady her nerves. Hilda, sensitive about her romantic relationship with a man young enough to be her son, usually objected to Jimbo's nickname for Tino. She must really be upset if she was letting it slide.

"What did he get picked up for?" asked practical Grant. "And can we get him out? Have they set bail?" Between them, Grant and Hilda had enough money to settle the national debt.

"He said the charge was making a public disturbance," she said. "But he was apparently already on probation, and of course he had an unregistered firearm—"

"Only one?" I interjected, earning a dark look.

She continued.

"—so he's not sure what they'll do. He'll go in front of a judge in the morning."

Grant shook his head. "Poor Tino. I guess his meeting didn't go too well."

"What meeting?" Sukey had returned to the bar in the middle of the sentence. "Did something happen to Tino?"

As Grant and Hilda got Sukey caught up, I considered Tino's predicament. According to Grant, running a successful street gang required all the skills of a CEO of a good-sized corporation. Apparently negotiating one's retirement from the position was equally complicated. Tino was hoping for what the business world called a "seamless transfer of leadership," with all the same goals: no interruption in productivity or cash flow, no loss of prestige in the surrounding community, and a nice severance package. Oh, yeah, and without the retiring executive officer having his head blown off.

"Whatever it is, we'll take care of it, Hilda." Grant patted her on the back, and she tilted her perfectly coiffed head up to look at him. I thought for perhaps the hundredth time how much they looked like a couple. "All we have to do is get him a good lawyer. With the court system so jammed, they'll be more than happy to deal. It's not like Tino cares about having a criminal record."

"Will it prevent him from getting his real estate license?" asked Sukey.

Hilda snorted. "Honey, if having a felony record prevented you from getting a real estate license in this state, half of my neighbors wouldn't be able to make their car payments." Hilda lived in a Lido Island bayfront mansion, and her neighborhood association list included many of the most influential businesspeople in Orange County.

"Oh, by the way, Hilda—" Sukey's tone was unnatural, designed to get my attention "—we're not having the birthday party. Mercy won't let us."

Not this again.

"Excuse me." I got up to go to the bathroom, my earlier annoyance with the place returning. I used the toilet, even though I didn't have to, then spent a long time washing my hands. I scanned the floor-to-ceiling graffiti for something new. I was about to give up when I made out some unfamiliar script low on the back of the door.

If you really learn from your mistakes, then I'm getting a fantastic education.

"You and me both," I muttered to myself. I looked at my reflection and winced—I'd forgotten to put on makeup, as usual, and there were circles under my eyes, making them look even darker. The long dark hair framing my face hung straight, but at least it was clean.

I'd come in to relax and have a good time. I hadn't even had a beer yet. Being annoyed with Sukey was pointless. She loved parties and she loved me, and I appreciated her desire to want to do something nice. Just not enough to smile through an evening of bad jokes and worse gag gifts. But I could thank her for trying and enjoy her company tonight. Girding myself with a deep breath, I exited the restroom and ran directly into a brick wall.

Actually, it was too yielding for a wall. And it was covered in plaid flannel.

"Why 'oncha watch where yer goin'?" I winced from beer fumes as the obstacle, which was resolving itself into the shape of a very drunk frat boy, enveloped me. He looked at me blearily, hostile in the truculent manner of the mean drunk.

"Get the fuck *away* from me," I said, trying to push past him. I looked up in time to see his face go from slack to very, very alert. His eyes widened, and a beer mug fell from one hand and a pool cue from the other as he backed away. He scurried around the pool table and out the door, throwing me one last look as he passed through the neon red glow from the exit sign.

Shit, shit, shit. I'd done it again.

I looked around to see a couple of puzzled faces— probably frat boy's friends—and then realized I had better go after him and try to undo whatever damage I'd done. In a blink, I was out the door and in Jimbo's well-lit parking lot, but my moment of hesitation must have lasted longer than I thought, because there was no sign of him. Could he have driven away? He was in no condition.

One of the guy's friends—I didn't recognize him,

which would never have happened on a weeknight—stepped out of the door behind me. "What did you do to Doug?"

I tensed, but there was no hostility in the tone, just curiosity.

Well, actually, I thought, I used my superhuman powers to compel a man I've never met to get as far away from me as possible, as quickly as possible.

I ignored the question, since my answer wouldn't make any sense to the kid anyway. "Your friend wasn't driving, was he?" I asked.

The guy shook his head. "No. Do you know where he was going?" This kid didn't look as buzzed as his buddy, but he might be high enough that I could avoid giving him an explanation. Maybe.

"No idea," I said, torn between checking down the alleys and side streets, and retreating into the bar.

"*Man*, that was freaky. You told Doug to get away from you, and he just…obeyed."

Fuck. This kid was sharper than he looked.

Of course, one way to get him to stop asking questions was to do to him on purpose what I'd done to his friend by accident. Which was, of course, against those principles I mentioned earlier.

Oh, hell, who was I kidding? I knew what I was going to do.

I glanced around to make sure we were alone, then looked into the kid's face. "You will remember the last few minutes as I am about to describe them. Your friend Doug told you he…he felt like taking a walk to…to sober up. He left of his own free will and didn't seem to be in a hurry." As I spoke, I put that special emphasis behind my words to ensure that he would obey them. Or, as I usually thought of it, I *pressed* him. "Do you understand?"

"Sure," he said, then smiled. "Hey, can I buy you a shot or something?" His eyes slid down to my breasts, and I was so relieved I almost smiled. This I could handle without resorting to the supernatural.

"Look, kid, I have *jeans* older than you. Thanks, but no thanks."

"Whatever you say," he replied, grinning. "But you still look good in those jeans, however old they are." He gestured toward the door and followed me amiably inside, but broke off and returned to the pool table once past the entrance. I made my way to where Sukey had returned to the bar and sank onto an empty stool.

She eyed me critically. "What happened?"

"A guy about the size of Kansas got in my face. I pressed him and he took off."

"That's okay then," she said. "It *is* okay, isn't it?"

"Not really, no." I looked for my beer, then remembered I hadn't ordered one yet. I signaled the bartender.

"Why not?" Sukey was insistent.

"Well…" I glanced around to make sure Grant and Hilda weren't paying any attention. They weren't. "I didn't press him on purpose. It just popped out."

"Sounds like it might have happened just in time."

"Maybe," I admitted. "But I wasn't expecting it. And I didn't think about it first. I told the guy to get away from me, and he ran out the door. I went after him, to try to slow him down, but I was too late. He was gone."

Sukey grinned—inappropriately, I thought. "You mean—"

"Yeah. I have a feeling he's going to keep running. At his size, he'll probably have a coronary two miles down Balboa Boulevard."

"Oh my God!" She started to laugh. "That's too funny."

"No, it's not, Sukey. He could run out into traffic or something."

Instead of making her stop, this statement had the opposite effect. She gave a shriek and put her hand over her mouth. "Was it that big guy dressed like a wanna-be lumberjack? In the flannel shirt with the sleeves cut off?"

When I nodded, she laughed even harder. "I can just see it," she managed to pant. "He must look like a crazed buffalo in…in—*red flannel!*"

"Sukey…" I tried to hold on to my annoyance, but it was hard when she was braying like a donkey. I could feel my facial muscles forming into something suspiciously like a grin. "You're missing the point. I lost control of the press." *Again*, I added silently.

This sobered her somewhat, and the mirth in her face gave way to concern. Well, sort of gave way. She took my hand, which I remembered not to pull away.

"I know. And I know how much you hate that."

"Plus, I had to press his buddy. He was getting suspicious."

"And you hate that even more." She nodded, understanding. "But it's like we talked about before. When you use the press, it's a good thing." At my dark look, she amended, "*Usually* a good thing. It's losing control of it that's the problem. Once we find your birth family, they'll be able to help you learn to control it, and then everything will be okay."

"*If* I find my birth family, *and* if they're willing to help me, *and* if they even know any more about controlling this thing than I do. Or if they even know what the hell it is to begin with."

Sukey's brow creased, and she released my hand. Guilt gnawed at me. She always tried to put a positive spin on things, and, as often as not, I shot her down. But she didn't know everything that had been going on with me in the past couple of weeks.

"And it's getting worse, Sukey. I've...I've lost control during a session."

This got her eyebrows up. "With one of your hypnotherapy clients?"

I nodded. "I caught it in time, and it was the last appointment of the day and I was tired, but still... And the telepathy has been getting worse, too."

"You mean stronger," she countered.

"Huh?"

"You said 'worse.' You meant stronger. Telepathy isn't a bad thing."

I wasn't sure I agreed. I didn't mind the link Sukey and I shared; it was easy to control, and I could turn it off when I didn't want to be disturbed. Plus, it came in handy at work, since I hadn't bothered to install an intercom.

"What's going on over here?" asked Grant. "You were laughing so hard I thought I was going to have to get you a paper bag to breathe into."

"Hypnotherapy humor," said Sukey. "You had to be there."

"I guess I probably wouldn't get it, since Mercy's never hypnotized me."

I winced. Little did he know.

Sukey's face changed, and I saw she was looking over my shoulder. She seemed pleased to see someone, but there was something else in her expression, too.

Puzzled, I turned, and Sukey's ambivalence made sense.

Sam Falls had just walked in the door.

Could my night get any more fucking perfect?

2

I'd never before tried to be friends with an ex-boyfriend. First, I'd never had friends before. Second, I'd never had a boyfriend before Sam, not a real one. Therefore, it was to be expected that I wasn't any more comfortable with this relationship than I was with any of my others.

It didn't help that he looked totally at ease. "Hi, Mercy. I see the gang's all here. Except—" He scanned the room.

"Tino's in jail," supplied Sukey. "Something about a probation violation." She got up and hugged Sam unselfconsciously. "Where've you been, stranger? We never see you anymore."

"I've been sailing a bit. And Dad's caregiver quit. I'm using a service now, but until they find someone he's comfortable with, I need to be over there a lot." Sam's father had Alzheimer's disease, and had good days and bad days.

"Hi, Sam," I said more quietly. However awkward the situation had seemed a moment before, it was worse now. Sukey had gotten off her bar stool to hug my exboyfriend. What was I supposed to do, shake his hand?

"Here, take my seat. I want to get the rest of the scoop on Tino from Hilda." She gave me a look that was far from subtle. She'd been almost more upset than I was over the breakup, and she made no secret of the fact that she thought I should be doing something to "get him back." Which sounded a little too Scarlett O'Hara for me.

Sam hesitated. "Do you mind?" He nodded at the seat.

"Go ahead." His arm brushed against me, and I smelled his familiar scent. Salt water, soap, with a hint of marine fuel. He owned the local gas dock and boat rental, and usually slept on his own sailboat a few nights a week.

A rush of longing caught me unaware. I wanted to touch his face, to tousle his sun-streaked hair, to lean into him and let him put his arms around me. I wanted to put my nose against the back of his neck and inhale.

Not that I had ever done any such thing in public, even when we were together. I kept my eyes averted in case the raw hunger showed.

"What's this about Tino?" he asked, as Jimbo brought him a beer without the necessity of ordering.

"I'm just hearing about it. Apparently he went over to try to talk to the gang about leaving. Negotiations must have gotten out of hand, and he's in jail. Hilda and Grant plan to pay his bail in the morning."

Sam nodded, unperturbed. Jimbo had probably been right that Tino was no stranger to the inside of a cell. I waited for Sam to take up the conversation—he had chosen to sit next to me, after all—but he didn't. I was usually comfortable with silence, but nothing about tonight was making me relaxed.

"What were you saying about your father?" I asked, sticking to a topic that felt safe.

"Ramón, the man who was staying at the house on weekends, quit. Which is too bad, because he was really good with Dad." Sam took a pull on the beer. "I'm having a hard time finding someone to replace him."

Another twinge of guilt pricked me. I'd never met Sam's father, despite the fact he'd invited me to meet him about one week into our acquaintance. I'd made plans to go to his house several times, but with one thing and another, I'd always ended up cancelling. It had never been intentional. I hadn't been avoiding the meeting. Had I?

"I've heard rumors," Sam went on quietly, "about a birthday party. It's supposed to be a surprise party, but I didn't think you'd like that much."

"I wouldn't." I was annoyed. I knew Sukey disapproved of the breakup, but I hadn't thought she would go so far as to invite Sam to a party she was throwing for me. "But don't worry, I already guessed what the Balboa Scooby-Doo gang was up to and headed them off."

As soon as the words were out of my mouth, I winced inwardly. Sam was the one who had coined the group's nickname when he, Hilda, Grant and Tino had teamed up to find out where Sukey was being held by a man who had kidnapped her in order to get to me. I guess he wasn't really a member of the gang anymore.

If he was bothered, he didn't show it. "I don't imagine Sukey's taking that too well," he said.

"She'll get over it," I replied.

He nodded, but it was an acknowledgement rather than an agreement. "She will, but you should be aware how excited she was about it. You know she lives to do things for the people she cares about."

This time my wince wasn't entirely internal. I *did* know. And I felt bad about disappointing her, really I did. But not bad enough to sit through a birthday party in my honor, watching a bunch of people get drunk who I liked better sober.

"She'll forgive me," I said, trying to keep my voice light.

"She always does."

Meaning what? I wondered, and tilted my head to look at him sideways, but his expression didn't hold any clues. Meaning I did a lot of things that required forgiveness, maybe? Probably.

"Well, I just agreed to something else she's been trying to get me to do," I said sourly.

"What?"

I surprised myself by telling him.

"I'm going to see my parents. My adoptive parents."

He put down his beer and turned to face me fully. "The ones who gave you up?"

"They're the only ones I've got." I knew I sounded sarcastic, but he was used to that. He didn't say anything right away, but he viewed me with slightly narrowed eyes, as if he were trying to figure something out about me. Which he probably was.

"Does this have anything to do," he started, speaking

slowly, "with what's been holding you back from telling me your secret?"

There it was. The topic I had most hoped to avoid. Sam knew I had a secret, I'd admitted as much. I'd also told him I had my reasons for keeping it, at least until I "took care of something." Which meant "determine whether I'm human." Because if I weren't, it was one hell of a relationship issue.

"It's something I need to do, that's all." Ambiguous enough?

"It's like she's an alien or something. Talk about not speaking the same language—I'm not even sure she's human anymore."

Georgette Clausen had opted for the couch rather than the recliner. The therapy room in the minute office that housed my practice included several seating options, and clients seemed to choose them about equally. Georgette was still in the introductory phase of her first hypnotherapy session—the part where I made damned sure her stated objectives for the visit were no more than they seemed to be.

In light of the fact that my clients followed my posthypnotic suggestions to the letter, starting each session with a little Q & A, in which I used a mild press to induce total honesty, had turned out to be a good thing. For example, one woman who claimed to need help staying on a diet turned out to have an eating disorder that needed medical help. Another who purported to always be making careless mistakes was actually a battered wife. And my personal favorite, a man who had come in for help remaining faithful to his wife, had turned out to be a bigamist. When I'd asked him which wife he was referring to, he'd told me, "Both of them." I'd resisted the urge to instruct him to perform a few anatomically impossible acts and sent him on his way.

Georgette, however, was another matter. She claimed to be having a difficult time controlling her temper when dealing with her not-quite-teenaged daughter.

"What happens," I began, wanting to make sure I understood the extent of the problem, "when you lose your temper?" I'd dealt with a horrific child abuse case a month earlier and had no desire to wade back into those waters.

"I yell at her. I completely forget all the calm, rational things I planned to say and just start screaming." Even though I had started by instructing Georgette to get into a relaxed state similar to real hypnosis, her tone and expression showed distress. "I've even called her names. I—I used profanity to my own twelve-year-old daughter."

Based on some of the behavior she'd described— lying, stealing, skipping school—I might have used a little profanity myself. On the other hand, I'd done all those things as a kid, too. But in my case it had been *after* I became a ward of the state. After Bobbie and Thomas Hollings gave up on me.

"I don't want to give up on her," said Georgette.

The hairs on my arms rose. Could she have heard me telepathically? I'd been hearing thoughts more regularly, especially from people I'd pressed in the past. I sincerely hoped it wasn't working both ways.

Sukey had a theory she referred to as "the Drano Phenomenon." She claimed using the press opened up a channel by sort of unclogging psychic pipes. I was not at all comfortable with the idea.

I forced myself back to the matter at hand.

"How would you handle the situation between yourself and your daughter if your temper was not a factor?" I asked. I was probably going to do as she had asked—I couldn't imagine any scenario where controlling one's temper would be a bad thing—but I was curious. Roberta Hollings had certainly done her share of screaming and name-calling with me. She'd called me "freak" long before the schoolyard kids took up the chant.

Georgette looked eager. "All the things the books say to do. Ask questions. Listen. Let her know it's the behavior I have a problem with, not Tina herself. And," she sighed, "stay firm on the boundaries. Stop giving in just because I can't stand arguing anymore and want to end the tantrum."

I nodded. "It sounds like you know what to do."

Georgette slumped against the back of the sofa. "After she ran away last year, the school suggested a counselor. We went to see her, and the advice was really good. If I could just not get so *mad*…" She smiled. "My husband's talked about sending her to a boarding school for difficult kids. But it doesn't feel right. I mean, she's my daughter. It doesn't matter what she's done—I'm in it for the long haul. I'm not quitting just because things are a little rough right now. You know what I mean?"

Not really, no.

"Okay, Georgette, I want you to relax a little more and breathe deeply, okay?"

"Okay."

"We're going to talk about what it feels like when you're about to lose your temper with Tina, and what you're going to do next time you start to have that feeling."

By the time we were finished, I was satisfied that we'd accomplished what Georgette had asked for.

"I feel much better," she said, after writing a check at Sukey's instruction. "Now if I could just get Tina to come in and visit you. Maybe you could hypnotize her and get her to tell you what she's so mad about all the time."

"I'd be happy to, but she's got to be in total agreement." Parents were always trying to get me to fix their kids. I'd decided I wasn't going to fix anyone who didn't want to be fixed, *especially* not a kid.

"That's it for the day," said Sukey. after the door closed behind Georgette. "How'd that last one go?"

I laughed. "She wanted help controlling her temper, and I'm pretty sure my instructions will work."

Sukey's freckled brow wrinkled. "So why is that funny?"

I sighed. "It isn't, really. It's just that sometimes I wish I could press myself. I can't always control my *own* temper, and here I am telling someone else how to do it.

"Your temper's not so bad," she said. When I raised my eyebrows, she added, "Well, it wouldn't be if bad things didn't happen when you get mad."

"Bad things" was a serious understatement.

"Anyway, I rearranged your schedule like you asked, and you now have a three-and-a-half-day weekend, starting Friday at noon."

I didn't really like taking extra days off—I'd already done so too many times in the few months since I'd opened my office. "I should probably fly," I speculated aloud. "But what if they aren't home, and I have to turn right around and catch a flight back?"

"You're not thinking about changing your mind again, are you?"

I shook my head. "No, if I wait until the time is right, I'll never do it. I've been avoiding this for eighteen years."

"Why?" asked Sukey. "I mean, I get that it's going to be pretty weird. But if it was me, I would have gone to see them a long time ago, even if it was only to tell them to kiss my ass."

I laughed. "I can't imagine you telling *anyone* to kiss your ass, Sukey."

"You'd be surprised. But seriously, I think I know why you haven't gone to see them."

"Why's that?" I was genuinely curious, because I wasn't sure I knew myself.

"It's back to that losing-your-temper thing. You're afraid you'll get mad and do something to them."

Pretty much what Grant had said, and close. But there was something I feared even more.

I was afraid I would press them and tell them to love me. And that was a line I would never cross. *Never.*

"Anyway, can you take Cupcake home with you again? I have a…a thing tonight."

At the sound of his name, the large black blob sleeping in the corner of the office awakened, yawned and coalesced into Cupcake. I held out my fingers, and he got to his feet, lumbering over to have his big head scratched.

"Sure. What thing?"

Sukey's freckled cheeks flushed prettily. "I'm taking a class at Orange Coast College two nights a week. It started Tuesday."

"That's great, Sukey." Sukey hadn't gone to college—in my opinion, mostly because her otherwise loving family had subtly convinced her that she didn't really have the brains for higher education. Which anyone else who'd known her for more than a few weeks knew was bullshit. "What kind of class?"

The flush on her cheeks deepened. "Introduction to Private Investigation," she said, her eyes on her handbag.

I resisted the urge to grin. Sukey had gotten interested in the subject specifically to help me get some answers about my past. I guess she'd decided to take it a bit further. I was glad she was taking the initiative, but the idea raised my hackles a bit, too.

"So," I asked, "do you think you want to become a P.I.?" I had a flash of Sukey creeping through a dark alley in a trench coat, stalking some shadowy, dangerous-looking figure. I grimaced before I had a chance to stop myself.

"I just might," she said; then, misinterpreting my expression, she hurried on. "Part-time. I'd still run the office."

"You've already got everything so automated, I know it's not really full-time for you," I said. I didn't want her to think I wasn't being supportive, and I knew P.I. work was really only dangerous in the movies. Wasn't it mostly done on computers these days?

"The instructor is a friend of Bob's."

"Bob Gerson?" Sukey sometimes dated the Newport Beach Police detective.

She nodded.

"He opened his own agency after he retired from the police department. We've only had the one class, so it's too soon to know if I'll be any good at it...."

I managed not to snort. She was obviously fishing for a compliment, and I happily took the hook. "You're good at everything you decide to do, Sukey. If you really want to be a P.I., then you'll be a great one." It may have been flattery, but I meant it.

She beamed. "If I do, I promise you'll be my number-one case."

"Thanks a lot," I said dryly. I didn't especially like to think of myself as a "case," but my sarcasm was lost on her.

"My pleasure. Besides, I may need to get you to press someone for me sometime, as part of an investigation." My expression must have darkened, because she added, "Only if it was really, really an emergency, of course."

Like the song says, I figured we'd burn that bridge when we got there.

3

I've never thought of myself as claustrophobic. I've even found small enclosed spaces oddly comforting at times, like the bottom bunk in the bedroom at a crowded foster home, where I used to hang a blanket curtain and read with a flashlight. I've been stuck in an elevator and experienced only annoyance that I would be late for an appointment. And I've made love in the tiny cabin of Sam's sailboat.

So if small spaces don't bother me, why does the wide-open sky of the desert at midday make me feel like the air is being sucked from my lungs?

Before that weekend, I'd driven across the Mojave a few times, or at least the small section between Riverside and Palm Springs. I guess there had always been too much traffic for me to notice the sky.

I'd always heard people say the sky was bigger in the desert, but I hadn't thought too much about it until the trip to Tucson. The sky was whatever size it was. I understood that the absence of trees and buildings made a difference, but I'd been out on the ocean, miles from shore, without a thing to interrupt the horizon in any direction. It was beautiful, but it was the vastness of the Pacific that had actually comforted me.

This desert was different than the Mojave. The air was crystal clear all the way to the limits of my perception, without any of the haze that was almost always present, even if not visible to the naked eye, along the California coast and, as often as not, a few miles inland. The open vista should have made me feel free, unobstructed. But I felt like all that open space was pressing down on me, feebly protected in my little Honda.

When the sun had finally set, I'd never been so glad of darkness.

The dawn sky wasn't as bad, at least not from the little patio outside the back door of my motel room. I sipped my coffee, scalding hot from the tiny pot and undiluted by cream—I draw the line at standard hotel issue foil packets of generic powdered nondairy creamer—but better than I would have hoped. I'd slept better than I'd expected, too, as nervous as I was. I'd been afraid that I wouldn't be able to stop mentally rehearsing what I was going to say to Bobbie and Thomas.

"Tom. Bobbie." I tried the names out loud. I hadn't spoken them many times before, although I'd used them in my imagination, at least when I was still a kid. Before the hearing when I'd been remanded into the custody of the state, I'd called them Mom and Dad.

Sukey had done some online research and found out that in New Jersey, the state court had the right to dissolve any adoption at any time, although it was usually only done in extreme circumstances. I remembered the hearing, although most of it took place without my presence in the courtroom. I didn't know what the Hollingses had stated as a reason for requesting that I be turned over to state custody. But I knew why the judge had ruled to honor their wishes.

It was because I'd pressed him.

A lot of the details were vague, but I remembered sitting in a chair facing the judge. It had been a small courtroom, nothing like what I'd expected from television. There was no witness stand, no bailiff with a Bible. We were sworn in as a group, sitting in a row: Bobbie and Thomas, a woman from child services who functioned as my representative, the psychologist who had examined me, and an attorney hired by my parents. Because they'd still been my parents when we walked into that room, although I'd been staying in a group home while the hearing was pending.

I'd almost looked forward to the hearing, because by that time I'd begun to understand the strange ability that had started to grow about the time my body began to show the signs of impending womanhood. I'd become mostly silent, because I'd learned my words could be weapons, even when I didn't intend for them to be. I had started to recognize the difference that putting that special emphasis behind my commands made. I imagined myself pushing down, pressing the intent into the listener's brain like shapes into soft clay. Then they had to do what I said.

There were still some problems. It often happened

unintentionally, that much was immediately obvious. It had only taken a couple of schoolyard arguments, with disastrous results to my opponents, to teach me that lesson. I was too young to completely grasp the more subtle issues of euphemism and hyperbole. Those I pressed didn't necessarily do what I wanted—they did what they *perceived* that I wanted. A "flying leap" meant different things to different people. In one case, a boy my age had taken it to mean he should throw himself in front of a moving vehicle.

He was lucky to have lived.

I might not have understood the intricacies of my gift or, as I was more likely to think of it, my curse, but I knew I had to be very careful in the courtroom. I'd likely have only one chance to speak my piece, and I had to get it right. So I'd practiced what I was going to say.

I was going to tell the judge to send me home. Make him tell the Hollingses I was their responsibility and legally enjoin them to take care of me until I grew up. To treat me well.

And to love me. I was going to press them to love me.

But as I sat there in the small paneled room, looking at the profiles of two people who were afraid to turn their heads and look directly at me, I had an epiphany.

Even I couldn't make someone love me.

Oh, I could make them *think* they loved me. Like they had tried to do since bringing me home. But even at eleven years, I knew the feelings they had for me weren't the same as those I had observed in the parents of my schoolmates. That effortless warmth and complete ease with one another was a mystery to me.

I might even be doing them a favor. They could stop being guilty about what they didn't—couldn't—feel.

But I would always know.

So, instead of launching into my carefully rehearsed script, I'd looked the judge right in the eye and pressed deliberately and unsubtly.

"Do what Mr. and Mrs. Hollings have requested," I said, the formal names strange and bitter on my tongue. "Make it so they aren't my parents anymore."

And he had. Invoking the authority of the state of New Jersey, he'd legally made me an orphan.

Of course, I'd regretted the words as soon as they'd left my eleven-year-old mouth, but the moment I'd felt the desolation and despair begin to well in me like a warm fountain, I'd clamped my teeth shut and fought both the nausea and the desperate words that threatened to erupt. I knew anything I said at that moment would be uncontrolled and dangerous. Even though, at eleven, I couldn't have articulated it, I was afraid of the devastation my words could leave in their wake.

So I remained silent, turning my head so I couldn't see the people I'd thought of as my parents for as long as I could remember walk out the door. And I'd stayed that way for weeks.

And now I was about to see them again. Despite three packets of sugar, the coffee I was drinking was suddenly as bitter as a child's worst memory. And the sun had risen high enough above the outline of Catalina Mountain that the strange, suffocating feeling of the desert was returning.

Funny that the mountain that hid the sunrise here had the same name as the island behind which the setting sun fell back at home. With a last glance at the brilliant disk of light, I fled into the hotel room and closed the sliding glass door.

I felt better in the car, navigating the curving streets with the help of an online map. Tom and Bobbie Hollings lived in one of Tucson's northern suburbs. The houses in Tortolita, while not exactly alike, seemed to have all been built in the same style by the same contractor. The Mexican hacienda-style cottages with their red tile roofs were familiar—Orange County was full of them—but no one here had a lawn. Rock gardens and cacti seemed to be the order of the day. With summer temperatures routinely reaching 115 degrees Fahrenheit, it was probably a sensible choice.

It was Saturday, so I had a pretty good chance of catching them both at home. I'd timed my arrival for 8:15 a.m., which I figured was late enough for them to be out of bed and early enough not to have left for shopping or whatever they did on Saturdays. I tried to remember how we'd spent Saturday mornings when I was a kid and only came up with a vague memory of watching cartoons and eating cereal. Had Tom worked on weekends? Had Bobbie slept late? I had no idea.

I turned onto Saguaro Court, which turned out to be a cul-de-sac. Damn. No way to cruise by casually a few times. I couldn't find street numbers on the houses and felt panic rise sourly in my throat—was I going to have to knock on doors until one of them answered?—then realized the street numbers were painted on the curb beside each driveway. I slowed, reading each number until I came to the beginning of the spoon-shaped turn-around that marked the end of the road. There it was.

The house looked much like the others on the street—a little more run-down, perhaps, but nothing for the neighbors to complain about. The front yard was sand, with concrete stepping stones set in a curving path. A few sun-burnt weeds grew up between the stones, but not so many that it looked uninhabited. The end of the driveway was flanked by reflectors set on rusty iron fili-greed stakes, the kind that have spikes on the end that stick into the ground. One was slightly askew, as if someone had dinged it with a fender. I pulled past the empty driveway and parked on the street.

I turned off the engine but hesitated before getting out. The garage door was closed, so I couldn't tell if anyone was home. The windows had some kind of re-flective film that turned them to mirrors. Probably the only way to survive in this heat without keeping the shades drawn twenty-four-hours a day. In the few seconds since the air-conditioning had stopped blowing out its frigid air, I was already getting a preview of what any vehicle left out in the sun probably felt like after only minutes. I turned the key back to the on position and rolled down my windows, hoping to alle-viate the sauna effect. The neighborhood looked benign enough, and there wasn't anything in the car to steal except the duffel bag in the trunk, which held only a change of clothes and my toothbrush. I had a couple of sun shades under the passenger seat, although I seldom used them, but I pulled them out now. Otherwise I would probably burn my fingers on the steering wheel when I got back to the car.

If, of course, I ever actually got out of it. Fighting a sudden urge to yank the sun shades off the windshield, start the engine and drive away in a cloud of burning rubber, I took the keys out of the ignition, pocketed them and opened the door.

The front door was recessed, with one side against the garage, which jutted out a good six feet from the front of the house. An iron security grille had been installed and was locked, making it impossible to reach the door to knock. They probably went in and out through the garage, because it didn't look like the front door was opened very often—withered leaves were blown up against it, adding to the general bleakness. There was a button mounted next to the grille's hinges, and I pressed it. If it rang a bell or buzzer within, I couldn't hear it.

I held very still, trying to discern whether there were sounds of movement behind the impenetrable windows. I couldn't even tell if there were curtains, never mind if someone was pushing them aside. I hesitated, unsure of whether to try the button a second time. Again the urge to flee rose hard and strong in my chest. But I'd driven eight hours to be here, and spent at least eight hundred hours talking myself into it.

I pressed the button again, holding it down for long seconds. Wake up, dammit, I ordered them. I considered trying to project my thoughts but didn't know how to do it without a familiar target. The Hollingses had ceased to be familiar a long time ago.

I considered what I would do if no one answered the door. The obvious move would be to return to the hotel or find someplace to walk around, then come back later. They had to come home sometime. But I was afraid that if I got back into the car, I'd drive straight to the I-10 and head west, even with the prospect of a second day under the crushing desert sky to daunt me. As for walking around, it was already at least 85 degrees out, and this was November. What must August be like?

I jumped when the door opened with a sucking noise, as if coming unstuck. It opened maybe ten inches.

"Yes?" The woman's voice didn't strike a chord of familiarity, and I could barely make out the figure in the gloom, standing in dazzling sunlight as I was. "What is it?"

"Bobbie, is that you?" I asked.

"Who are you? What do you want?" It wasn't an answer, but the tone was sharper, and I felt a frisson of recognition. It was Bobbie, all right.

"It's Mercy," I said flatly. "Come on, Bobbie, let me in." I resisted the urge to press her, but I would if I had to.

There was an intake of breath, followed by a beat of silence. I expected the door to slam shut, but instead it opened a couple of inches farther. "M-Mercy?"

"Yes, Bobbie, Mercy. Are you going to let me in?"

This time the hesitation lasted a little longer. I took a deep breath, ready to command her to open the door, and then she said, "Just a minute. I have to get the key."

The door closed, and in the silence that followed I could hear my heart beating. Stay calm, I told myself. Remember to breathe. After a few seconds the door reopened and Bobbie Hollings stepped into the sunlight.

She was smaller than I remembered, no more than five feet, four inches. Her hair was dishwater blond and tied back with a rubber band, and I could see a good half-inch of salt-and-pepper roots as she leaned forward to insert the key in the lock on the iron gate. How old would she be now—fifty-eight? Fifty-nine?

The grille opened on squeaking hinges, and she stepped aside to let me pass. She didn't look at me.

I walked through the entryway and into the dim interior beyond. There was a short hallway leading into a small living room. I saw a matching chintz sofa and love seat in a faded rose print, and I only hesitated for a minute before sitting down on the latter. The magazines and full ashtray on the table at the opposite end of the sofa identified her regular seat. I'd forgotten that she smoked. When I was a kid, she'd always gone outside with her cigarettes.

She sat down and looked at me. "I always knew you'd come. I didn't think it would take this long, though." Her face was calm, but there was a barely discernible tremor in her voice.

I reminded myself that however unsettling this was

for me, it had to be worse for her. The thought didn't displease me.

"Where's Tom?" I asked. Other than her niche on the sofa, the rest of the room didn't look like it got much use.

She shrugged. "I'm not sure. We've been divorced for almost twelve years."

Twelve years? "But his name's on the title," I said and, when her eyebrows rose, added, "That's how I found you. Property search."

She nodded. "We were going to sell it. You know, split the assets. But he had a good job, didn't need the equity. The mortgage payments were low, so I took it over."

Divorced. I hadn't considered this possibility, even though it seemed obvious now. I had planned what I wanted to say to the two of them. Would Tom's absence make a difference?

"You really don't know where he is?" I asked.

"Florida somewhere. Tampa, maybe. I get a Christmas card from his sister. Do you remember your Aunt Kate?" I shook my head, and she went on. "She generally jots a note, says if he's moved or anything."

She picked up a tooled leather cigarette case from the table and shook a cigarette out of it, put it between her lips and lit it. As she inhaled, I studied the deep vertical lines that transected her mouth. She wore no makeup, but I remembered her always applying bright red lipstick before leaving the house. I shuddered at what that would look like now.

"So," she said, "why did you come? To tell me to kiss

your ass after all these years?" Her tone was hard, bitter. This wasn't how I remembered her. I thought about what Sukey had said last week in the office and realized that, no, I had no such intention.

"I didn't come to try to make you feel bad," I said. This was part of my rehearsed speech. "I do have a few questions about the dissolution of the adoption, but that's only because my memory of the whole thing isn't very clear."

She took that in, regarding me through a haze of blue smoke. The place was air-conditioned to a degree of frigidity that must have cost her a mint, but the air didn't seem to move much in this room. As my eyes adjusted to the gloom, I could see that the ceiling was stained yellow from nicotine.

"Ask your questions, then," she said. Her tone had lost its harshness, but there was still something unsettling in her expression. Fear, I suddenly realized. She was afraid of me.

Well, of course she was. I felt like an idiot for not anticipating this. Now the realization took all the nervous tension out of me like a suddenly deflating tire.

Reservations gone, I pressed her. "Relax, Bobbie. You don't need to be afraid of me. You can be assured I don't mean you harm."

She almost slumped in relief. I wondered if she knew I'd pressed her not to be afraid, the way Madame Minéshti, a gypsy woman who had met others like me, had immediately recognized the feeling of being compelled. I didn't think so.

I went on, no longer pressing. "I've become interested in trying to find my birth parents. I'm wondering if you have any paperwork or anything relating to the adoption."

She thought for a moment, unconsciously lighting a new cigarette from the old. "Maybe," she said finally. "There's a box in the garage with old records. We—Tom and I—lugged it around for a few moves. I haven't looked in it in years. I'll go get it." She started to rise, but I stilled her with a gesture.

"You can get it before I leave," I said. "I have a few more questions first."

She settled back. "Shoot."

I almost smiled. I had a sudden vivid picture of a younger Bobbie, the skin on her face unravaged by time and cigarettes, wearing shorts and serving potato salad at a backyard barbecue. A man—a neighbor, maybe—had said, "Can I ask you a question, Bobbie?" She'd turned her head, grinning flirtatiously, and said, "Shoot." I'd thought it clever and cool at the time.

"When you adopted me, did you know where I'd come from? You told me I'd been abandoned. Was that true?"

She winced. "Yes, it was true. I probably could have phrased it better, though."

"You may have—I don't really remember. But go on, what do you know?"

"You were in some kind of orphanage run by a church, but they only took care of the babies. They didn't have anything to do with the actual adoption, which was all done through the state."

"What church? Where was it?"

She shrugged. "I'm not sure—it's probably in the paperwork. We didn't go to the orphanage to see you. Once we made it to the top of the list, they showed us pictures, and then a woman who worked for child services—a social worker, I guess she was—brought you to meet us."

"How old was I?"

"Seven or eight weeks old," she said. Her face took on a wistful expression. "You were *so* beautiful. Everyone says that about babies, I know, but you were like some exotic doll. A full head of dark hair, and eyes already brown—not a hint of blue, like with a lot of newborns. You didn't even seem like a real baby. I couldn't believe you *were* real, that they would actually let me keep anything so perfect."

"She brought me to your house?" My throat was beginning to feel oddly constricted.

"It was an apartment, back then. But yes, they brought you there. You were supposed to stay for a couple of nights before everything was decided. But the moment I saw you, I already knew I was going to keep you."

"And did you—" I searched for words. This wasn't going the way I'd planned. I'd grown used to the idea that they'd never loved me. But that wasn't what I was hearing here, not exactly. "Did you still feel the same way…later?"

She got very still. "I wanted to," she said, her voice small. "I held you and kissed you and played with you. You never cried, were never a problem. You slept through the night."

I was hearing an unspoken "but" here. I didn't have to wait long.

"I kept expecting this…this *zing* to happen, and all at once I'd really feel like you were mine. My little girl. That we loved each other. I read books. They said sometimes a mother can take a while to bond with her baby, even her natural child."

"And did it? Ever happen, I mean?" I already knew the answer, but I needed to hear her say it.

She looked at me, then away. "No," she said, finally. "I mean, I was fond of you, and I didn't want anything bad to happen to you. But you'd watch me with those big brown eyes like *you* were expecting something, too. Something that never came. I knew some of the other mothers from day care, and their babies would look at them and just burst into a smile. Like they were connected. I wanted that *so bad*…."

Her voice broke, and I looked away, giving her time to collect herself.

"What about Tom?" I asked eventually. "Did he notice anything wrong, do you think?"

She snorted. "Tom? He thought you were some kind of toy to take out and play with, and then put away when he was done. He liked showing you off—you were so pretty and, once you got a little older, so smart. But Tom was old-school. Children were the mother's business. The father was responsible for their financial well-being, making sure they had a roof over their head and a college fund, but, beyond that, he didn't pay much attention to what was going on."

I nodded. My memories of Bobbie were more vivid than those of Tom, who seemed like a background figure. I waited for her to say more, but she'd apparently come to a stopping point.

"Tell me about having the adoption dissolved," I said. "When did you start thinking about that?"

She lit another cigarette. "When you started to… get odd."

"Odd?" I, of course, knew what had been different about me, but only from my own point of view. I wanted to know what it had been like for her.

"I think other people noticed before I did, because I started hearing whispers. From other mothers. They didn't want their kids to play with you. They were afraid."

"The mothers?" I hadn't known this, but it made sense. Certainly the kids had started to be afraid.

"One of your teachers called me, asked for a meeting. But she couldn't really explain what was wrong, and I got pretty nasty with her."

"You did?" I was surprised.

Bobbie smiled for the first time since I'd arrived. "I may have had my doubts, but that didn't mean anyone else was allowed to mess with you. You were my kid, even if it didn't always feel like it."

For a moment there, I almost liked her.

"But then something happened that scared the bejesus out of me," she said. "And I started wondering if what everyone was saying was true."

I had no memory of a specific incident. "What was it?"

"You were in your room, probably reading. You always had your nose in a book. Anyway, you were supposed to be taking out the trash—we'd given you some chores—and I'd already reminded you once. So I called in, and told you to get your butt out there and take out the damned trash." She looked at me funny then.

I nodded, and she went on.

"You didn't come out, though. You yelled back at me and said 'Wait a minute, I'm busy.' I was really pissed, because you'd been ignoring me, and I was going to march in to your room and yank the book out of your hands. But I couldn't."

"Couldn't?" I echoed. I was pretty sure I knew what she meant.

"Nope. I was rooted to the floor. I couldn't make my feet move. Not until—" She took a deep drag on her cigarette. "Not until a full minute was up. I was terrified. I ran to the bathroom, shut the door behind me and locked it."

"I don't remember." I was surprised to hear that my voice was almost a whisper.

"No reason for you to," she said. "It was just a normal eleven-year-old thing for you, not wanting to interrupt your book to do your chores. Afterward, once I calmed down some, I realized you didn't even know you'd done it. Whatever *it* was."

"Why didn't you ask me about it? I mean, if it was the first time."

She shook her head vigorously. "But it wasn't. It

was just the first time I noticed." She stood up, moving toward the kitchen. "You want some water? A Coke or something?"

"Water's fine." I heard her open cabinets, heard the sound of a refrigerator door opening and closing, of ice cubes clinking and tap water pouring. She returned with two tumblers and handed me one before resuming her seat. She lit another cigarette before continuing. I wondered if she always smoked this much.

"That night I lay in bed awake and thought about it. Tom was out of town somewhere. I started remembering things. Watching you play with other children. Not that you had a lot of friends, but there were a couple of girls who came around sometimes. Beth or Betsy or something. Her father was a car salesman. And the girl from the next block—I forget her name."

"Candy," I said. I remembered her because she'd been one of the first to stop coming around, once my abilities started to show up with regularity. "Her name was Candy."

Bobbie nodded. "That's right, Candy. I remember now. You were out in the backyard, sitting at the picnic table, playing some kind of card game. I remember she was a real brat. She was trying to cheat or something, and you got pissed off and told her to 'straighten up.' She dropped her cards and stood up, straight as a board. She looked like some kind of cartoon character or something."

"She might have been joking around," I protested, but I knew better, even if I didn't really remember.

Bobbie grinned mirthlessly. "She might have been, but she wasn't. I could see her eyes. She was terrified.

She didn't have a choice. Then you told her to sit back down and 'play right,' and she did it, meek as a lamb. I could tell she wanted to bolt home, but she stayed there and played until you said you had to go in to dinner and she could leave. You had to tell her to go a couple of times—she wouldn't get up and leave until you got a little mad."

I nodded. This had probably happened well before I figured out that I had some control, albeit shaky, over my ability. I wouldn't have been able to press someone at will yet—might not have even known why Candy wouldn't leave, or why she'd finally done so once I got annoyed.

"And I remembered other stuff—the doctor who wouldn't give you a shot after you told him not to. He had to bring in a nurse, which seemed strange at the time. Tom backing right down when you didn't want to help him wash the car."

"Did Tom know? Later, I mean."

"Not until I told him. And even then he didn't believe me. At least not until after that boy almost died. You remember."

The flying-leap kid. Yeah, I remembered.

"So that's when you decided you wanted to try to have the adoption dissolved," I said, then stopped. Bobbie was shaking her head again.

"No, I never wanted that."

I was confused. "But you said—"

"I said I *thought* about having the adoption dissolved. I never *wanted* to do it."

"Then why," I asked, completely perplexed, "did you go through with it?"

She put out her cigarette and gave me an odd look. "You really don't remember, do you?"

I shook my head, mystified. "Remember *what?*"

She sighed. "Look, Mercy, you were no piece of cake. I didn't know how to love you. Hell, I was even a little afraid of you. But I had no intention of giving you up. Neither did your father—Tom, I mean."

"Then why did you?" I repeated. My pulse was hammering in my eardrums, as if my body was trying to drown out what I was about to hear.

"Because you told us to, Mercy. You told us to get out of your life and leave you alone. You *made* us do it."

4

"You just need to walk away. You're starting a new life, Tino—concentrate on that." Grant's tone was reasonable, as, I thought, were his words. But Tino wasn't buying it.

"You still singing that same song? I'm tired of it." Tino gave Grant what was probably his most menacing look. It had no doubt silenced a few hundred gangsters, druggies and the odd bystander over the years. It had no effect whatsoever on Grant.

Mitzi's Diner was one of the few Balboa businesses not dependent on seasonal tourist traffic. Between the wobbly counter seats and the battered vinyl of the booths, it had a maximum capacity of about forty. The only difference in the summer was the duration of the wait for a table on a weekend morning. There was no waiting list—Mitzi seated patrons according to the honor system, hollering to waiting customers whenever a table became available.

It was usually possible to snag a single counter seat but, this morning, none had been available. I'd been about to join the small crowd waiting on the sidewalk when Tino and Grant, already seated at a window booth, called me over to join them.

Other than the scowl, Tino didn't look any the worse for wear for someone who had recently survived a gang brawl and a night in the Santa Ana city lockup, although over a week had passed, so any bruises had had time to heal. In fact, Tino looked good enough that the waitress taking an order at a nearby table was paying more attention to him than to her customers. The middle-aged man and his wife, obviously rare off-season tourists, looked annoyed.

Grant sighed and shifted his gaze from Tino, seated on my left, to me. "Talk to this kid, Mercy," he appealed. "You're good at persuading people."

"I've got no dog in this fight, Grant." I resisted the urge to squirm, although it was probably the ancient bench seat's busted springs making me uncomfortable rather than the argument. I was actually kind of enjoying listening to Grant and Tino bicker. They were both good negotiators, despite a vast difference in style.

"I like that—'No dog in this fight.'" Tino grinned, a gold tooth flashing. "Mercy don't fuck around in other people's business. Unlike this old rich white dude I know."

Grant snorted. "Mercy gets *paid* to fuck around in other people's business. It's how she makes her living."

"That's different," said Tino. "Those people, those *clients*—" Tino pronounced the word carefully "—they, like, volunteer. They ask her to hypnotize them. It ain't like she decides to get all up in their shit."

My inward wince was somewhat tempered by amusement. Tino's speech patterns were becoming more incongruous by the day. The *barrio* expressions and subtle Chicano rhythm were still there, but Tino's language had become speckled with business terms learned from Grant, his real estate textbooks and the social circle he had entered through his liaison with Hilda.

"Mercy is your friend," said Grant, ostensibly talking to Tino but looking pointedly at me. "I'm sure she wouldn't be happy if you got shot because you're too damned stubborn to cut your losses and let someone else take over the *Hombres*."

I didn't know much about the *Hombres Locos*, although I'd seen the stylized "HL" graffiti on a few of the overpasses, street signs and buildings in Santa Ana. The *Hombres* called their leader "Mad Tino," a sobriquet of which he was proud. Although I hadn't weighed in with my opinion, I agreed with Grant that Tino's attempts to negotiate his retirement as the group's leader had small chance of success.

More for my own edification than Grant's, I decided to play devil's advocate.

"Just what are you trying to accomplish in these meetings?" I asked.

Before Tino could answer, we were interrupted by Mitzi herself.

"You want some more coffee, honey?"

I nodded, and she poured, filling my cup, as well as Tino's and Grant's. She usually didn't venture out from behind the counter, so she must be short-staffed today. I hadn't noticed, probably because the Tino and Grant floor show was keeping me occupied. She moved on, squeezing her fireplug frame between the corner of the booth and the back of a customer's chair. It was the same man who had already looked unhappy with his distracted waitress, and he now aimed a scowl at Mitzi's back. My eye followed her to where a sign was posted on the wall above her short gray hair, next to the fifties-era wall clock.

This isn't Burger King. You get it my way or you don't get the sonovabitch.

Mitzi had no doubt hand-lettered the sign herself. She meant it, too. I'd once heard her call a tourist, who had tried to argue with her about the proper way to make corned beef hash, a "cocksucker."

Mitzi's interruption had given Tino time to formulate his answer.

"There's three things. One—" Tino pointed an index finger to illustrate "—I gotta make sure the different stuff that brings in the money...the whatchoo call them, Grant?"

"Revenue streams."

"Yeah, the revenue streams. They keep operating, you know what I'm saying? I set them up. There's people outside the *Hombres* ain't never dealt with no one but me. I step out, that money may stop coming in."

"What do you care?" asked Grant. "You're not going to be making your money from chop shops or drug sales anymore."

"Hold it down, man!" Tino glanced around nervously, but no one seemed to be taking any notice. Nevertheless, he lowered his tone, and Grant had to lean forward to listen. "It ain't just me, Grant. And it ain't just the *Hombres*. The garages do legit stuff, too. People got families to feed, you know?"

"And they'll go on doing business, legit and otherwise, whether you're there or not. Supply and demand, like we talked about. Just because someone else is in charge of supply, the demand doesn't change. Things may shake up a little, but they'll settle down quickly enough."

"But I wouldn't get my cut."

This time Grant's snort morphed into a guffaw. "Since when does someone leave a gang and still get a piece of the action? If you're not taking any of the risk, why should they give you any of the profits?"

"Like I said, I set them up. Those—those revenue streams wouldn't even exist if it wasn't for me. And it ain't like I'm expecting my full cut. Just a little *sabor*— a little taste. We get this new thing started, I'm gonna have expenses, man."

"That's what the venture capital is for," argued Grant.

Venture capital? I knew Grant had been helping Tino sketch out a business plan of some sort, but I didn't know any of the details. I could have used some venture capital when I started my business, but I hadn't known Grant back then. And even if I had, there was no way I would have explained to any potential investors exactly why my hypnotherapy practice had a better-than-average chance of turning a tidy profit.

Or would if I stopped taking time off to deal with personal issues.

Not that I was planning on any more time off in the near future. My adoption records, which had indeed been gathering dust in Bobbie's garage, were still in the sealed manila envelope she'd given me. Sukey had asked me about them at least six times in six days, and I'd put her off each time.

You told us to get out of your life and leave you alone. You made us do it.

For me, those words had been the emotional seismic equivalent of the big one—the inevitable earthquake that would eventually reduce Balboa and most of the surrounding towns to a shaken sandbox, if you listened to the experts. We were in what was known as a "liquefaction zone." That meant all the soil and, presumably, the roads, buildings and people on top of it, would become suspended in liquid, in this case the Pacific Ocean.

I'd believed that my horrific, loveless teenaged years had been at least partially Tom and Bobbie's fault, a belief that was built on bedrock. It turns out I'd constructed a whole set of memories on my own little liquefaction zone.

You made us do it. As soon as she'd said it, the memory had sprung whole in my mind, vivid with color and sound and scent. It could have happened last week, not eighteen years ago.

How could I not have remembered? And, more to the point, what else had I forgotten?

"Mercy, are you listening to me?"

My eyes refocused on Tino, who was holding up a second finger, indicating he had made point number two. I remembered that he was answering my question—that Grant had already heard this, so he was enumerating for my benefit.

"Sorry, Tino. I was remembering something I need to talk to Sukey about. What was the second thing again?"

He rolled his eyes but continued. "Number two is the leaders. I got *vatos*, they been down for me, you know what I'm saying?"

"I think so. When you say 'down for you,' you mean loyal, right?"

"More than that," he said. "When someone's down, that means they do anything they got to. Whatever it takes—they don't argue, don't worry about getting hurt. They're just down."

I nodded. "And you want to make sure these guys—what? Move up the corporate ladder?"

He grinned, appreciating the metaphor without being offended by the sarcasm. "Exactly. I don't want some outsider coming in, taking everything over. One of them, what do you call it, Grant?"

"Hostile takeovers." Grant sipped his coffee, hiding a smile. I could tell that, even though he disapproved in principle of the context, he was enjoying Tino's understanding of big-business parallels. "Sometimes followed by breakup and asset liquidation."

"Yeah, that thing. And that's the third thing. 'Cause

when you break up the business and liquidate the assets, people get fired." This time his pirate's grin looked mean. "And in Ghost Town, when you fire someone, you shoot him."

This last statement confused me. "Ghost Town? I thought the *Hombres* operated in Santa Ana? Isn't Ghost Town part of Long Beach?" Long Beach was just above the Los Angeles county line, a real city, and about as different from Newport Beach as a beach town could be.

Grant explained. "The *Hombres Locos* are loosely affiliated with the *Hermandad*. They operate out of Ghost Town and give other gangs a de facto permit to operate in certain territories. The *Hombres* are mostly autonomous, but they kick up a percentage of their profits, and any major decision, like the promotion of a new gang leader, isn't going to work out in the long run without the *Hermandad's* blessing."

"Wow. So the *Hombres* have a parent corporation."

"You could look at it that way," Grant said, and Tino nodded his agreement.

"I tried to work it out with the *Hombres* first," he added. "Get one of my *vatos* in, then go to the *Hermandad* with the thing already done. One of those—" He gestured, searching for the term.

"Fait accompli," Grant and I supplied in unison. Tino went on.

"But the *Tiburónes*, these guys outta L.A., they already come down, start sniffin' around. You know *Tiburón* means shark, right?" I knew the word, and inclined my head. "Yeah, well, they smell blood in the water. I'm not around so much, they figure they can step in. My boys don't like it, but they ain't used to handling stuff without checking with me. Which was okay when I was, you know, right there all the time. But now…"

He shrugged, trailing off. Even before formulating his plan to go legit, Tino had been spending more and more time in Hilda's marble-floored palace and on Grant's sleek sailboat, and less time in *bodegas* and smelly Santa Ana barrooms, like the one where we'd met. He wore more linen than leather these days, and his prison tattoos were usually concealed by long sleeves.

The only thing that hadn't changed was his baby-blue Impala convertible. It was parked in the nearby municipal lot—I'd noticed its highly polished tint from a block away. Its gaudiness stood out less in Balboa than on conservative Lido Island, among the upscale sedans and SUVs that dominated the neighborhood, although I'd seen more than one of Hilda's neighbors stop to admire it on the rare occasions it was parked in the driveway rather than the garage.

"So I'm thinking I need to go straight to the *Hermandad.* They got the juice to make everybody sit down and talk. The *Hombres*, the *Tiburónes*—everyone."

"How often," I asked, "does one of these group sit-downs take place?"

"Not very," he admitted. "Maybe couple times I can remember, when things got really bad. When everyone was, like, at war."

"Doesn't sound promising," I said, earning a frown.

"It's not," said Grant, his expression smug. I'd apparently reinforced a point he'd been trying to make. "Sit-downs are an extreme measure, not something they do just because someone wants to leave, even if it is someone as respected as Tino. And even when they do it, it doesn't always work out. These guys aren't exactly known for their self-restraint."

"Just 'cause they don't normally do it this way, that ain't no reason not to try it now. You're always telling me to think outside the box."

"I was talking about creating a business plan that's unique enough to get investors excited, Tino, not about this gang business."

"Same thing. I get the *Hermandad* excited enough, maybe they gonna listen."

"If investors don't buy your idea, they just walk away with their money. If the *Hermandad* doesn't, you could end up dead."

Tino responded to this statement with another of his patented glares, but Grant was no stranger to intimidation and matched it with a lowered-eyebrow expression that would have frightened children.

"Who's got the waffles?" Our waitress, looking harassed, hovered over us, arms full of carefully balanced dishes. Tino raised his hand, and she plopped the fruit-laden plate in front of him. Grant and I had ordered the same thing, and she slid the identical omelettes in front of us.

"Could I get some water?" I asked before she had a chance to rush off.

"Sure," she replied, reaching for a pitcher on the nearby wait station. "Oh, and I forgot your blueberry syrup." She smiled brilliantly at Tino, who had stopped glaring at Grant long enough to favor her with his best Antonio Banderas grin.

"Just a minute," said a voice behind her. "We were here before those people, and we don't have our breakfast yet." It was the tourist from the next table, and he pointed to the pass-through window, where several plates sat under heat lamps. "I think those are ours. If you let them sit there, the eggs will get rubbery."

"I'll get them right away, sir," she said, breaking eye contact with Tino with apparent reluctance. "As soon as I get this gentleman's syrup."

She started to turn toward the counter, away from the pass-through, when the man's hand shot out to restrain her. "You'll get it now, or I'll complain to the owner." The man's voice took on a tone I associated with some of the more abusive foster parents I'd known over the years.

"Please let go of my arm, sir."

The asshole ignored her and, in fact, seemed to be trying to compel her to turn toward the pass-through. "I don't know why our hotel recommended this place," he went on. "This has got to be the worst service I've ever seen."

"I asked you to let go of my arm, sir." The waitress's voice had grown shrill, and heads were starting to turn in our direction. Both Tino and Grant seemed about to get out of their seats and intervene, but the jerk was oblivious.

"And at these prices, you'd expect a little class. Not some bimbo waitress who can't even—*hey!*"

The man shrieked as the waitress dumped the pitcher of ice water, which she was still holding in her other hand, directly into his lap. A collective gasp went up from the rest of the customers, and I caught a flash of movement as Mitzi, now standing behind the register, quickly lowered her head to stare into the cash drawer. I caught the hint of a grin before her face took on a neutral expression.

The outraged man was on his feet, spluttering, completely ignoring his hapless wife's efforts to calm him down. He pushed past the waitress, who narrowly missed landing in Grant's lap, and stomped over to stand in front of Mitzi. She didn't look at him.

"Did you *see* that? What that idiot waitress did to me?"

"Nope." Mitzi continued counting her money, her concentration on the bills.

"She dumped a pitcher of ice water on me!" The man fairly vibrated with rage.

Mitzi's fingers never paused as she shuffled worn bills, and she still didn't look up. "You must have pissed her off."

The entire room broke into laughter, and the outraged customer seemed to reach a level of anger that rendered him speechless. Gesturing to his wife, he pointed to the door and then stomped out of it. She followed him silently.

Mitzi finished her counting and closed the cash drawer, then finally lifted her head. Walking around the end of the counter, she went to the still open door, then shouted down the sidewalk in the direction of the departing couple, "Have a nice day, asshole!" Then, turning to the small crowd waiting near the door, she gestured toward the now-empty table. "Next."

The laughter inside the restaurant had died down, but the short-order cook and the dishwasher were still peering around the kitchen door, grinning at the fracas.

"What are you motherfuckers looking at? Get back to work." The two heads ducked back inside the kitchen, and Mitzi shuffled back behind the counter. "You want some free eggs, honey?" she asked a shabbily bearded man nursing a cup of coffee at the counter. "I'll just have to throw 'em out."

The old guy nodded, and the waitress, who had regained both her balance and her composure, retrieved one of the plates and set it in front of him. Then she grabbed a small pitcher from the counter and brought it over to Tino.

"Here's your syrup. Sorry about the wait," she said. I noticed tears standing in the corners of her eyes.

"You okay?" I asked her.

"Fine," she replied. "I love that old bitch, that's all."

"You gonna stand around all day or pour some fresh coffee?" the bitch in question called from her post at the counter.

"I'm coming, I'm coming." The waitress swiped at tears as she reached for the pot.

"Oh, God, I'm sorry I missed it." Sukey was still laughing as I finished up my attempt to relate the tale of Mitzi and her hapless customer. "I can just see her, too. 'You must have pissed her off.' Priceless."

"Yeah, she's one of a kind. People are always asking me how someone so rude can run such a successful business. I tell them it's because the food is amazing."

"That's just part of it. I think Mitzi's is successful *because* she's so nasty. People go in there hoping something will set her off. It's part of the experience. And you gotta love that she backed up her waitress."

My first client was late, which was not unusual for a Saturday, and Sukey and I were sitting in the two rocking chairs she had recently purchased at a garage sale. The second-floor walkway extended about ten feet past our office door, making a sort of a balcony. The morning sun could make the spot uncomfortably warm in the summer. This time of year, it was perfect.

"Hey, did you remember to bring in those adoption records? I'm itching to get a look at them."

"I forgot to put them in the car."

"Mercy! I've been reminding you all week."

"I know, I'm sorry. I meant to bring them today, but it took longer than I expected at Mitzi's, so when I got back to the apartment, I never went inside. I just got in the car and came straight here."

"Oh, well. I'll just go by and pick them up after work."

I was about to say I wasn't planning to be home after work—untrue—but realized it wouldn't make a difference. She had a key. I'd given it to her so she could drop off and pick up Cupcake without having to schedule in advance.

I wasn't sure why I was dragging my feet. Yes, the realization that I had been the architect of my own misery had rocked me to my core. But did that really change my need to find my birth parents? If anything, my decision to separate myself from the only family I'd ever known was even stronger evidence that I was something other than strictly human. I had probably, on some level, been trying to protect them.

"Yeah, okay," I told her. "They're in a brown envelope—I stuck them behind the wet bar."

"Great. I got these worksheets in class last week for researching public and private records. They're way more comprehensive than the ones in *The Exciting World of Private Investigation.*"

I was careful to hide my smile. The well-worn manual, purchased a few months back when Sukey decided to help me look into my past, still held pride of place on the end of the reception desk. Sukey studied the thing constantly and quoted it like the Bible. Managing my office was far from a full-time job, but I was glad she chose to spend most days studying and doing research here. It was more professional for clients to talk to a live person rather than a machine during business hours, and besides, it kept her out of trouble.

Actually, since I'd made her my first unofficial client, she didn't need nearly as much looking after. She still liked to hang out in bars and was always on the lookout for a good party. But Sukey's most self-destructive behavior had always centered on men. With a little press-induced boost to her self-esteem, she was no longer an asshole magnet.

This morning I'd noticed that *The Exciting World of Private Investigation* had been joined by a less gaudy textbook and what must be a corresponding workbook.

"I don't mind you researching my adoption records as a class exercise, Sukey, but I hope that doesn't mean the whole group, or even the instructor, will have access to my private information."

"I'll make sure anything that gets posted in class is anonymous. Don't worry—I know how important your privacy is to you."

Of course she did.

Footsteps on the metal stairs told me that my client had finally arrived, and we stood up to greet the heavyset woman who panted her way to the top. I was actually pleased to see that she was substantially overweight. Many of the people who called requesting hypnotherapy for help with weight loss were, in my opinion, not overweight at all. It was a lot more satisfying to help someone for whom weight posed an actual health risk than someone who was trying to look like a supermodel.

My recent slipups using the press had made me hypercautious, and even though the session was routine, I was still relieved when it ended without incident, as did the next two in my busy morning schedule. I never let Sukey book more than three clients without at least a half-hour break, because I got mentally tired, a state I couldn't afford even when I wasn't having control issues.

When the break came, she and I walked across the street to Alta Coffee, even though our state-of-the-art coffee machine made this custom more of a treat than a necessity. Cupcake needed to be walked, anyway, and enjoyed the inevitable attention he got from the staff and other customers.

"Oh, I forgot to tell you," Sukey said when we settled in the cafe's cozy garden area with our twin lattes. "Tino called. He wanted to know if you could come by Hilda's after work."

I was puzzled. "I saw him two hours ago, at breakfast. I wonder what he wants."

She shrugged. "Maybe something he didn't want to say in front of Grant."

I shook my head. "Tino's a lot closer to Grant than he is to me. Probably Hilda asked him to call."

"If it had been Hilda, he would have invited both of us."

"True." Hilda probably liked Sukey more than she liked me. Hell, everyone liked Sukey—why wouldn't they?

"Besides, he sounded different. Normally he's all 'hey, baby, how you doing?' but he seemed kind of, I don't know, edgy. I got the impression he was going to ask you for a favor."

I felt a twinge of annoyance, then immediately mentally chastised myself. I'd recently given some thought to the idea of karmic debt. Tino had done me a lot of favors in our short acquaintance, only the first couple of which had been because I'd pressed him. If he wanted a favor, I owed it to him.

I just couldn't imagine what it might be.

5

"Is there a point to this discussion?"

Tino had been talking for twenty minutes, and I still had no idea why he had asked me to stop by. Hilda had, uncharacteristically, withdrawn to another room, leaving Tino and me to our own devices in her spacious kitchen. I was sitting at the breakfast nook, watching him avoid eye contact.

"I'm getting to it," he said, a hint of annoyance in his tone. "You should drink your beer before it gets warm."

I picked up the Corona bottle, wet from condensation, and obediently took a sip. I gave him what I hoped was a pointed look, and he sighed and sort of shrugged, as if he knew he had used up his stalling time.

"Look, most of that stuff Grant said this morning was a bunch of shit, but he was right about one thing. You're good at getting people to do stuff."

I had gotten pretty adept at keeping my face neutral when people said things that hit too close to home, so I just nodded.

"There's someone…I mean, I know it ain't your

problem, but it'd be a solid if you would talk to him for me, man."

I felt a tightening in my lower abdomen, as if my body were trying to suck itself in defensively. "Not one of the *Hermandades*." I may be persuasive, but I'm generally not suicidal.

"No, no," he assured me. "At least not now." Before I could voice an objection, he went on. "It's just this guy. A kid."

"Kid?" Tino had never mentioned any children, at least not to me.

"Yeah, he's still a kid, even though he thinks he's a man. It's my brother."

"Your *brother?*" I don't know why I was so surprised. Tino was a Chicano, a U.S.-born citizen of Mexican descent. As a group, they weren't known for their small families. And yet I'd always thought of Tino as a lone wolf, an image he definitely cultivated. For some reason, it was funny to picture him having siblings.

"Yeah, Gustavo. Gus, we call him."

"What do you want me to talk to him about?"

"The *Hombres*. I want him out. He don't want to go."

"You let your little brother join the gang? Jeez, Tino, how old is this kid?"

"Older than I was when I joined," he said, defensive. "Fourteen. Fifteen next month."

My disapproval must have been apparent, because he took a sip of his beer, set it down carefully, then spread his hands on the table and looked at them.

"When I was a kid, the *Hombres* ran the *barrio*—the neighborhood. Not the police, not the government, the *Hombres*. Your house gets broke in to? No point calling the cops. If they even show up, they stay about five minutes, write down what's missing, tell you probably you'll never see it again and go."

I nodded. Most of the cops I knew were good people, but, in the neighborhood where Tino had grown up, they were stretched pretty thin.

"So about the twentieth time it happened to us—I was nine—my Mami, she walks down to the *bodega*. Takes me with her. I'm trying to act cool, you know? She talks to a guy there, goes by the name of Flaco. He asks Mami, 'What house you live in? What they take?' and she tells him they took the radio—the TV's gone from two times ago—and the new air conditioner she just got."

He took another sip of his beer, his eyes glazing with memories. His accent had gotten stronger, his words more redolent of *barrio* rhythms. He was nine again, following his mother down the gritty street and into the *bodega*. I knew the neighborhood—could smell the *chicarrónes* and cigar smoke that dominated those neighborhood stores.

"Flaco, when he finds out what block we live on, his jaw kind of tightens up and his eyes get real small. We're in the middle of his *barrio*. No one's supposed to commit no crimes unless he gives them the say-so. I guess whoever broke in to our place didn't talk to him first, and I can see he's pissed. He tells Mami go on home, don't worry about it. So we go.

"Next morning, there's a knock on the door, real early. Mami, she's scared—don't no one come to the door that early unless there's a problem. But she opens up, and these three guys are standing there. One's got a big fucking TV, way better than the one got stolen. The other two, they got a brand-new air conditioner, still in the box, and this boom box, got speakers big enough to rattle the windows, you know what I'm sayin'?"

I nodded, finding it easy to picture the scene.

"They say Flaco sent them, and he wants to send his apologies for not having better security in the building. And he says they got to apologize, too. I take a better look at the guys, see they're all beat up—got black eyes, cuts, bruises and shit. The one carrying the boom box got a bad limp." I caught a flash of gold as he grinned at the image and finished off the beer.

"That day, I skip school and go to the *bodega*. I ask to talk to Flaco, tell him thank you for the new stuff, and thanks for making my Mami feel safer. He looks me up and down, says 'How old are you?' I tell him thirteen, and he just laughs—he knows I'm lying. And he asks how'd I like to really help out my Mami. I ask him what I need to do, and he tells me to come around the next morning, he'll find something. After that…" He shrugged.

It wasn't a surprising story, but it was the first time I'd really thought about how normal it was for someone like Tino to enter gang life. Not long ago, I'd chastised Hilda for referring to him as "an entrepreneur." Maybe she wasn't that far off.

I picked up the story where Tino had left off.

"So you started working for the *Hombres* at nine. How much longer did you stay in school?"

He gave me a look that would have chilled someone who didn't know him as well as I did and of whom he hadn't just asked a favor.

"Couple years. By then, I was probably making more money than some of the teachers."

"So," I went on, "when your brother got a little older, it was only natural for him to follow in your footsteps." I didn't quite keep the accusation out of my voice.

"That was a long time later. Gus wasn't even born then—I was almost thirteen when he came along."

I thought about that. Tino hadn't mentioned a father in his earlier story, and presumably his mother wouldn't have had to go see Flaco on her own if there'd been a man in the picture.

This was tricky ground. You don't impugn a Chicano's mother. Period.

"You and Gus," I said carefully. "Do you have the same father?"

I saw his jaw tighten, but it wasn't me he was mad at. He avoided my eyes and didn't say anything. I waited. I was good at this game.

He got up and put the empty bottle into a recycle bin—Hilda had really civilized this guy, whether he realized it or not—and got a couple of fresh beers out of the refrigerator, even though mine was still half-full.

He sat back down, sighed, and finally made eye contact.

"When you go to a guy like Flaco and ask for help, he's gonna remember. He may come around later asking you for a favor. Something you can do. Like if you're a tailor and his kid needs a suit for his confirmation, maybe you make something special." He stopped again, and I waited. It didn't take long.

"Papi was gone, died of cancer real young. Mami, she worked at a dry cleaners. She didn't have anything Flaco needed. But, you know, she was pretty. Hot-tempered, fight like a *tigre* for her kids. When she was down at the *bodega*, yelling because of all the times the place got broken in to, how she doesn't feel we're safe in our own beds, Flaco was looking at her, really paying attention. And then, when I started working for him, she came around sometimes. Made him a cake to thank him for taking care of me, shit like that."

Realization dawned. "Flaco is Gus's father?"

"Was." He took a long pull of his Corona. "Got killed—shot—about four, five years back."

The other shoe dropped. "And you took over the *Hombres*. Just like that."

"No, not 'just like that.'" He sounded offended. "There were other guys thought maybe they should be in charge. 'Cause they were older, or their brothers or fathers were in the *Hombres*. But I was Flaco's *teniente*, man, his lieutenant. I know the people, who to call, where the money's coming from, how it gets up the ladder. And I moved fast. Had to settle a couple of people down, you know what I'm saying? But, yeah, that's when I took over."

"And Gus wants to be just like his big brother. *And* his father."

"He's stubborn."

"And you're not?"

Tino inclined his head, conceding the point. "Gus is even worse than I am. He gets it from both sides."

He was fidgety, nervous, and I realized how hard it was for him to ask me for a favor.

"So I assume you've already talked to him about this."

"Talked. Yelled. Threatened. Not just me. Mami, too. But he says I'm letting the *Hombres* down, even the *barrio*."

"And you think he'll listen to me?"

"People do."

He was right about that. But, as he had accurately pointed out to Grant, my clients volunteered to listen. Technically, they didn't know about the press, so they couldn't really give me permission to use it, so for the purposes of my business, I had rationalized that asking to be hypnotized amounted to consent.

I was pretty sure Gus wasn't going to volunteer.

But I couldn't explain all that to Tino, so I bowed to the inevitable.

"When do we go? *Where* do we go?"

"I been thinking about that," he said, relief in the set of his shoulders. "I can find him anytime—I know where he goes. But mornings are probably better. He won't be doing business, you know what I'm saying?"

I did. "Business" was almost certainly something dangerous or illegal or both, and I was all for avoiding peak work hours.

"You want to go tomorrow morning?" I asked. My office would be closed—it was Sunday—and I would just as soon get this over with.

"Yeah, that would be good. We can get him before anything's happening."

"Does he still live with your mother?"

Tino shook his head. "He's supposed to, but lately he's been crashing with some of the *Hombres*. Mami don't like it, but if I'm not around, there's not much she can do about it. She's not going to go into the projects looking for him, or at least I hope not. Like I said, she's got a temper."

"But you know where he is?"

"Yeah, I know. I figure we get there early—wake him up. Get him outta there before he knows what hit him."

I didn't much like the prospect of walking into a housing project, entering an apartment inhabited by a bunch of gangbangers and dragging out an unwilling teenager. If the rest of the *Hombres* were anything like Tino, they probably slept with guns under their pillows.

I couldn't press a bullet.

"Tino," I began cautiously, "if he doesn't want to go, or some of the *Hombres* object, just what do you think I can do that you can't?"

He shrugged. "I don't know. Hypnotize them, I guess."

I almost laughed, then realized he was dead serious.

"Tino, you don't just hypnotize someone in the middle of…of…" I was going to say "a gunfight," but I didn't really think it would come to that. "In the middle of a crowd, on the fly. It takes time, and privacy."

He looked genuinely puzzled. "I seen this guy on TV, he was in a big nightclub or something. Hundreds of people in the place, all drinking and yelling. He didn't have no problem hypnotizing people." He smiled, remembering. "Man, he had those people doing all kindsa crazy stuff. It was hilarious."

Shit. I should have realized that Tino's only exposure to hypnotism came from the movies and TV. He'd never been to my office, and the times I'd pressed him, he'd had no idea I was doing it.

"Tino, that guy was an entertainer. A hypno*tist*. I'm a hypno*therapist*. It's totally different. I can't just walk up to someone on the street, hypnotize him and make him do something he wouldn't normally do."

"Sure you can. You did it to me."

I almost choked on my beer. *Holy shit.* All this time I'd thought he was completely oblivious, he'd probably been wondering why he'd agreed to help a complete stranger, a *gringa*, after a five-minute conversation. When he found out I had a hypnotherapy office, he must have come to the logical conclusion that I'd hypnotized him, like the guy on TV, who no doubt made people bark like dogs or cluck like chickens.

He misinterpreted the horror on my face. "Don't worry, *mamacita*, Tino's gonna take good care of you. You think I'd let you get hurt?"

I was surprisingly comforted. This was the Tino I'd first met—posturing, macho and oddly endearing. I'd liked him from the beginning, even when I'd thought he was no more than a thug, someone I would use for information and never see again. I didn't think—then or now—that by pressing him I'd actually done him any harm.

And if he thought what I did was hypnosis, I'd better let that particular sleeping dog stay comatose for as long as possible.

"Okay, Tino. How do you want to do this?"

"I'll come by your place in the morning, pick you up."

"You mean I finally get to ride in the Tino-mobile? I feel honored."

"You should. A lot of women would sell their mothers to be seen in that car."

"I'll bet."

Cruising the Pacific Coast Highway in a Malibu convertible on a sunny summer afternoon might be the subject of legend and the odd Beach Boys song, but it wasn't nearly as glamorous on a chilly November morning on the 55 Freeway. I was cold, and, despite my best efforts to tie it back, strands of my hair escaped their bonds and whipped my face. I could taste grit from the exhaust of passing trucks.

"Don't you ever put the top up?" I shouted to Tino over the din of an OCTA bus.

"It don't work that good!" he yelled back. "Beside, once we get there, I got to be seen."

"It's seven-thirty in the morning, Tino. Aren't all the good little gangbangers still tucked in their beds?"

He grinned but held his silence for the time being.

A few minutes later, we finally turned off the freeway and onto the streets of Santa Ana. We cruised through working-class neighborhoods, respectable enough on a Sunday morning. There was foot traffic, but its character was nothing like Balboa's, which was dominated by joggers and dog-walkers. Here, cars were being washed and laundry hung. A few hands were raised as we drove by, and Tino waved in return.

We turned up Main Street, and the mostly single-family homes gave way to apartment buildings, and mom-and-pop businesses. The waves became more frequent—the fruit vendor, a guy selling the Spanish-language edition of the local paper on the corner and kids. Not yet eight in the morning, and already, the streets were full of kids, mostly on bicycles. Tino seemed to make a special point of acknowledging them, and I saw envy in the gazes that flickered from Tino to the chrome-laden Malibu to me. Yeah, they were definitely curious about me.

We crossed an intersection and suddenly were on a part of Main Street I hadn't seen in a long time. I was surprised at the changes.

It was as if the downtown from a prosperous, trendy beach town had been lifted and transplanted to the middle of this working-class city. Palm trees sprouted from the median, and street lamps hung over park benches. The ubiquitous graffiti was mostly absent, although the speed limit sign and the bus stop had what looked like fresh tags. Tino pointed to where the familiar *HL* of the *Hombres Locos* had been painted over with a styled *T* that trailed into the outline of a shark's fin.

."When did they do all this?" I asked him, gesturing at the new storefronts and landscaping.

He shrugged. "Few months ago," he said. "Nice, huh?"

"I guess." It did look nice, but I couldn't help but notice that most of the shops were empty, with "available for lease" signs propped inside their windows. "What happened to all the businesses that were here before?" I remembered a *taquería*, a hairdresser and a place that sold party supplies.

"Couldn't afford the rent," he said. "Which means they move somewhere else, which means I don't make no money off them. All this so-called 'restoration' is just code for 'get the poor people out.'"

He had a point. Whoever had signed off on this project from the city's side must have hoped to attract more upscale tenants. They have to have known the existing businesses wouldn't be able to afford higher rents. A new branch of a national bank had moved onto one corner, opposite a major chain drugstore. But I couldn't see Starbucks or Pottery Barn making a go of it in this neighborhood, though admittedly, it was too early in the day for much foot traffic. A few people were going in and out of a brightly lit bakery, I noticed, and silently wished the owners good luck—they would have to sell a lot of *pastelitos* to afford those accommodations.

When Tino steered the big car onto a side street, all signs of gentrification vanished within a block. At least half the businesses were boarded up, and the other half had ancient neon signs glowing through dirty glass behind barred windows. We passed a high fence on which the multilayered graffiti showed several examples of both *Hombres* and *Tiburónes* tags, with the latter appearing to be more recent. I could make out the shapes of windowless cars between the fence boards, and then through a rusty iron gate behind which a sign read *Piezas Usadas*. A translation was crookedly scrawled below the Spanish: Used Auto Parts. A smaller sign warned *Peligro—Perro feroz*. I peered through the bars but saw no trace of a dog, ferocious or otherwise. It didn't mean he wasn't there. When Cupcake—then known as Cujo—was doing guard duty for his previous owner, he hadn't made any noise at all until the trespasser was within a few feet of him. I knew this from an incident when I'd been the trespasser in question.

Immediately past the salvage yard, a group of apartment buildings rose. They were all alike and had probably not looked too bad—once. There was something subtly different between them and the other buildings we'd passed that made them easily recognizable as government-subsidized housing. Welcome to the projects, I thought. The convertible slowed, and my stomach tensed. Somewhere in this beige-and-brown warren, Gustavo slept, along with who knew how many other *Hombres*. If I ended up having to press someone, how the hell was I going to pull it off without making Tino more suspicious that he already was?

There was a parking lot that didn't have room for as many cars as there were doors in the building, but Tino didn't park there. Instead, he pulled the big car up against the curb, in front of the *No Parking to Corner* sign. We were on the wrong side of the arrow, but that didn't seem like a detail worth mentioning.

"We're gonna walk between those two buildings." He pointed, I nodded, and he went on. "The *Hombres* will have a lookout. Sometimes they have someone inside an apartment, but I don't think they have a place they can use in that building, and the other one's got no windows on this side. There'll be a spotter, though, maybe by the Dumpster or the swing sets or something. Keep an eye out. I want to talk to him before he goes and tells anyone I'm here."

"Aren't you still the boss?"

He shot me a quick glare but must have realized I was just asking, not trying to score a point.

"Yeah, I'm the boss. But people like to know if the boss is looking over their shoulder. I'd rather see how things look when they don't expect me, you know what I'm saying?"

He got out of the car, and I followed suit. I felt eyes on us as we moved through the parking lot, but if Tino felt the same, nothing in his gait showed it. How someone managed to look stealthy and swagger at the same time was beyond me, but he pulled it off. A tiger in his element. I shivered.

He nodded for me to get behind him as he entered the narrow alley between the two buildings, and I fell into step. He unzipped his leather jacket, and I didn't have to look to know why—he would have a gun in the top of his jeans. He might never have been a Boy Scout, but Tino liked to be prepared.

I followed him into the labyrinth, conscious of eyes that may or may not have been on us. We wound between a few buildings, past a series of back doors that opened onto tiny yards. Most were dismal, littered with broken lawn furniture, shabby children's toys and the occasional threadbare couch or easy chair, abandoned to the elements. A few, however, were cheery, with potted plants and brightly painted statuary, mostly depicting religious figures. I recognized the Virgin of Guadalupe and one enormous Jesus, arms spread and garishly tinted red heart exposed.

There was another narrow passage, and then we came out into a courtyard. Swing sets, mostly innocent of swings, were on one side, and what was probably meant to be a pavilion area was on the other, with a few concrete tables and benches still in usable condition. Every surface displayed gang tags, and I didn't see any examples of the *Tiburónes'* characteristic symbol. All the sharks in these waters were familiar.

After seeing so many kids on the streets, I had expected to see a few here, but they were curiously absent, with the exception of one adolescent boy, who sat slumped at one of the tables wearing a pair of dark sunglasses that were unnecessary in the shade cast by the surrounding buildings. His head swiveled our way, and I saw him stiffen as he recognized Tino. It only lasted for a moment before he reassumed his oh-so-casual posture, although I could sense his eyes darting behind the lenses, assessing his chances of getting out of the courtyard before Tino could stop him. They weren't good, and the kid must have been smart enough to see that, because he didn't move an inch as Tino and I came up to stand before him.

He darted a glance at me, and even through the tinted lenses I could see the curiosity in it, but he was way too focused on Tino to give me much thought just yet. Which indicated good judgment on his part.

I expected Tino to speak, but he didn't; he just stood. Although the kid didn't actually move, something changed subtly in his posture, making his slump seem less careless and more cringing. Tino waited, and finally the boy took off his glasses and met his eye.

"'Zup, Tino?"

"You tell me, Hector. Who you sittin' lookout for?"

"I'm not—"

"You wanna think before you lie to me, Hector."

I hadn't seen Tino move, but he was at least a foot closer to Hector, who was starting to squirm, his macho attitude completely abandoned. His head dropped, and he spoke quietly.

"Joaquin."

The answer was apparently one that Tino had expected, because he nodded.

"I thought so. Thing is, Hector, I'm gonna stop by Joaquin's place this morning, and I don't want to wake him up."

"But—" The kid seemed to be getting younger by the minute, and now he looked as if he were about to panic.

I got a vivid flash of a nine-year-old Tino, carrying messages for Flaco. Had he ever sat sentry in a project courtyard on a cool morning, trying desperately to look tough and ready for whatever might happen?

"Don't worry, Hector. This goes down the way I want, he won't even know I was here. You won't get in trouble."

The words didn't seem to reassure Hector.

"He kill me, man."

"He ain't gonna kill you, Hector. Your *abuela* won't let him." Tino grinned, and just like that, the tension was gone. He broke eye contact with the hapless Hector and turned toward me.

"Hector's Joaquin's cousin. Joaquin's a fierce dude, but he's afraid of his grandmother. Shit, *I'm* afraid of Hector's *abuela*."

I smiled, as I was expected to. I was impressed at how Tino had first put Hector on the defensive, then put him at ease. Very effective management.

"Look, I'm gonna pick up Gustavo, take him over to see Mami. He sleeping on Joaquin's sofa?"

"Yeah, I think so."

"Who else is staying there?"

"Marisol. And I think Nestor."

Tino nodded, then pulled a bill out of his pocket and handed it to Hector.

"Okay, *amigo*, you do me a favor. Go down to the corner, get some *pastelitos*, couple of *chorizos,* bring them over to Joaquin's. I'll be gone by the time you get back, but you tell him I came by and Gustavo'll be helping me with something for a few days. Say I'll catch him next time."

Hector was on his feet, nodding and moving, relieved to be sent out of the line of fire. Metaphorical fire—I hoped. Tino watched him long enough to make sure he was heading in the direction of the bakery, then turned to me.

"Marisol is Joaquin's woman, so they'll be in the bedroom with the door closed. I been there before, and they got two bedrooms, so Nestor probably has the second and Gus is alone in the living room."

I tried to picture it. "How are we getting in?"

"I got a key."

"How the hell did you get that?"

He grinned his pirate's grin. "Who you think got this crib for Joaquin in the first place? You forget, he works for me."

"Aren't they going to wake up when we go in?"

"Not if we do it right. But if they do, no big deal. I'm the boss. But I wanna get Gus out of there before he starts arguing. Everyone else don't need to hear that, you know what I mean?"

I did. In Tino's position, he couldn't let members of the *Hombres* get away with challenging his orders. Not even his little brother—at least not in front of other gang members.

"What do you want me to do?"

"Stay behind me. I go in, we leave the door open. It's on the second floor, there's like a bridge that runs between the two buildings." He pointed up at the second-floor landing. "Like that. You stand in the doorway, make sure it stays open, see if anyone's coming up the steps on either side. Just watch me—I tell you if I need you to do something different, okay?"

"Okay." I figured it was better not to mention that I suddenly had to pee very badly.

My apprehension must have shown, because Tino reached out and touched my arm, an uncharacteristic move.

"Relax, *mamacita.* You're with Tino. Nobody gonna fuck with you in this neighborhood."

"Okay," I repeated. I still had to pee.

I followed him to one of the staircases, metal with concrete risers. Following his silent progress, I winced at the metallic echo my own feet made on the first couple of steps. I tried to match his grace, and the sound diminished, but even so, I envisioned eyes opening and heads lifting from pillows in the surrounding apartments.

Tino went straight to the left-hand door. I saw a glint of metal as he pulled the key from a pocket; then, after a quick glance at me, he had the door open and stepped inside. I followed him despite the fierce hammering of my pulse in my ears.

It took only a moment for my eyes to adjust to the dimness of the room. The ragged Venetian blinds, although closed, still let in enough light to reveal the details. Bare walls—why didn't men ever hang pictures?—and mismatched, shabby furniture, incongruous next to an enormous plasma TV. The floor was littered with clothes, an empty pizza box, beer bottles and an assortment of DVDs. Tino crossed quickly to the sofa, blocking most of my view of its occupant. I could see a pair of white socks, bare brown legs sticking out above the cotton.

"What the fuck! Tino?"

"*Silencio, hermano.*" Tino's tone was terse, barely above a whisper. "Get up, man, we going for a ride."

"I got to—"

"You don't got to do nothing but put on your damn pants and come with me. Come on, man, I don't like leaving my ride out on the street for long."

"Nobody's gonna fuck with your ride, Tino." The legs disappeared as the sofa's occupant sat up. A hand snaked down and groped at the heap of clothing on the floor, lifting a pair of jeans.

"Keep your voice down, man. And hurry up. I don't feel like talking to Joaquin and Nestor right now, and they wake up, they gonna want to discuss business."

"Where we goin'?" Gustavo got to his feet, and I was surprised to see he was taller than Tino. I could see his eyebrows over the top of the shorter man's head, caught a flicker of pupils as he registered my presence. "And who the fuck is that?"

"She's a friend of mine, man. Come on, we're going." He stepped back, and I got my first full view of Tino's little brother as he picked up a leather jacket from the floor and shrugged into it.

The resemblance was strong, but where Tino was compact and muscular, Gus was lanky. The face was still a boy's, and he had buckled his oversized jeans so that they barely clung to his mostly nonexistent hips.

"She the one you been staying with?"

A laugh burst into my throat and almost made it out of my mouth before I managed to stifle it into sort of a snort. Tino obviously hadn't revealed much about Hilda to his family. He ignored his younger brother's question.

"Come on, we gotta go. That your shit?" Tino indicated a battered knapsack, and Gus nodded. That surprised me—I couldn't picture a gang kid carrying a backpack, even if he was only fourteen. But Gus slung it over one shoulder and shuffled toward the door, yawning. Maybe this was going to be easy after all.

"Tino, when did you get here?"

Snapping my head around to see who had spoken, I felt a jolt of adrenaline travel from my stomach to my scalp, making it tingle.

A young woman stood in the bedroom doorway, disheveled and bleary-eyed.

"*Silencio,* Marisol. I don't want to wake up Joaquin." Tino's voice was steady and low, but I could almost feel electricity coming from it.

"But—" A vertical line bisected Marisol's brow, and I could see she was trying to shake herself awake enough to know what to do. She gestured vaguely back toward the darkened bedroom. "Joaquin said—"

"Mercy, *now* would be a good time."

Tino's words snapped me out of my shock, and I acted quickly.

"Marisol, close the bedroom door very quietly and

come to the kitchen with me." I pressed her, hoping her half-asleep state would make her instant compliance seem less bizarre to Tino and Gus, who was staring at me.

Marisol did as I said, and I followed her around the corner into the kitchen.

"Pour yourself a glass of water and go back to bed," I told her, keeping my voice low. "Be careful not to wake Joaquin. And there's no reason to mention later that you saw Tino, okay, Marisol?"

"Okay." She got a glass with a picture of Mickey Mouse on it out of the cabinet and poured some tap water into it, then took it and shuffled back toward the bedroom. She never even looked at Tino or Gus as she quietly shut the door behind her.

Gus was openly gaping, and Tino spoke sharply. "Get going." He pointed toward the still-open front door, and Gus complied, with one last puzzled look at the closed bedroom door.

I felt shaky, probably mostly from relief, as I followed Gus out onto the landing and down the stairs. I felt, rather than heard, Tino behind me.

Gus didn't ask where we were parked, but he headed in the right direction. Again I felt eyes on us as we threaded our way back between the buildings. A few kids now hung out at the swing set, and a little girl kicked a ball in a weedy area that might have once been a volleyball court. Hector was nowhere to be seen.

When we got to the car, Gus reached for the front passenger door when Tino stopped him.

"Get in the back, man. What's wrong with you?"

Gus shot me a sullen look, but opened the back door and slid into the seat, where he slumped. I almost said I didn't mind riding in back, but I held my tongue and got into the front next to Tino.

"Where we going, anyway? There's stuff I'm supposed to do for Joaquin today."

"You work for me, and so does Joaquin. I tell him I need you for a few days, he's not gonna argue."

"A few *days?* What the fuck you talking about, Tino? And you still didn't tell me where we're going."

The Malibu was moving now. "Take it easy, *hermano*. We're gonna get a little breakfast. I was hungry for *chilaquiles* and thought you might like to go to Guapo's.

"Yeah, okay." I heard the world-weariness in Gus's voice and was glad I had my back to him, so he couldn't see my involuntary smirk.

"You gonna get some real Mexican food this morning, Mercy," Tino said. "And I hope you like it spicy."

6

"I'm down for the *barrio*. You ain't anymore." Gus's chin was more pointed that Tino's, and it stuck out in a way that substantiated the "stubborn" description.

"You keep your voice down." Tino's voice was a growl. "I still run the *Hombres*, and I'm still your big brother. You don't disrespect me."

Gus's expression remained sullen, but Tino still carried enough authority to silence him, because he dropped his eyes and returned his attention to the plate in front of him.

The food *was* amazing, and Tino hadn't lied about the spiciness. My lips tingled from the salsa, which was fresh, and redolent of smoky chipotle peppers and tomatoes sweeter than any I could buy at the local supermarket.

I'd heard of Guapo's, but this was my first visit. The place stayed open twenty-four hours and, despite the marginal neighborhood, was a popular destination after the bars and nightclubs around South Coast Plaza, only a few miles to the south, closed.

Guapo's occupied a stand-alone building behind a

cratered parking lot and could have fallen out of a Mexico City suburb, or so I had once been informed by Sukey—I'd never been farther south than Tijuana. Colorful hand lettering decorated the windows of two front doors, set a few feet apart. One side said *Carnicería* and the other *Restaurante*.

When we arrived, there were no lights on in the butcher shop side, but a long line snaked from the restaurant door. I got out of the car and automatically walked toward the end of the queue, then realized my mistake when Tino headed through the other door. I hurried to follow.

Once inside, Tino and Gus never hesitated, walking behind the unmanned butcher's counter and through a doorless arch into the restaurant kitchen. Hair-netted women looked up, recognized Tino, then refocused on their work. Meat was sliced, tortillas folded, sauces dribbled. The air held the tang of hot peppers, freshly chopped cilantro, lime and onion. My stomach gave a rumble that would have been audible if the din of the place hadn't drowned it out.

"Tino! You didn't tell me to expect you." A short balding man in a salsa-stained apron approached us. We were blocking traffic in the busy kitchen, and I itched to back out of the way, but Tino and Gus seemed unconcerned, as did the man now heartily shaking Tino's hand.

"You got a table for us, Guapo?"

"Always." I didn't see how—every seat was occupied, with some people standing and eating at a counter that ran along the front window. Guapo turned and spoke rapid-fire Spanish to a young man carrying a tub of dirty dishes. The busboy nodded, dumped his burden into a sink, then went around the counter and between the tables. Approaching the largest booth, he bent and spoke into the ear of a man seated with his back to us. The man glanced over his shoulder, zeroing in on Tino. He nodded to the busboy; then, gesturing to the rest of his party, he stood up and walked back toward the door, where he stood at the front of the line. No one grumbled. I wondered if their deference was out of fear or respect.

I looked over to see if Tino had noticed the interplay, but he was conversing with Guapo in Spanish, asking questions about the man's family, from what I could follow. Guapo led us to the table as the busboy finished clearing and resetting it.

The other customers nodded at Tino and practically gaped at me. It took real effort to keep my gait natural—the sensation of being stared at evoked strong memories of my adolescence, and those final weeks when I still lived with the Hollingses and attended public school in a tree-filled New Jersey suburb. The kids had called me "freak." Sometimes I still heard their singsong voices in my dreams, but I drowned them out now with the reminder that the only reason these people were looking at me was because I was with Tino.

I wondered if, before his liaison with Hilda, he'd ever shown up here with a woman in tow. I would have bet not. His was a macho world, where women had their place. No matter how good the food smelled, I knew that Tino's appearance here had more to do with being seen than the *chilaquiles*. A casual girlfriend would never make it through the door, although I could imagine him bringing his mother here.

He was, however, probably questioning the wisdom of choosing this as a venue for his conversation with Gus, who was not being cooperative. Luckily the restaurant was noisy on this busy Sunday morning, and I doubted anyone could make out Gus's defiant words, although his expression was thunderous.

"You don't need to worry about the neighborhood," Tino was saying to his brother now, his voice quiet and intense. "That's my job, and I'll make sure everybody gets taken care of. But I got other plans. For you, too. Things are gonna be better, you'll see."

"What I'm supposed to do, I'm not in the *Hombres?* Be all, 'you want fries with that?' Shit, Tino, I got *respect*. Joaquin say—"

"Joaquin ain't in charge. I am." Tino's voice rose enough to draw glances from a couple of nearby tables, and he lowered it again. "Joaquin's a good *soldado*, but he ain't even a *teniente*. Not until I say so."

Gus snorted. "When you been around to say so? Things been getting crazy, man. Those *hijos de putas*, those *Tiburónes*, man, they been all up in the *Hombres* business. Half the time, you don't even answer your phone. Someone had to step up for the *barrio*. Joaquin, he don't take no shit from nobody."

"When I'm not around, Joaquin's supposed to talk to Gordo."

"Gordo don't do nothin', man. Man can't take a piss unless he check with you first."

Tino's jaw worked. I figured he probably wanted to reach across the table and grab his brother by the throat. Maybe he'd chosen a public place in order to curb his impulses.

"I gotta take a piss." Gus got to his feet and, at Tino's "go ahead" gesture, slouched off toward the back of the restaurant.

"He ain't a bad kid," he said, his focus split between me and the restroom door. "Just too much like his old man."

And his big brother, I thought.

"So why am I here?" I asked. "So far, I haven't done anything. I thought you wanted me to talk to him."

"Yeah, well, I figured I'd give it another shot." He gestured toward the counter, and Guapo came around with coffee refills. When he was gone, Tino went on in a lowered voice. "He got a point about Gordo, though. Grant says the problem with type A personalities is we don't empower our subordinates. Gordo ain't in the habit of making quick decisions on his own. I wanted him to take over when I'm gone, 'cause I know he's loyal. But maybe he ain't the right choice."

"What about this Joaquin that Gus keeps talking about? He a candidate?"

Tino took a sip of coffee and winced, and not at the taste. "Joaquin's a *cabeza caliente*—a hothead. He's smart, though. A good earner. But when he gets mad, he can't control his mouth. One day, he gonna piss of the wrong person, and…" Tino mimed pulling a trigger.

"Gus seems to look up to him."

"Yeah, well, I guess I haven't been around as much as I should. He—"

"*Perdón,* Tino." A man had come up behind me and now stood next to the table. "I am sorry," he bowed a little toward me, then turned back to Tino. "Can I speak with you for a *momento?*"

Rather than looking annoyed at the interruption, Tino gave the man his full attention.

"*Hola,* Ramon. How is Yoli? Is she better?"

"*Sí, sí,* much better." Again the man looked at me, apologetic. "My English not so good."

"It's okay, Ramon. Tell me in Spanish—Mercy will not mind."

As the man quickly outlined some problem to do with, I thought, parking in front of his store, I watched them, fascinated. Tino kept his seat, and the man, who was probably in his sixties, remained standing, his head lowered. Tino was a benevolent dictator doing a favor for a humble subject, and both men were completely at ease in their respective roles.

"*Shit.*" Something caught my eye outside the front window, and I looked up just in time to see the back of a familiar leather jacket crossing the parking lot and heading for the intersection beyond. I interrupted the conversation. "Gus is taking off." I got to my feet, and Ramon backed out of my way. Tino was already up.

"What the *fuck?* Where?"

I pointed, and Tino shot out the door. I followed, but he was through the parking lot and halfway across the intersection before I'd squeezed past the people waiting at the door.

"Gus! Get back here, *pendejo!*" Tino stopped to let a bus go by, and Gus darted down an alley.

I ran to the edge of the street and stopped. There was no way I could catch up with them, but I figured the alley must run parallel to the street. I scanned the building facing the sidewalk and saw no gaps big enough for a teenager to squeeze through. If the same held true on the other side, he would have to come out on the next block. I ran down the sidewalk and waited for a break in the traffic to scoot across the street.

I didn't have to catch him, only get close enough so he could hear me. Luckily, I had my running shoes on.

When I made it to the end of the block, Gus was heading down the side street away from me. I concentrated. Physical proximity shouldn't make a difference when I pressed, as long as he could hear me. At least I didn't think so.

"Gus!" I shouted. *"Wait for me!"*

I felt a wave of relief as he slowed to a stop and turned toward me. I could see he was panting and, although I couldn't make out his expression from this distance, could sense his puzzlement.

Tino shot out of the alley and, belatedly, I realized my mistake. Gus would probably refuse to move until I got there, and the two men had half a block on me. Despite my own breathlessness, I hurried to catch up to Tino, who was pounding down the sidewalk in Gus's direction.

"Wait for *your brother*," I managed to shout, knowing it would seem strange to Tino, since Gus was obviously already waiting, bent over with his hands on his knees, trying to catch his breath.

Tino didn't seem winded at all. He grabbed Gus by the upper arm and steered him back into the alley.

"What the fuck is wrong with you, man? Making me run after you in front of all those people."

"Let go of me!" Gustavo tried to shrug Tino off but failed. My press had forced him to wait, but it didn't make him cooperative. I considered adding an instruction to listen to his brother, but I was still moving, out of breath, and it looked like Tino had things under control.

When I finally caught up with them, I tried not to pant like Cupcake after a beach run but didn't have much success.

"I thought you were smart enough to be cool, so I figured 'Hey, get a little breakfast with my *hermano*— say hello to Guapo,' but I can see you ain't gonna be reasonable."

"Tino, I—"

"*Silencio, infante,* I'm talking now." Tino's tone had dropped, and something in it must have gotten Gus's attention, because he shut his mouth, and looked a little less sullen and a little more scared.

"Since you can't act right in public, we'll go somewhere we got some privacy. Now, you gonna walk back to the car like a man, or I got to drag you like a boy?"

With a look that was so much like Tino's familiar glare that I had to stifle a snort, Gus straightened both his posture and his leather jacket, and walked back down the alley. Tino walked behind him, and I fell into step.

"You see what I mean? Like a *burro,* this one." Tino spoke loudly enough that I knew the comment was for Gus's sake, not mine. "Maybe you can talk some sense into him."

Gus faltered slightly as he walked, but he recovered instantly. He still didn't know who I was, or why I'd been brought along on this particular field trip, but he knew something was up with me.

"Where are we going?" I asked. Tino made a hand motion that meant he didn't want to say in front of Gus, and I backed off.

We went straight to the car. My stomach gave a longing grumble in the direction of the unfinished meal, presumably still waiting on the table. I wondered briefly about the check—we'd left without paying. Considering Guapo's obsequious manner toward Tino, I doubted there would be a bill. Still…

"Tino, I'm just going to step back inside for a minute."

He looked annoyed. "What, you got to use the bathroom? We ain't going far."

"I want to leave some money."

"Mercy, it's taken care of."

I shook my head. "I know, but I want to leave a tip." I'd worked my way through hypnotherapy school as a waitress and knew if I didn't put some money on the table, it would bug me for hours, if not days.

"Wait." Tino dug in his pocket for a twenty. "Here. I'm the one brought you down here." I took the bill and went inside, unable to avoid one last, longing glance at the remains of my food as I dropped the twenty on the table.

"*Doña! Esperete.*" Guapo hurried over, a large paper bag in his hand, grease spots forming on its otherwise pristine surface. "To take with you." At my puzzled look, he added, "Tamales. Fresh this morning."

I thanked him and returned to the car, getting in and placing the precious bag carefully between my ankles. If Tino noticed it, he gave no sign.

Tino steered back onto Main Street, in the direction of the more genteel neighborhood we'd come though on the way here. When he turned the big car onto St. Gertrude Place, Gus broke his silence.

"No, man, Tino, not here. I don't wanna—"

"Did I ask you what you wanted?" Tino snapped, and Gus lapsed back into silence.

We pulled up in front of a small two-story house with a spotlessly groomed yard. A variety of flowers bloomed in beds along its walls, dominated by sunflowers. The house had been painted in the last couple of years and would have fit well into a more prosperous neighborhood, if not for the bars at the windows and a forbidding fence with lethal-looking spikes at the top.

Tino got out, and nodded for Gus and me to follow. The gate had a modern-looking electronic locking mechanism with a keypad, shiny against oxidized surroundings.

Tino punched in a six-digit code, and I heard the metallic click of the lock disengaging. He gestured for Gus and me to go in front of him. Gus's posture had degenerated to a slump so low that he looked like a turtle trying to recede into his shell. He no longer seemed noticeably taller than Tino.

The front door opened, the doorway framing someone I couldn't quite make out. Then a figure rushed forward. I had barely enough time to register long hair and a swirl of bright yellow fabric when the person came to an abrupt halt in front of Gus. The woman, for a woman it was, threw her arms around him, and he seemed to shrink even further.

"*Ay, niño.* Where the hell have you been? I've been crazy worrying!" She stepped back from the embrace and swung an arm fast enough to blur, and I heard the resounding smack of the slap before I knew it had happened.

"Why don't you come home? You think I don't know where you been, hanging around with those *putas y cabrónes?*" She switched into full Spanish, the words coming out much faster than I could follow, although it was clear why Gus had wanted to avoid this confrontation.

After a moment or two, Tino, who appeared to be enjoying this, stepped between his little brother and the woman.

"It's okay. He's okay. Let's go inside," he said, and her focus changed to him.

"So, Tino, you finally got time to stop by." She spoke forcefully, but with less heat. "You too busy for me now, Mr. Businessman? You too important?"

"Not for you, Mami," said Tino, grinning and taking her into his arms. "Never for you."

The kitchen was old-fashioned, dominated by a central table where an enormous bouquet of sunflowers stood. Religious figures competed for wall space with more sunflowers of every description—paintings, metal sculptures, plaster pieces that might have been made by children. The theme was continued with refrigerator magnets, assorted gadgets and plastic placemats, the sunny yellow flowers with their dark centers everywhere.

And the place was *clean.* Not like Hilda's kitchen, which looked like a page from *Architectural Digest.* This was the kind of lived-in spotlessness that bespoke the pride of constant maintenance. I could smell soap and cleanser and Lemon Pledge, an oddly pleasant combination. Teresa, as she had asked me to call her, was serious about her housekeeping. As I had yet another cup of coffee—I would be vibrating all day—I tried not to stare at my hostess.

According to Hilda, Tino was twenty-seven, which meant Teresa had to be at least in her forties, and her eyes seemed at least that old. Nevertheless, she was an astonishingly beautiful woman, as vibrant as the bright colors in her kitchen. Tino had described her as pretty, but he had been talking about when he was nine and had first accompanied her to the *bodega* to see Flaco. I'd pictured "Mami" as matronly and stolid, like the women I saw waiting at the bus stop in maids' uniforms, having walked from their jobs on Lido Island to the corner near my office. Estela, the woman who cleaned for Hilda, was cut along those lines, although sometimes I could see the serene beauty of a Mayan princess lurking behind her plain features.

Teresa was another creature entirely. She was fine-boned, with a proud arch to her neck that made me think of a Thoroughbred horse. Her hands were long and graceful, although they looked strong, her nails short and without polish, and she gestured constantly as she spoke. Her figure was still lush, and her hair, shot with silver, was thick and black and full of wild curls. I could easily imagine a younger Teresa, filled with indignation at the violation of her home, raising holy hell in the *bodega.* When Tino had originally told his story, I'd thought of Flaco as taking advantage of a vulnerable single mother. I had a feeling that any man who tried to take advantage of Teresa did so at his own risk.

"So," she said, turning to me. "Tino tells me you are a friend. *Not,*" she said, her eyes flicking briefly toward her older son, "the one he stays with."

I nodded. Teresa intimidated me in a way her son never had. Out of the corner of my eye, I saw Gus's chin lift. So far, he'd been pretending to ignore us. Teresa went on.

"This other woman, this Hilda, do you know her?"

"Yes, I know her." When I didn't elaborate, she lifted

her eyebrows and waited. I just barely managed to resist this tactic and keep my mouth shut.

"I see," she said, finally. "And what about you? How do you know my son?"

This was tricky. I'd met Tino in a bar while looking for information about Dominic, a drug dealer who'd been threatening my friends. Tino had known Dominic through his own drug connections, and I'd pressed him into doing some information gathering on my behalf. I'd thought, at the time, that would be the end of our relationship.

"Tino helped me out with a…personal matter a while back. We got to be friends."

"And you introduced him to Hilda?"

I shot a look at Tino, but he avoided my gaze. I was surprised he'd told his mother this much.

"Yes," I said, carefully. "He met a few of my friends, including Hilda."

"While he was helping you out."

"Yes."

Tino finally came to my rescue. "Mami, don't give Mercy a hard time. I got some stuff to talk to Gustavo about, and I asked her to come with me. In fact, maybe you could, you know—" he shrugged apologetically "—give us a little privacy."

Her eyebrows rose higher. "You got something to talk to Gus about and *she* can listen, but his own mother can't?"

"It's *Hombres* business."

"*Hombres business! Hombres business!*" she mimicked. "You know how many times I heard that excuse, Tino? First Flaco, then you. And you're worse that he was—he didn't bring his business into my kitchen, not unless there was some kind of emergency."

"If it wasn't for *Hombres* business, you wouldn't have this kitchen *or* this house."

Her eyes flashed, and I froze. I felt like a coyote witnessing a confrontation between mountain lions.

"However I got this kitchen," she said, her words measured, "it's mine, and no one can order me out of it. You may be the *jefe* of the *Hombres*, but you're still my son."

They stared at one another for a long moment. Then, to my surprise, Tino conceded. He put his hands up in a gesture of peace. "*Tranquila*, Mami. You're right, it's your kitchen, and I can't make you leave. I'd like it if Gus, Mercy and me can talk in private, but it's up to you."

She looked from Tino to me and back again, then nodded and got to her feet.

"Since you *ask*, I'll go. I got some work to do in the garden, anyway. But—" she narrowed her eyes in my direction "—in eighteen years, this is the first time I heard anything about a *gringa* having anything to do with *Hombres Locos* business." Putting her own coffee cup in the sink, she gave me one last glare before leaving the room.

What was it with this family and the evil looks?

The back door slammed, and Gus immediately came to life, talking fast.

"I know what you're gonna say, and I ain't moving back in here."

"That's right, you're not." Tino folded his arms, smug.

"I'm not?" Gus was so surprised, he forgot to sound tough. His voice squeaked a little, and I remembered that, despite his height, he was still just a kid, and his voice was still changing.

"Wouldn't do no good. You already shown you won't listen to Mami—"

"Like *you* ever listened to her."

Tino reached over and smacked him on the back of the head. "Listen, *hermano*, at your age, I listened to her plenty. Flaco woulda kicked my ass if I didn't."

Gus's expression changed, and he mumbled something under his breath.

"What was that?" Tino asked sharply.

"I said Flaco wasn't your father."

Tino threw back his head and laughed, and not in a pleasant way. "No, he wasn't. And if he didn't let *me* disrespect Mami, how do you think he'd feel if he saw *you* doing it?"

I could see that Gus was hurt, but he turned his head, and I wasn't sure Tino saw it, too.

"So why you don't want me to stay here?"

"I thought *you* didn't want to stay here."

"I don't." This time Gus really did squeak. "Why you playing with me, man?"

Tino reached out again, and Gus cringed, but this time he ruffled his hair. "Look, Gus, I was hoping you'd stay with Mami, take care of things when I'm not here—"

"You're never here."

"—but I know Joaquin and Nestor will just come

over here and pick you up. And if Mami and Joaquin ever get in to it, I don't wanna be around to see what happens."

Gus's snarl was, momentarily, almost supplanted by a grin.

"I can keep Joaquin away from Mami."

"Yeah, but can you keep Mami away from Joaquin? You know if she gets fed up, she gonna go down to the projects looking for you."

This time the grin was open, if brief. "Yeah, that could turn out bad."

"So I think it'd be better for everyone if you come down to Newport Beach, stay with a friend of mine."

Gus nodded toward me.

"With her?"

What? I wanted to shout, but I managed to keep quiet.

Tino snorted. "With Mercy? No, that would be worse than Mami. *Believe* me." He rolled his eyes at me to let me know he meant no insult. "I got other friends down there."

"I can't go to no Newport Beach, man. The *Hombres* are here. In the *barrio*. You forgetting that?"

Gus's voice rose, and I saw a muscle bunch in Tino's jaw. They stared at each other for a moment, at a standoff.

A telephone—an old-fashioned wall mount with a real bell—rang loudly about a foot behind my ear, and I jumped.

Tino and Gus continued to stare at each other, not moving. The phone rang again, and I felt a growing inner disquiet. What is it about an unanswered telephone that makes people jumpy? A third trill, and I almost reached for it myself.

The door swung open and Teresa stepped in, removing a pair of sunflower-patterned garden gloves. She glared at her two sons, then marched over next to me and picked up the receiver.

"*Díme.*"

Teresa listened for a moment, then looked over her shoulder at Gus. "He's not here."

"Is that for me?" Gus was on his feet, reaching for the receiver, but Tino was too fast and jumped into his path.

"I don't care what you think you heard, I said he's not here," Teresa said into the receiver. She started to hang it up, but Gus managed to get one hand on the cord and tried to yank it away from her. Tino pushed him back from the phone but didn't dislodge the cord. The receiver was pulled from Teresa's hand, hitting the floor with a loud clunk.

I backed quickly out of the way.

"Joaquin, is that you?" Gus yelled in the general direction of the receiver, which was still a good three feet away from his mouth. "Don't hang up, I'm—"

His words were cut off as Tino, who had gotten both arms around him, lifted him completely off his feet and dropped him back into the chair.

Gus looked as if he were about to bolt, then thought better of it. Tino bent and picked the receiver up from the black-and-white checkerboard linoleum.

"Who's this?" He listened briefly, then replied.

"Didn't you get my message? You did? Then why you calling here, man?" I could make out an argumentative tone coming tinnily from the earpiece, but not the words.

"We just stopped here to pick up some stuff for Gus. He's gonna be busy for a few days." Gus started to speak, but Tino held up a hand. "None of your fuckin' business doing what. Something I need him to do. That's not good enough for you all of a sudden?"

It must have been, because the voice on the phone got quieter, and Tino's face lost some of its menace.

"Yeah, I know we got to meet, but I gotta take care of Gus."

"You don't have to—"

Again the hand went up, and again Gus subsided with an exasperated expression. Hell, it was more than an expression—his whole body registered annoyance, from the eye-roll to the exaggerated slump to the big exhale. Quite a performance.

"No, I didn't talk to Gordo since last night. He said what?" Tino listened intently, nodding his head.

"Yeah. Yeah, okay. Okay. I said, I'm agreeing with you. You can stop arguing with me now. Look, man, I'll call you back in five minutes."

He hung up and turned toward me.

"Mercy, I need you to take Tino to Hilda's. I got some business I need to take care of. I'll catch a ride down there later."

"Hilda's?" I blurted, simultaneously with Teresa. He addressed his answer to her.

"Yeah, Mami, she's got a lot of room at her house. And none of the *Hombres* ever been there. Gus stays here, you gonna have guys coming around looking for him."

"I don't like it. I'm supposed to let this woman I've never met take care of my son?"

"I can take care of myself."

"*¡Silencio!*" snapped Tino and Teresa simultaneously. Neither looked at Gus, who performed another of his full-body sighs.

"Look at it this way, Mami. I don't keep an eye on him, he's gonna end up back over at Joaquin and Nestor's. And you know what they do there."

She pursed her lips and crossed her arms. "Maybe I should go with them, make sure everything's okay."

As a successful gang leader, Tino had mastered controlling his features long ago. But even though his face remained stoic, I *felt* the moment of pure panic as he contemplated a meeting between Teresa and Hilda.

"Mami, Mercy's taking my car and not coming back here."

"You're going to let her drive your *ride?*" The astonishment in Gus's face must have been mirrored on my own, because Tino grinned.

"Yeah, Gus. See the kinda shit you make me do?"

After a little coaxing—which sounded remarkably like threatening—Gus and Teresa left the room, ostensibly to pack a bag. I sat back down at the kitchen table and eavesdropped on a phone call. Tino used the old wall phone and, from what I could follow, arranged a meeting between Gordo, Joaquin, Nestor and a bunch of other names I didn't recognize. The *Tiburónes* were mentioned several times, and I assumed the business had something to do with the rival gang.

"It's like *West Side Story,*" I told him. He looked completely blank. "You know, the old musical?"

"I don't like musicals," he protested. "Especially not those old ones."

"You've got to have heard of *West Side Story.* It's all about street gangs in New York. The Anglo gang was called the Jets, and the Puerto Ricans were the Sharks."

"The *Tiburónes* ain't no Puerto Ricans. They're Chicanos, mostly. A few Mexicans—I mean born in Mexico. Thing is, most of them don't even live in Santa Ana."

"So all this—" I made a vague gesture indicating the neighborhood, if not the entire city "—is *Hombres* territory?"

He shook his head. "No, no way. We got the projects, that end of Main Street, a few blocks north, all the way to Orange. Other side of town, over by Garden Grove, the Vietnamese got that neighborhood—gang called the Golden Tigers. A couple of white guys, not really a gang, handle most of the action on the Tustin side. I do business with them—we got an agreement, you know what I'm saying?" I nodded, fascinated. "A few black dealers across the line in Orange, call themselves the BB. Supposed to stand for Blood Brothers or some shit. They claim they part of the Bloods, but they don't fuck with anyone outside a couple of blocks. We stay outta each other's way, mostly. But I hear the *Tiburónes* been bothering them, too."

Even I had heard of the Bloods. "The *Tiburónes* are powerful enough to want to piss off a big L.A. gang like the Bloods?"

"Not really." He shrugged. "Which is one of the reasons I don't think those BB guys are really Bloods. Either that or the *Tiburónes* are crazy stupid."

"Who runs the territory we're in now?"

"No one, man. This street, the whole thing, is neutral, everything south of Edinger, all the way to South Coast Plaza. You maybe see a little action, a couple of places on Warner, but not much." He nodded around at the walls. "First thing Flaco did, when he hooked up with Mami, was move her out of the *barrio*."

He got up and stretched, then looked at his watch. It was an expensive one that Hilda had bought for him. He called out in the direction of the doorway, "Hurry up! I want you out of here before I leave to go talk to the *Hombres*."

"I'm coming," said Gus from the stairs. He came into the kitchen with his backpack, now looking considerably fuller, and dragging a duffel bag. "And *I'm* an *Hombre*. I should go to the meeting."

"I'm not meeting with everyone," said Tino. "Just key people."

Gus wrinkled his brow at a term that must have come directly from one of Grant's business lessons, and Tino clapped him on the back. "Ready to go, *hermano?*"

"No," said Gus, but he slumped toward the door,

making more noise with his feet than was necessary. Tino followed us to the curb, where he gazed apprehensively at the Malibu, its baby-blue paint the same color as the sky.

He turned to Gus. "I better not hear you tried to pull any shit, jumping out of the car at an intersection, something like that. You hear me?"

Gus gave an infinitesimal nod, and Tino went on. "Give me your cell phone."

"Tino—"

"Just give it to me." He held out his hand, and Gus fished the cell phone out of the knapsack. "The pager, too."

Gus handed it over, and Tino returned to his perusal of the convertible. Sighing, he fished in his pocket and pulled out a pair of keys attached to a rabbit's foot chain. After a moment's hesitation, he handed them to me.

"Not a scratch. You got that?"

I nodded, careful to keep my expression solemn. I wasn't sure whether he was talking about the car or Gus. And, truth be told, it didn't really matter.

7

"Look, he likes you." Sukey paused in the act of adding another log to Hilda's outdoor fireplace. "See, I told you he wouldn't hurt a fly."

Don't laugh at him, I warned her silently.

I won't. It is pretty funny, though. He's actually shaking.

She was right. Gus's expression of pure terror when the French doors had opened and Cupcake had galloped onto the patio had afforded me a certain spiteful glee. He hadn't had time to extricate himself from the chaise longue where he'd been slumped before the dog was practically on top of him.

Gus had scrambled backward so suddenly that the chair had nearly toppled over, and Cupcake had decided the newcomer was playing a game. Barking joyously, he'd climbed up on the lounge, resulting in the chair tilting even farther. The two had ended up in a heap, with the dog, who probably had ten pounds on wiry Gus, on top.

I'd called the big mutt off, but he'd been staying close to Gus ever since, hoping his new playmate would start another game. Once he'd more or less recovered his dignity, Gus had tried to appear nonchalant, but he was obviously afraid of dogs. Or at least dogs the size of Volkswagens.

Cupcake now had his head almost in Gus's lap, his whole back end wagging furiously. I could see the whites of Gus's eyes and felt a mean little twinge of satisfaction. The kid had been a pain in my ass since the moment I'd pulled away from the curb in front of Teresa's house. He'd complained, sulked, whined and argued. I'd had to press him again—twice, because I'd been too specific the first time—which I wouldn't have done if I hadn't promised Tino I'd get him to Hilda's. Before Sukey and Cupcake showed up, he'd been bitching because neither Hilda nor I would let him have a beer.

"Good dog," tried Gus. "Maybe you want to lie down now."

The words *lie down*, if spoken with tone of authority, would normally generate instant compliance in Cupcake. Gus's tone was so tentative that it sounded more like a question than a command, and the dog ignored it.

"He just wants you to rub his head a little," coaxed Sukey. "Right between the ears. Go ahead."

Not wanting to look afraid in front of a bunch of women, although Hilda had fled to the house's interior and her housekeeper, Estela, had gone home for the day, Gus lifted a hand and placed it oh, so carefully on the enormous skull. "Here?"

Sukey didn't have to answer, because Cupcake lifted his chin in order to push his head more firmly against the hand. Gus gave an experimental scratch, and Cupcake moaned with pleasure. The motion became more deliberate, and the big dog sighed and lowered his head against Gus's knees. I could see the boy's shoulders relax. "Good dog," he repeated. This time it sounded like he actually meant it.

I was annoyed to still be sitting there, my whole day gone, but Tino had called and said his business was going to take longer than expected. Hilda had looked so aghast at the prospect of being left alone with Gus—Estela took one look at the boy and decided it was time to dust the insides of all of the closets—that I hadn't had the heart to abandon her, even after Sukey showed up.

I craned my neck to see if Hilda was still in the kitchen. She liked to joke that the only thing she was any good at making for dinner was reservations, but Estela often put something together that could be warmed in the oven or heated in the microwave, and Hilda could at least manage a salad. She'd asked Gus what he would like to eat, but he'd only shrugged and mumbled. Even my suggestion of pizza hadn't raised a flicker of interest. I'd told Hilda she should just make dinner for herself, and Gus, if he was going to be an asshole about it, could just go hungry.

"But I told Tino I'd take care of him," she protested. "What will he say if I can't even give him a decent meal?"

"Tino just wants the kid out of Santa Ana until he gets his gang business resolved. I don't think he expects you to do anything other than provide a bed and a roof."

"Yes, that's what he said," Hilda said. "Grant offered to take him, and I should have kept my mouth shut. But oh, no, I had to stick my nose in the middle of it."

"It's not too late, you know. Tino would understand if you called Grant and asked him to pick up the kid."

She shook her head. "No, then Tino would just be running over there every five minutes, making sure he was okay. I thought it would be better to have Gus here, where his brother could keep an eye on him. Of course," she added, asperity in her tone, "I thought Tino would actually *be* here."

Now the sun had gone down, and there were lights in the windows of the breakfast nook. It was starting to get too cool on the patio, even with the fireplace going, and I decided it was time to check on dinner.

"I'm going to go see if Hilda needs any help. It's probably almost time to eat."

"I'm not hungry," said Gus.

He's lying, said Sukey, the telepathic comment unnecessary. It had been more than nine hours since the breakfast Gus hadn't even finished, and teenagers' stomachs needed regular feeding.

"Even so, I want you come in and sit at the table. You don't have to eat," I told him.

"What if I don't want to?"

Gus's tone was starting to make me feel as if I were chewing aluminum foil, and I didn't bother to answer him.

You can always press him, Sukey's voice sounded in my head.

To eat dinner? Let the little fucker starve. The silent sound of Sukey's laughter filled my mind as I opened the French doors and headed into the kitchen.

"Ten minutes," said Hilda the moment I came around the corner. "I don't need any help."

"You sure?"

"It's calming me down," she said. "Ten minutes and I'll be perfect."

"Okay."

Back on the patio, Sukey was sitting in the chaise opposite Gus. Cupcake had transferred his attentions to her, and the kid looked relieved. "Rottweilers are really very gentle, if they're well-trained. They were bred to herd sheep, you know," she was telling him.

"I thought they were all like, you know, attack dogs. Like in *The Omen,* man, when they were possessed by the devil, and that kid was making them eat people and shit."

Trust Sukey to finally get Gus interested in something.

"Well, they *are* often trained as guard dogs," she admitted. "The Romans brought their ancestors to Germany as war dogs, trained to fight in battle right alongside the soldiers."

"No shit?"

"Nope. And Cupcake here *was* trained as an attack dog. He just doesn't attack unless someone commands him to."

"Will he, like, kill someone?"

Sukey gave me a troubled look. We really didn't know *what* Cupcake would do. The transfer of ownership from his previous master had been done in a rush, and Sergio, the asshole in question, had neglected to give us the voice commands, all of which seemed to be randomly selected. We'd since learned a few, and not in particularly convenient circumstances.

Nail file would make Cupcake block someone by standing in front of them, growling and snapping. The word *bumblebee* would cause him to grab someone by the arm with his teeth and grip them just tightly enough so they couldn't escape. And *piston* elicited a takedown followed by a throat hold—a spectacular but, so far, nonfatal move.

We hadn't stumbled across a *kill* command. Yet.

"I don't know if he would—" Sukey started.

A cell phone played the opening bars of a Bob Marley tune. Gus's expression, which had become almost pleasant, returned to a scowl—he'd probably been reminded that Tino had instructed Hilda and me not to let him use our cell phones. We wouldn't be able to keep him away from Hilda's house phones forever, but he didn't feel comfortable enough yet to sneak off and make a call.

"Hi, Grant!" Sukey seemed relieved at the interruption and turned her back on Gus. "No, I'm at Hilda's. We're getting ready for dinner and last time I checked, there was enough for an army. You want to come by? I'll tell her…." She headed in the direction of the French doors, Cupcake trailing in her wake.

Gus didn't seem any more thrilled to be alone with

me than I was to be with him. He sighed for about the
thousandth time.

"When is Tino gonna get here, man?"

"Soon, I hope." I didn't want to stay for dinner but
couldn't see how I was going to get out of it.

Gus looked at me. "What are you, anyway?"

I froze. "What do you mean?"

"You ain't Tino's woman, but he let you drive his car.
And he brought you to Mami's. Tino don't bring *nobody*
to Mami's."

I relaxed a tiny bit.

"I like your mother." I'd said it to change the subject,
but it was true.

"She liked you, too." I was surprised, both at what
he'd said and that he'd said it at all. I'd hardly had time
to make an impression at Teresa's house, and Gus didn't
seem too interested in making friends with me.

"But the way Tino was talking to you at Joaquin's,
it was like—" he shrugged "—like you were backup
or something. If he thought he needed backup, why'd
he bring a woman? Why not bring Gordo? Gordo's
his *teniente*."

"Because Gordo's got more important things to do
than help me talk some sense into my *burro* of a little
brother."

Tino stood at the edge of the patio, framed by the
light streaming from the dining room. I'd never been so
glad to see him.

"Come on, we're eating," he said.

I expected Gus to start whining about his lack of

hunger, but he got up and headed into the dining room without comment. He was probably more relieved at Tino's arrival than I was.

"Hey, it's the Newport Bitch!"

I was actually comforted by both the strident voice and the insult—Jimbo only gave rude nicknames to those he liked. Sunday nights were too quiet to pay someone else to tend the bar, so the man himself was holding court for his small audience.

"Hey, Jimbo." A draft beer arrived on the bar in front of me at almost the exact moment I settled onto the bar stool.

"This is on Butchie." Jimbo nodded toward the opposite end of the bar, and I turned to see one of my favorite local fixtures. Butchie had sold Sam his gas dock and boat rental business when he retired.

"Thanks, Butchie. How've you been? I haven't seen you around for a while?"

"Oh, I've been staying with a friend a few nights a week." Butchie indicated a tall man with a full head of white hair sitting next to him. "You know Roger, don't you?" He clapped the man on the back, and he turned toward me.

"No, I don't think we've met." As the man got up from his bar stool and took a couple of steps toward me, hand extended, I recognized him.

I was right—we hadn't met. I just knew those impossibly blue eyes, although I'd previously only seen them in a different face.

"Hi, I'm Roger Falls. And you are…?"

"Mercy Hollings." As I shook his hand, I waited for recognition and, possibly, disapproval to flood his features. But his expression remained cheerful.

"I'm sure I'd remember meeting such a pretty girl. But I'll bet you know my son, Sam."

I managed not to stammer. "Yes, I know Sam. He looks a lot like you."

"So they tell me." The eyes sparkled with innocent good will. I wondered whether Sam had never mentioned my name, or if Roger had forgotten it.

I searched for something to say. I hadn't been around a lot of people with Alzheimer's and didn't know how to act. Roger seemed perfectly alert, and was tanned and healthy-looking. His slight stoop seemed more a product of leaning over to talk to shorter people—which would be just about everyone on the planet. He had to be six foot eight.

Butchie rescued us. "Roger was kinda under the weather a little while back, but he's been feeling so good lately that I thought a trip down to the beach today would be nice. We even got a sail in—Sam took us out for a while this afternoon. Good wind today."

"By God, yes!" Roger enthused. "Blue water sailing—nothing like it. You ever see Sam's boat?"

"It's beautiful," I told him, sincerely. "I took my first sail on that boat."

"Did you? Tell you what, I'll talk to him about doing it again. Great weather this time of year…" He faltered for the first time, and I wondered if he really knew what time of year it was. He went on, sounding more confident. "I'd enjoy having a beautiful woman on board, and I'd bet Sam would, too."

He tilted an eyebrow and canted his head to one side, as if to say, "Don't you agree?" I'd seen Sam execute that exact mannerism a thousand times.

"Won't you come sit with us?" Roger gestured toward the other end of the bar. I hesitated. I only had to shift about five stools to be next to him, but I had a feeling Sam would show up any minute. I was starting to lose the all's-right-with-the-world feeling I'd gotten when I first walked in the door and heard Jimbo's squawk.

But I couldn't think of an excuse, and besides, I'd wanted to meet this man for a long time, so I moved the few feet and resettled.

"Another beer, innkeeper." Roger nodded at Jimbo, who looked at Butchie.

"You haven't finished your last drink, Rog." Butchie pushed over a glass with something red in it. Sam's father looked at the glass and grimaced, then winked at me.

"Cranberry juice," he said, lowering his voice in a mock-conspiratorial voice. "Not at all a fit drink for a sailor, not at all." Despite his words, he took a sip. "This old fart—" he nodded at Butchie "—claims that beer interferes with my medication or some such nonsense."

"According to Sam, the doctor says you can have one beer or one glass of wine a day," said Butchie. "And, far as I know, you ain't had it yet. So go ahead, Jimbo, give the man a beer so he'll quit bitching."

"Thank you, barkeep," Roger said as Jimbo placed a mug in front of him. He took a long draw. "Ah, there we go. Nectar of the gods."

I relaxed a bit. Despite the strong resemblance, Sam's father had a quality I seldom saw in his son. It was a sense of fun. Not that Sam was incapable of being lighthearted, it was just that he always seemed to be holding something back, as if he were watching and waiting. I supposed the same could have been said of me.

"Where is Sam?" I asked.

"He's fueling up the *Reef Runner*," Butchie supplied. "They usually fill up earlier, but they were doing some engine work—took them a little longer than they thought."

I nodded. The *Reef Runner* was one of several charter fishing boats that did overnight runs. I often saw it returning to the harbor in the late mornings or early afternoons, decks filled with life-jacketed men, a few of whom proudly held up tuna or mahimahi. According to Matt, the *Reef Runner*'s captain, at least a quarter of his customers got seasick, but most came back again anyway. Although the gas dock normally closed at sunset, the commercial captains all knew where to find Sam if they needed fuel after hours.

"You know Sam?" asked Roger, and I saw Butchie wince.

"Sure," I told him. "Sam's a great guy."

"Yes, he is. I'm damned proud of that boy. Damned proud. I'm glad he's found something he likes to do, too. He needed something low-key, after that terrible time in Iraq. Bad business, that. Sam blamed himself, but I never believed—"

"Roger," said Butchie sharply, "don't go boring Mercy with all that ancient history. Drink your beer."

Iraq? Bad business?

Roger looked flustered but obeyed Butchie, taking another swig from the mug. "Sorry," he said. "Was I repeating myself?"

Butchie clapped him on the back. "No, Roger, you were doing just fine. I just thought it was time to change the subject. You know Sam doesn't like everyone hearing about that stuff."

"Right, right." Roger looked contrite. "Sorry, my dear. Being in the presence of a lovely young lady has obviously gone to my head. Forgive me."

"Nothing to forgive," I told him. Not by me, anyway.

So Sam had been in Iraq. It must not have been in the latest war, based on what I knew of his recent history. I wasn't really all that surprised. Sam obviously had secrets, and there were a few facts that had never added up. He'd discussed martial arts with Tino in a way that led me to believe he had more than academic knowledge of the discipline. I'd once seen him scale a telephone pole like a monkey, and he'd busted down a door with too much precision for it to have been his first time. And he'd conversed with the Tunisian owner of a local restaurant in his own tongue. Fluently, according to the restaurateur.

There was some activity at the back door, and I

turned to see Lifeguard Skip and a couple of his cronies
come in. Skip was probably in his late fifties but, from
what I'd been told, had in fact once been a Newport
Beach lifeguard. There were about six guys named
"Skip" local to Balboa, and they each had a nickname.

The newcomers were happy to see Butchie, and
came over to say hello and be introduced to Roger.
Lifeguard Skip wasn't quite homeless or quite a bum.
He had, at the moment, a one-room apartment, and he
worked odd jobs for cash. Sam sometimes employed
him, as did several of the other local business owners.
I didn't know his two friends as well, but they were cut
from similar cloth. Usually at least one of the three had
enough cash in his pocket to buy a few beers, but they
were always glad if someone with more regular income
was willing to stand a round, as Butchie could usually
be relied upon to do.

I was mentally debating a second beer when the bar
stool behind me scraped against the cement floor.

"Hello, Mercy."

"Hi, Sam."

"Hey, Egghead. Beer?" Jimbo liked Sam, too, although
I'd never thought the handle with which he'd christened
him was a good fit. Of course, Jimbo still subscribed to a
school of thought in which "egghead" meant anyone
educated. When Sam had first arrived in Newport last
spring, knowing few people, he'd sometimes sat at the bar
with a book. He favored large, impressive-looking
volumes on military history or novels with seafaring
heroes. Not too many people brought books to Jimbo's bar.

"Sam, my boy," said Roger, having spotted his son. "Have you met this pretty girl here?"

"Yes, Dad, I know Mercy."

"Ah, yes, Mercy," repeated Roger, and I wondered if he'd forgotten my name. "So, Sam, did you get your business all squared away?"

"Yup. After I drink this, we'll head on home, okay?"

Roger looked at his own glass, which was nearly empty. "Perhaps I'll join you in another mug."

"You're only supposed to have one."

"Well, yes," Roger said, "but these mugs are really quite small…." He looked appealingly at his son.

Sam smiled, and I saw both pain and affection in his expression. "Yeah, they are. Okay, just one more. Jimbo?"

Jimbo, who had been observing from a distance, drew a fresh beer and brought it over. Roger thanked him and turned back to Butchie, who was in the middle of a riotous and off-color tale.

"I'm glad I finally got to meet him," I told Sam. "He's a nice man, Sam. And very proud of you."

"I know." Sam was quiet, not looking at me. "He's been—well, he hasn't been good lately. I was beginning to think I wouldn't be able to keep him home much longer. Then, a few days ago, he just woke up one day, almost his old self. I know it can't last, but it's sure great to see him like this."

Sam inclined his head toward his father, and I saw that Rog had joined in the tale, even getting off his bar stool to act out part of the account as the others laughed uproariously. "I always said that no one could tell a story like Dad. He was a journalist for the Navy, you know, before he became a college professor."

"How did he feel about you going into the military?"

Sam's head snapped around, his cheerful expression gone. "I've never actually said I was in military." His voice was perfectly calm, but there was something underneath it. Something unsettling.

"Roger mentioned Iraq."

Sam put his beer down and turned toward me with deliberation. He seemed to be choosing his words carefully.

"Dad sometimes forgets that there are certain things he isn't supposed to talk about. I know he's said more to Butchie than he should have, but Butchie's an old Navy man and knows how to keep his mouth shut. But—" I saw a vein twitch in his temple. "If you've taken advantage of his illness to ask questions about things that I've already told you I'm not at liberty to discuss…"

Adrenaline coursed through my veins and made my scalp tingle. How *dare* he?

"Do you actually believe that I would take advantage—that I would use your father to—to…" I shut my mouth and took a deep breath before the outrage could take hold of me and make me start yelling or, worse yet, pressing.

"Even if he brought it up on his own, you shouldn't have encouraged him—"

"I didn't encourage him!" My voice had risen, and Butchie's head swiveled toward me, eyes bright with

curiosity. I turned my back to him and looked straight at Sam. Struggling against the rising tide of my temper, I measured my words carefully.

"I didn't encourage him," I managed to say more quietly. "And Butchie interrupted him before he had the chance to say much. But, Sam, after all the grief you've given me about keeping secrets from you, you have to admit that you've been keeping a pretty damn big secret yourself. Do you blame me for taking notice?"

"Grief?" The derision in Sam's tone could have cut diamonds. "You think I gave you *grief?* I *let* you keep your secrets, Mercy."

"Until you broke up with me," I shot back.

Sam glanced over my shoulder, and I realized he was looking to see how much attention the other men were paying to us. Jimbo, a veteran of thousands of barroom arguments, had remained discreetly at the other end of the bar, attuned enough to our body language to know we would rather not be overheard.

The only thing to do was make myself scarce. I'd come into this place to avoid tension, and this conversation was the last thing I needed after a day that had started off stressful and progressed to nerve-wracking. I'd wanted to wind down before bedtime, and at this rate I would be up half the night.

I stood up. "This is not the time or the place for this discussion," I said, sounding pompous even to my own ears. Would there ever be a time and a place? "I'm going home."

I was out the door and halfway across the parking lot when I heard his voice.

"Mercy, wait." I almost kept on going, but I stopped. Sam caught up.

"I'm sorry I accused you of—of manipulating Dad. You're right, you would never do that. You just caught me off guard when you bought up Iraq."

I folded my arms, a barrier between us. "I'm sorry, too. That I brought it up. I should have kept my mouth shut."

He shook his head. "No, actually, I need to know if Dad is being indiscreet." He looked back over his shoulder at the light streaming from the bar's back door. "He doesn't really know all that much himself, but—" He bit his lip.

"Can I walk you home?" he asked, surprising me.

"I'm fine—it's only a couple of blocks."

"I know. I just want to say something to you."

I nodded, and we turned down the alley. He waited until we'd crossed Balboa Boulevard and were almost on the boardwalk before speaking.

"We—you and I—only talked about this once before. I told you I had taken an oath, and that was why I couldn't tell you everything."

"Yes."

"Yeah, well, I could have told you some things without violating that oath. Not much, but enough to— to explain a little bit about why I can't talk about it. I should have trusted you that much."

Here it was, my opening. Time for me to admit that I should have trusted him more, too. Time for me to tell him—what? That I didn't know who or what I was? That the only other person I'd ever met who was anything like me had turned out to be a monster? Even Madame Minéshti, the gypsy woman who'd told me there were others like me and that her people had known about them for centuries, didn't know for sure whether I was human.

The moment stretched—and passed. Our secrets would remain secrets, at least for the time being.

It really was a short walk, and we were in front of my house before the silence had time to get uncomfortable. I suddenly realized how very, very badly I wanted to invite him in. I paused, uncertain, wondering if he knew what I was thinking.

"I have to get back to Dad. He was having a good time tonight, but things can change fast with him."

Relief and disappointment warred in my belly.

"Okay," I said. "Sam, I really did enjoy meeting your father. I'm glad I got to see him on one of his good days."

"I may bring him to work with me this week, since the weather's supposed to be good and I'm between regular caregivers. I think all the activity's good for him."

"I'm sure it is. Good night, Sam."

"Good night, Mercy. Stop by and say hello to Dad tomorrow, if you're around."

"I might do that. Mondays are quiet." I went inside without turning on the lights and moved to the living room window, where I could see through the blinds. I watched his form in the pools of light the street lamps shed on the boardwalk until he turned the corner to head back toward Jimbo's.

"Meow?" Fred sounded inquisitive as he rubbed against my ankle.

"No, he's not coming in." Sam was one of Fred's favorite people, with his calm voice and slow, deliberate movements. "And you'll be glad to know Cupcake's spending another night at Sukey's." The loud, rumbling purr allowed me to perpetuate my delusion that Fred understood every word I said.

I looked at the clock. It was almost eleven, and I needed to get ready for bed, but I feared that the day's events would swirl in my head like a carousel, preventing sleep. Sighing, I sank onto the sofa and picked up the remote control. I clicked over to the classic movie channel, where a black-and-white image of Olivia de Havilland's sweet, soulful features filled the screen, and Fred jumped up and settled on my lap. I toyed with the idea of getting the vodka bottle out of the freezer but never quite made it off the couch.

I let the sentimental old movie sweep me away, and when my eyes got heavy, I didn't fight the feeling. I was just trying to decide whether to get up and go to the bedroom when the pounding started.

8

"Mercy! Mercy, you still up?"

It was Sam's voice. I sat up groggily. "I'm coming." Fred was stalking back and forth in front of the door. I stumbled to the foyer and managed to get the lock disengaged.

The Sam illuminated by my entrance light was a different man from the one I'd seen...how long ago? I couldn't see the clock from where I stood. He was disheveled and sweating, his eyes wide.

"It's Dad," he said. "He wandered off. Butchie thought he was in the bathroom, and—"

"I'll call the police," I said.

He stopped me as I started to turn away. "Already done. They're looking in all the alleys and doorways, and along the bay front. I was heading over toward the pier, and I saw your light on, and thought—"

"Of course. Just let me put my shoes back on."

We headed straight across the dunes to the water's edge. The beach was wide here, and the lights from the closest parking lot did little to amplify the glow cast by a quarter moon. The tide was coming in but still pretty low, with six-foot wave faces breaking into inches of water. Farther north, man-made breakwaters made it easier for swimmers to get in and out of the surf. Here the diagonal shore break often caused body surfers who got caught in the bruising churn to say they'd "been maytagged."

I knew that the moonlight was deceptive, only pretending to illuminate the beach, and even small shadows could easily hide a man's form.

"Dad!" Sam called, cupped hands in front of his mouth. "Hello, Dad!" His shouts were largely drowned out by the sound of the waves.

I'd grabbed a flashlight, but its beam didn't really illuminate more than a tiny wavering circle on the sandy expanse. Nevertheless, I scanned it back and forth as I walked.

"Roger!" I shouted, aware of my voice being swallowed by wind and water. "Roger Falls!"

"I don't think he'd be on the beach after dark. Even if he wandered over this way, he'd go toward someplace with lights." He pointed toward the pier, now only a couple of blocks away, bright as a beacon.

As we increased our pace, I saw a police cruiser come around the corner and pull slowly onto the pier. A handheld spotlight shone from the passenger window, illuminating first the sand on either side, and then the water, as the car moved farther onto the pier.

"Roger Falls!" The amplified voice was definitely loud enough to cut through wind and wave noise, but nothing stirred on the pier except for a couple of late night fishermen, who turned curiously.

The base of the Balboa Pier is set back a long way from the water's edge and the pier itself rises high above the ocean waves. We altered our course to angle away from the water and back to the boardwalk, where stairs scaled the side of the pier. By the time we climbed the steps, a second police car had arrived, and now everything was illuminated except the area directly underneath the pier.

Sam waved to one of the cops, who stopped to wait for him. As they spoke, I went partway back down the staircase and directed my flashlight's beam into the shadowy recesses at the pier's base.

It was built farther back than the high tide normally reached, and I expected to see litter, but the sand looked pretty clean. Toward the water, several signs warned *No Swimming Under the Pier*. Wooden beams running between the enormous concrete pilings cast weird shadows and tricked the eye. Back near the base, something was sticking up just behind a pile of sand. I wanted a better look at it. First I turned off the flashlight, and then I took a couple of steps back up the staircase and shouted.

"Sam! I'm going to look under here." Sam turned and held one hand to his ear, his expression telling me he'd heard his name but not the rest of what I'd said. "I'm going to look down there," I yelled, gesturing. He nodded and returned to his conversation, and I went back down the stairs and, turning my inadequate flashlight back on, stepped into the shadows.

I searched for whatever had caught my eye before I'd spoken but couldn't see it from this angle. Just pitted sand—kids played here during the day, and the trucks that smoothed the sand on either side couldn't fit between the pilings to smooth the craters left over from the construction of castles and treasure-hunting excavations. The sand was soft and difficult to walk in.

I was about to head back into the light when I finally spotted the thing I'd noticed earlier. Something the same color as the sand but too smooth, too regular. I trudged over toward it, and as I got closer, its outlines became clearer.

It was a tan deck shoe.

My mind whirred into high gear. Sam almost always wore deck shoes—had his father been wearing them at Jimbo's? I couldn't remember. They were pretty common—the shoe could have been here for days. Still…

I swung my light around the space. "Roger! Roger Falls!" My voice was swallowed by the thunder of waves, much louder here as it echoed against the ceiling created by the pier above. Other than the shoe, I saw nothing that didn't belong here. I shone the beam toward the water, into the latticework of supports leading down to the pilings. Stupid—a monkey couldn't climb up there, never mind a senior citizen.

I looked at where the pilings emerged from the frothing ocean. The waves seemed larger and more violent under the pier, broken up by the pilings. A couple of people drowned or were severely injured under here every year, despite lifeguards' best efforts to keep swimmers away from the roiling chaos. I couldn't make out much in the beam of my household flashlight. What was needed was a spotlight, like the ones on the police cars.

Uncertain about what to do, I picked up the shoe. It was large, the right size for a tall man. As I headed back toward the stairs, I saw the flashing reflection from one of the cruisers' lights—it must be leaving the pier and heading back toward the street. I cursed the sand that impeded my progress when I finally reached the base of the stairs and watched the second cruiser also pull away from the pier and cruise back toward Balboa's main intersection.

"Wait! Come back!" I shouted, but I knew I couldn't be heard. I practically ran up the steep steps, which didn't feel difficult after the drag of the sand. I ran to the middle of the pier, where I was illuminated by lights on either side, and waved my arms in the air, the deck shoe in one hand. "Come back!" Maybe they would see me in their rearview mirrors. I jumped up and down, but first one cruiser and then the other turned the corner onto Balboa Boulevard and disappeared.

Frustrated, I turned toward the end of the pier. Sam had spotted me and was running. I could tell he was shouting but couldn't hear his words. One of the fishermen, seeing the commotion, was coming my way, too, although he was still forty or fifty feet behind Sam.

I ran to meet Sam and held out the shoe. "Is this…?"

He grabbed it, eyes wild. "Where did you find this?"

"Under the pier. But I can't see anything with this

stupid flashlight. We need to get the police car back here with the spotlight. Can you call 9-1-1?"

"No, I don't have my cell phone." His frustration seemed to vibrate through his entire body, and he raked the hand not holding the shoe through his hair.

I hadn't picked my phone up on the way out the apartment, either. I pointed to the fisherman, who had almost reached us. "Maybe he has one."

The man drew up, out of breath and panting.

"Did…you…find…something?" he asked me, and Sam waved the shoe at him.

"Yeah, she found this. We need the police back here. Do you have a phone?"

The man shook his head, and I looked toward where the cruiser had disappeared. "I'll go after them," I said, and would have started running if Sam hadn't grabbed my arm.

"No, I need you to show me where you found the shoe. You—" He pointed toward the panting fisherman. "Can you run after the police car, flag them down?" The man nodded and, despite being winded, started to move. "Tell them we'll be under the pier. Tell them to bring one of those dune buggies. Tell them—" The man nodded, even as he ran, and Sam turned back to me. "Show me."

He followed me down the stairs, and I used my flashlight to illuminate the spot where the shoe had been. "There. But he's not under here now. I looked everywhere. I'm afraid that—" I didn't want to say it, but I nodded toward the churning water. A larger wave crashed, the noise deafening.

"Give me that." Sam took the flashlight and tried, as I had, to shine it over the constantly moving waves. It was like staring into an explosion of water—the surface constantly dissolving and reforming, making it impossible to find anything on which to focus. *"Dad? Dad!"*

As the beam moved back and forth, I thought I saw something at the edge of one of the big pilings, and I clutched Sam's arm. "There," I said pointing. "On the right side of the piling, up high. I thought I saw—"

He swung the flashlight and steadied it, focusing on the piling's pitted and barnacled surface. It had to be six feet in diameter, and it gleamed wetly in the light. Dark metal rungs protruded from its rounded surface, the remains of a series of footholds that had probably once been used to access the crosshatch of beams. As the flashlight beam moved up the rungs, something white appeared at the edge of the light.

A hand, pressed against wet concrete.

"Dad!" Sam charged down the sand and around to the right, stopping when he was ankle deep in the surf. I was right behind him, and, as he shone the light from this new angle, I could see that another ladder was attached to the opposite side of the pillar. There, perched above the waves, Roger Falls clung. The shock of white hair, wet and wild, glowed in the flashlight's beam. The blue eyes were rimmed by a wide circle of terrified white.

"Hold on, Dad! I'm coming. Here—" Sam reached for my hand, pulling it up to the flashlight. "Hold it steady on him."

"Sam, you can't—"

"Just hold it." He released his grip on the flashlight, and the pool of light dipped, then resolved again on Roger as I faltered and then steadied my arm.

Sam was already pulling off his shoes and wading into the water. A wave almost toppled him.

Then another monster wave came along, and this one did knock him down. I held my breath, the flashlight beam wavering, as the wave's backward motion threatened to sweep him into the maelstrom between the pilings, but he got to his feet and trudged back toward me.

He coughed and spat, then yelled back to his father, "Hold on, Dad, I'll be right there."

I thought Roger might have nodded, but I couldn't really tell.

"I can't go straight in," he shouted into my ear. "I'll have to swim out on the north side, then let the wave carry me back toward the pier." He pointed, and I tried to picture it.

"He's on the wrong side of the pier," I protested. "You'll have to let the waves carry you between the pilings."

"I know." He moved quickly along the water's edge, and I followed, crablike, trying to keep the beam steady on Roger. "There's no other way."

"Shouldn't you wait for the police?" I shouted, but he shook his head.

"No time. He could fall any second." As if to validate his words, an especially large wave smashed through the pilings, throwing a sheet of spray over the frightened man, who turned his head away from the brunt of the water. I thought I could see him shaking, but from this distance it was impossible to tell.

"Sam, are you sure—"

"I can do this," he shouted, already wading into the cold water. "I was a fucking Navy SEAL."

Well, of course you were, I thought.

Even a few feet away from the pier, the waves were less chaotic, and Sam was able to time the right moment to dive under the approaching wave and pop up on the other side. I tried to watch him and hold the flashlight on Roger at the same time, but it didn't really work. As he dove under the next wave in the set, I returned my full focus to keeping the beam steady, trusting that he knew what he was doing and would make it to the place where his father clung.

A Navy SEAL. I should have guessed.

It took all my discipline to keep my head from swiveling to search for Sam's dark form in the water as I watched wave after wave assault the pier. The tide was coming in, and it seemed as if each peak reached higher, spraying the soaked man perched on the corroded remains of the rungs. It was taking too long, and I wondered how a man with Alzheimer's could have the strength to hold himself up there for all this time. I wanted to press him to hold on tight, but I knew he couldn't hear me, and besides, he was obviously already doing that. Sam had told me that, in the early stages of the disease, patients often exhibited unusual physical vigor, making it harder to control them. I guessed I was looking at a prime example of what he'd described.

After what felt like an age, I saw a dark spot in the foam of one of the waves. It was moving too fast, caught in the pull, and heading toward a piling. The wrong piling—the one opposite Roger's. As it collided with the back of the piling, the side I couldn't see, I gasped. "Sam! *Sam!*" I aimed the beam at the roiling water around the base of the piling. If he'd been knocked unconscious…

I spotted him, a dark form in the water, using the momentary trough between the waves to stroke toward the opposite piling. I tried to keep the light just ahead of him, not sure how much it was helping, and I moved along the water's edge back toward the side of the pier. I had to dance back momentarily when I got too close to an incoming wave, then refocused the beam. Sam had reached the piling and had his hand on a rung. As he started to pull himself up, a wave slammed into him with such force that I felt sure he would be swept from his hold, but, as the froth subsided, I saw that he was still clutching the rusty steel. This time he made it up two rungs before another wave crashed against him, but he hung on and then scrambled up another three or four rungs. His face was even with his father's feet now, and he reached up a hand and patted a leg clad in soaking khaki. I trained the beam back up to Roger's face and saw that he was looking down, speaking. I had no way of hearing what passed between them, but, as Sam pulled himself up so that he was standing on the same rung as his father—would it hold their combined weight?—I could imagine the relief of the terrified man.

I moved back so that I was once again under the

edge of the pier. I couldn't get parallel with them—the pillar would have blocked the light. Sam turned toward me, one hand shielding his eyes. I could see his lips move—he was shouting—but I didn't know what he was trying to say. He gestured toward the opposite side of the pier, and I understood.

The waves, which were rolling in diagonally from north to south, were pulling away from the side of the pier where the two men now perched precariously above the rising tide. If they got back into the water, it would pull them toward the shore to the south of the pier. Sam wanted me and my flashlight beam over on that side.

"You should wait for the police!" I shouted uselessly. Not only couldn't he hear me, I didn't even know if I was right. Even if the fisherman had already found the police—although it felt like hours, it had in reality only been a few minutes—it would take them a while to get a rescue crew over here and set up. If they were bringing a boat, it would have to come around from the harbor or down from the Newport Pier, two miles north. And the tide was coming in.

I nodded in response to Sam's wild gestures and crossed under the pier to the south side, retraining my beam on the pillar. I couldn't see them as well from this angle, but I could see that Sam's head was close to his father's, and he was talking into the older man's ear. Roger was shaking his head, protesting, and one of Sam's hands let go of the rung above to squeeze his father's shoulder. The head shaking stopped and was replaced by a nod. Then Sam moved down one rung, followed, much more slowly, by his father. Sam spoke into Roger's ear again, and again I saw the headshake. I could imagine the conversation—Sam cajoling his father to descend closer to the waves, Roger protesting, Sam insisting.

They climbed down another rung, then another. Their progress stopped as a series of strong waves reached them, rising up to their knees. I saw Sam press close against his father, steadying him. Between the waves, I saw Sam's head turn, as if he were assessing whether the set had finished and how long he had before the next arrived. I wondered how much he could make out in the dim moonlight. Then the two men let go of the ladder and fell backward into the chaos of the waves.

Sam had timed it just right. The backwash of the final wave pulled them back a few feet from the piling, and I saw Sam's arm arch from the water as he pulled his father close in a lifeguard's cross-chest carry. A new wave lifted the two men out from under the pier and, finally, from its shadow. I threw my flashlight aside without turning it off and ran to the water's edge, trying to gauge where the waves would bring them ashore.

The reflection of red lights told me at least one of the police cruisers had finally returned. The beam of the spotlight swung around wildly and, after flashing by several times, found me. I flung out an arm, pointing, and the circle of the spotlight followed my direction, wavered, then settled around the two figures in the water.

The waves crashed in and rushed out, but each swell carried them a little closer to the shore. The bright light illuminated Roger's white hair and sharply outlined Sam's arm as it rose again and again from the waves, stroking resolutely toward the shore.

The flickering lights grew stronger, and figures ran past me. One was a policeman, and another, clad in khaki pants and a red T-shirt, was probably a fireman. I finally turned and saw that the two cruisers had been joined by a fire rescue paramedics' truck, and the base of the pier now blazed with lights.

I ran to catch up with the rescuers, who waded into the water to meet Sam and Roger, who were just getting to that tricky point where the shore break disintegrated into shallower water. By the time Sam got to his feet, trying to support his taller father, at least five other sets of hand reached out and pulled the two men through the surf and up onto the sand, where they both collapsed.

I managed to fight my way between broad shoulders to stand before them. "Sam…"

By now dozens of flashlights were trained on them, and he blinked, holding up a hand to shield his eyes. "I'm okay," he said, then coughed. "Dad—"

I turned to where the older man lay blinking on the sand, also coughing. "I think he's okay. Sam, I—"

"I'm sorry, miss, you'll have to step back." A big hand pulled me firmly from the circle of light, and I struggled only momentarily before complying. More figures, some in uniform, some not, rushed toward the prone men, and I took several steps back. Dark silhouettes, probably residents of the houses that faced the boardwalk south of the pier, were crossing the parking lot and heading toward us, drawn by the flashing lights from the emergency vehicles, more of which were arriving.

I stumbled back, found a dune and sat. I wondered briefly where my flashlight had ended up but dismissed the subject. Flashlights were cheap.

A few residents came to stand beside me, speculating out loud about what had happened. I overheard "drowning," and even "great white shark," but didn't bother to enlighten anyone. A couple of police ATVs arrived, pulling directly onto the sand and heading toward the growing crowd of law enforcement and rescue personnel, which swallowed them. After a few minutes the ATVs emerged from the ring of bodies. One supported a stretcher, paramedics walking alongside and steadying it. Roger was strapped in, covered by a blanket. Sam was seated on the back of the other, a similar blanket thrown over his shoulders. I got up and ran to catch them.

The crowd kept me from reaching them, but just as Sam was climbing into the back of an ambulance into which his father had already been loaded, I managed to get within a few yards.

"Sam!" I shouted, and his head turned toward me. "I'll meet you at the hospital." He heard me, or at least read my lips, because he nodded. The doors closed, and I ran back in the direction of my apartment and my car.

My cell phone was ringing as I came in the door. I snatched it up.

"Mercy?" It was Sukey. "Are you okay?"

"I'm fine," I told her. "Sam's father—"

"I know," she told me. "I'm on my way. I'll take you to the hospital. Change out of your wet clothes, and I'll be right there."

9

By the time I'd changed out of my sodden jeans, I'd calmed down enough to wonder about Sukey's call. How had she known about Sam's father? It made sense that I would want to go to the hospital, but she'd even known my clothes were wet.

She pulled up in the alley just as I locked the back door. I opened the passenger door to find Cupcake sitting in the front seat. He scrambled into the back, and I got in.

"How did you know—"

"Telepathy," she said.

"But I didn't hear you," I said, mystified. "And I didn't even think about trying to contact you. I didn't know you could hear my thoughts when I wasn't even aware of it."

"It wasn't your thoughts, it was everyone else's," she said, turning onto Balboa Boulevard. "Butchie, Jimbo, Lifeguard Skip, half the police force…"

As if in synch with her words, a couple of police cruisers passed us, lights no longer blinking, probably heading back to headquarters. Sukey continued her story.

"I was heading home from Hilda's—you skipped out pretty fast after dinner, by the way—and I started hearing this big, like, jumble of thoughts. I don't usually hear stuff like that unless someone's really agitated. Everyone was thinking 'Sam's Dad' or 'Roger' or 'missing'—stuff like that. I went to Jimbo's, but it was locked up. I think Jimbo was out helping them search."

"You heard all those people? Has that ever happened before?"

She shook her head. "Not like that. Not all at once, I mean. But I told you, I've been hearing more and more thoughts all the time."

The traffic light at Fifteenth Street was red, and we stopped. "I saw the ambulance head toward the pier, so I went that way. Then I saw you next to the ambulance, your jeans all wet, like you'd been wading in the ocean. When you headed back toward your apartment, I went and got my car from Jimbo's."

"Why'd you call me? I mean, instead of contacting me telepathically?"

"I tried. You had me blocked."

"Not on purpose."

She shrugged. "I guess you were just so focused on the situation, nothing else could get in."

Strange, but I couldn't concentrate on it right now. "It looked like Roger—Sam's father—was okay, but I couldn't really tell," I told her.

"I think he's fine. They're just taking him to the

hospital to check him out. Sam got a pretty bad bump on the head."

I stared at her. "Did you find that out from someone's thoughts, too?"

"Yeah. Sam's."

Whoa. Sukey could read my ex-boyfriend's mind. Wonderful.

We rode the rest of the way to Hoag Hospital in silence punctuated only by Cupcake's panting and parked in the palm-lined lot nearest the emergency entrance.

"Lie down, Cupcake, we'll be back in a while," Sukey said. The big dog complied, and we walked toward the doors. The ambulance was no longer in the bay, but a couple of police cars were parked in their designated spots.

I'd expected the waiting room to be chaotic, but it wasn't, and I realized that despite the panic I'd felt, one old man who was probably more scared than injured really wasn't much of an event. Also, Hoag was one of the best-run hospitals in California, and turnover in the E.R. was fast.

A young woman was speaking with one of the policemen, jotting in a notebook—probably a reporter from the *Orange County Register* or the *Daily Pilot*, both of which had big enough offices that someone was assigned to respond to police reports twenty-four hours a day. An Alzheimer's patient wandering off and being saved in an ocean rescue would probably make the front page in the local editions. Sam wouldn't like the publicity, but there wasn't anything he could do about it.

I approached the desk. "I'm looking for information on Roger Falls. He just came in with his son, with the fire rescue unit."

The woman behind the desk nodded. "Yes, they're both being checked out right now. Are you family?"

I shook my head. "No, but I was with Sam when he went into the water to rescue his father."

She smiled, warmly. "That must have been amazing. I take my kids down to the pier all the time in the summer, and the water coming in between those pilings is really scary." She glanced at the glass doors, over which a sign said *Hospital Personnel Only*, then back at me. "I can't let you go in, but I'll try to let them know you're here. Your name?"

"Mercy Hollings."

She made a note and indicated the mostly empty chairs in the waiting area. "I'll call you if there's any information."

I walked back to a shut-eyed Sukey, who opened her eyes briefly when I sat down, then closed them again.

"I'm trying to listen," she said.

"To what?"

"To anyone who's thinking about what's going on with Sam or his dad—a doctor or a nurse or something."

"You can do that?"

"Sometimes. Sshh!"

A vertical line appeared between her closed eyes, and I considered the implications of her ability to listen to strangers, including those who weren't even in her line of sight. Outside of my mental conversations with Sukey, I only heard thoughts occasionally and, pretty much without exception, only from people I knew. Either she really was more psychic than I was, or she practiced more.

Or both.

I closed my own eyes and tried to listen with my mind instead of my ears. All I heard was the ambient noise of the waiting room. A few people were waiting to be seen—an emergency room the size of Hoag's was never completely without patients—and they were conversing in quiet tones with friends or family members, mostly about questions on the paperwork. Could I make out any thoughts? There was something….

That's not him. Maybe…no. How about… Yes!

It was Sukey's voice, faint despite the fact that she was sitting eight inches away. I wondered if it seemed quiet because she wasn't directing her thoughts toward me.

I could tell she'd found someone whose thoughts were of interest, but I couldn't make out what she was hearing. It was as if I were standing across the room from someone who was on the phone, able to tell there was a voice coming through the earpiece but no more.

She opened her eyes. "It's really tricky, all the thoughts jumbled together. But I found Sam. He's talking to a doctor, who wants him to get his head x-rayed. He doesn't think he needs it, and he's annoyed because it's keeping him away from his father."

"Can you hear Roger at all?"

"I don't think so. But we've never met, so I might not recognize him. There is *someone* who feels confused and scared, but I can't zero in on it."

"Try again. Maybe you can hear a doctor."

"Oh, I hear plenty of doctors. But they all sound the same—administer this drug, order that test, how long until their shift ends." She shook her head. "I can't tell one from the other. If someone thought about Alzheimer's, it was before I was paying attention."

Interesting. "We haven't talked about the telepathy much lately," I said.

"We haven't talked about the telepathy much *ever*," Sukey retorted. "Every time we start, you change the subject."

I didn't bother to argue. "Well, I have a question. When I hear your thoughts—or anyone's, for that matter—they're in your or whoever's actual voice."

"Me too."

"Even if the person is a stranger and you've never heard their voice?"

She frowned, thinking. "I—I'm not sure. I hear people I know more than I do strangers."

"Did you ever hear someone thinking in another language?"

The frown deepened. "I don't think so. But I'm not around people who don't speak at least some English. What difference would another language make?"

I thought about it. "I can carry on a conversation in Spanish if I have to, but it's hard work. That's because I don't *think* in Spanish. In my head, I'm constantly translating. I have to think about what each thing means before I can formulate a sentence, then I have to translate that sentence. See what I mean?"

She nodded. "I think so. If I could understand someone's thoughts and they don't even speak English, or don't speak it fluently, that would be *massively* cool." She grinned. "Sukey's Psychic Translation Service. Whadaya think?"

"There might be a market," I said, laughing. "But back to my original question—if you heard someone's thoughts and the person sounded one way, and then later you heard them talk and they sounded totally different or even spoke a different language, then it means that the telepathy is picking up on…on *intent*. I've been trying to figure out if…" I lowered my voice. "If there's any relationship between the press and intent."

"What do you mean?"

"I've always assumed it was all perception. I mean, if I tell someone 'take a walk,' how they'll react depends on their idea of what a 'walk' is. One guy might head out for a nice stroll on the beach. The next might march out my door and keep walking until he passes out from exhaustion, or even walk in front of a bus rather than stop moving."

"So you have to be careful how you word things."

"Always. But you remember that time when I was at the porno movie shoot and someone knocked me out?"

"How could I forget? One minute we're in the middle of a telepathic conversation, and the next you go totally silent, like a phone line was cut. I, like, totally freaked!"

"Yeah, well, when I came to, I was tied to a chair and this guy was guarding me, and I told him—I pressed him—to untie me. But he didn't speak English."

"You told me this before. He couldn't understand you, so you couldn't press him."

"No, but I kept trying anyway, because I was desperate. And just before the police arrived, I thought I was making some headway."

Her gaze sharpened. "You didn't tell me that part."

"I wasn't sure if it was really happening or was just wishful thinking. But it seemed like, whether he could understand me or not, he was starting to perceive my *intent*. And even though I couldn't actually tell him what to do, he was showing signs of feeling compelled to obey me."

"That is *so cool!*" Sukey's voice rose, and heads turned toward us. At my gesture, she lowered her voice. "Sorry. But do you even get what that might mean?"

I shook my head, not following her train of thought.

"Mercy, this could be the biggest thing ever. It means you could press someone *telepathically*. You wouldn't even have to say anything. You could just—like, *project* the press into their minds, and they'd obey."

The room suddenly felt about thirty degrees colder.

"What?" asked Sukey. "Don't you think that would be cool?"

"I have enough trouble keeping my words under control. If I'm going to have to start monitoring my thoughts…" I shuddered.

"But it's exactly the same thing. Your words only

work when you add the press to them deliberately. I'm sure thoughts would work the same way."

"I'm not sure about anything," I replied. "First, you know it still happens by accident—"

"Hardly ever."

"—every once in a while. And second, I can't project thoughts to people at will."

"You can with me."

"That's different." I struggled for words. "That's more like just starting a conversation. It's like making the decision to just open my mouth and start speaking, only I'm using my mind instead. Plus, you're listening. I've never projected my thoughts into anyone else's mind."

Even as I said it, I wondered if it were true. I thought about Georgette, the client who'd come to me about managing her temper. Hadn't she voiced aloud a thought I'd just been having, like an echo? At the time, I'd managed to convince myself it was a coincidence, but now I wasn't as confident.

"That's because you don't practice. You should try it—talk to someone else, someone besides me, and see if they hear you."

I snorted. "And if they do, how do I explain it?" A thought occurred to me, and I purposely narrowed my eyes. "Sukey, you haven't been doing that, have you?"

She shrugged. "A few times. But I'm really careful." I glowered, and she hurried to continue. "Seriously, Mercy, I don't do anything that's going to get me caught."

"Like what?"

"Well, say I'm at the mall or something, with lots of people around. I pick out some guy, and I say—telepathically—something like, 'your fly's open' or 'your shoe's untied,' then I watch him to see if he looks."

I laughed in spite of myself. "Doesn't the guy look around to see who said it?"

"Sure. But I do it when a bunch of people are passing him, like on the other side of the escalator, and hope he just figures it was one of them. By that time, I'm looking in a different direction."

"Does it always work?"

"Almost. Not when I first started, but now, yeah. Which means..." She arched her eyebrows significantly.

"It gets stronger as you practice."

"Yup. And *you* don't practice."

I blew out my breath. I hated the whole idea of treating telepathy like a research subject. "I'm not sure I want to get better at it."

"Oh, come *on*." Her voice rose again, and, although fewer people remained in the waiting area by now to pay attention, I motioned for her to be quiet. She spoke more softly. "Look, Mercy, we both know that what gets you into trouble is when the press gets away from you. If there's any possibility that you can press someone telepathically, then you'd better be sure you know how to control it by trying it on purpose before it happens accidentally."

She had a point. "I can't really see myself making strangers in the mall check their zippers, like some psychic episode of *Punk'd*."

She grinned. "No, I can't see that, either. But I'm sure we can come up with something that works for—"

"Ms. Mercy Hollings, please come to the reception desk."

The public address system wasn't especially loud, but there's something about hearing your own name that always gets your attention.

"Shit, I forgot to listen to see if anything new was going on with Roger," Sukey said as I got up and headed toward the desk. She settled back into her chair and closed her eyes again.

"Mr. Falls—the son, I mean—asked if you could come in for a moment. If you could just follow me…?" the woman behind the desk said.

I'd been in Hoag's emergency room just a few months ago, to see Sukey, but she'd been transferred to Intensive Care by the time I'd arrived. This was the first time I'd entered the labyrinth of cubicles, rooms containing shining stainless steel tables and curtained alcoves with beds. I was glad I had a guide.

Roger Falls was in one of the alcoves, his eyes closed. A tube ran from a hanging bottle, clear liquid flowing to a needle in a hand that seemed much whiter than it had a few hours ago. Sam sat in a chair next to the bed but stood when I approached.

"They're going to keep him overnight," he said. "Just for observation. He was a little hypothermic and had a few scrapes, but other than that, I think he's just worn out. We're waiting for someone to take him to a room."

"Were you ever able to figure out how he got up on that piling?"

Sam shook his head. "I asked, but I didn't get a lot out of him. I don't know if he'll ever remember. He said something about trying to get to the lights."

I thought about the pier. "I guess if you didn't know where the staircase was and saw those rungs, it might look like a ladder up to the top of the pier."

"Especially to an old submarine man. He's still as strong as an ox," Sam went on. "I was afraid he wouldn't let go of the ladder and I'd have to do something to pry him off. Luckily he recognized me."

"Has he ever not? Has he reached that stage yet?"

"So far he's always known me, although sometimes I think he calls me 'son' because he can't quite remember my name. But he was so disoriented by the time I got to him, it took a few moments before he realized who was climbing up behind him."

He leaned forward and pushed a stray hair away from Roger's sleeping face, and as Sam moved into the light, I saw the bandage at his hairline.

"Are you sure you don't want to get that x-rayed?"

He looked at me sharply. "How do you know I didn't already?"

"I didn't think you'd been back here long enough," I said, relieved that I didn't stammer. He held my gaze for a long moment but looked away when his father moaned quietly in his sleep.

"Ready to go?" I hadn't heard the orderly arrive, and I stepped out of his way as he moved around the bed, which I now saw was on wheels, and released the brakes.

"You should go home," Sam told me. "I just wanted to let you know he was going to be okay, and that he'll be spending the night."

"Do you need a ride?" I asked, then remembered we were in Sukey's vintage Mustang, which didn't have much of a back seat.

"No, I'll stay with him. Butchie's going to open up for me in the morning, then get Skip to watch the gas dock while he gives us a ride home."

"Sounds like you're all set, then. 'Bye, Sam." I started to turn, but he touched my arm, and I stopped.

"Thank you, Mercy. I—I might never have found him if you hadn't been with me." His gaze was intense, focused. For a moment I thought he was going to hug me. A great throb of longing, as if I were the one in need of comfort, overtook me. Sam was exhausted, salt-rimed and covered with sand up to his knees, and I'd never wanted so much to be in his arms.

"We're ready to go, sir." At the orderly's voice, the moment disintegrated like so much smoke.

"Call me and let me know how he's doing," I said, and turned toward the maze that led back to the waiting room. I was halfway there before I realized I'd never said, "You're welcome."

"They agreed to the sit-down," said Tino. "Tomorrow night. I gotta figure out what to do with Gus to keep him from following me."

We were sitting on a concrete bench across from the beach near my office. It was still afternoon, and the sun was bright, but I was yawning. I'd made it to the office on time but was glad there hadn't been too many clients. By the time Tino showed up, Gus in tow, I was on about my fifth cup of coffee.

"Maybe you could hypnotize him, then tell him he's got to obey me. Like a regular customer."

"Client," I corrected. "And I already told you, I won't work with anyone who doesn't want to be hypnotized. I won't even do it for underage kids when their parents ask me to, not without the child's consent."

Of course, I'd already pressed Gus, but that had been in the heat of the moment, and I could justify it as an emergency, at least if I told myself he might have hurt himself trying to escape Tino or jumping out of the car.

Gus was, at that moment, acting more like a normal teenager than I would have thought possible. Sukey had gone to her private investigation class, leaving Cupcake to spend the night with me. This time of year, dogs were allowed on the public beach only in the late afternoons and early mornings. We were pushing it at this hour, but it was cool out, the beach was mostly empty, and the police were inclined to look the other way. They'd loved Cupcake since he's helped them capture some scumbags running a child pornography ring a couple of months back.

He'd gotten one of his favorite toys out of Sukey's car before she left—a much-chewed coconut. Gus was busy tossing it into the waves for the dog to retrieve.

Breakwaters positioned every few hundred yards helped the sand build up. Here, waves broke farther out and with less violence than at the Balboa Pier. Gus, who had taken off his basketball shoes and rolled up his jeans, appeared to be having almost as much fun as the dog. Laughter mingled with joyous barking as Gus held the coconut in the air, faked a throw in one direction, then hurled it in another in a perfect imitation of a spiral football pass.

"Has he made any attempt to leave?" I asked.

"Not yet. But I disconnected Hilda's phone line before we went to bed, and locked up all the cell phones and car keys."

"How long do you think you can keep that up?"

"Not long," he admitted. "But once I get this business settled with the *Hombres Locos*, he can go back to Mami's."

"What makes you think he won't go right back to Joaquin's?"

"Because he'll be out of the gang. I'm planning to make that a...condition of my withdrawal as *jefe*."

"You think that'll work?" I had a hard time imagining a bunch of gangbangers sitting around and going over a list of terms, never mind abiding by them afterward.

"If I do it just right, yeah. It'll work. The *Hombres* won't let him back in, especially not if Gordo's in charge."

"I thought you were having second thoughts about Gordo."

He shrugged. "He did good last night with the stuff

we had to take care of. I had a talk with him, told him the other guys need to see him stepping up. He gets it."

I shuddered inwardly at the thought of what "stuff" Tino and Gordo had been managing. "What's to prevent Gus from joining another gang?"

Tino shook his head. "No way. Once he's been in the *Hombres*, he can't even go near one of the other gangs. They'd think he was a spy and probably kill him. He knows that." He stood up and stretched. "I was thinking maybe Sam would let him help out down at the gas dock on weekends. Sam, he's quiet, but I bet no one fucks with him too much. He could be a badass, he wanted to."

Twenty-four hours ago, I might have disagreed, but not now.

"But even if he works for Sam during the day, 'til things are settled I still gotta keep him with me at night. That *niño* decides to go, no one's gonna stop him if I'm not around."

Yeah, once the kid got out, if he made it off the peninsula, there were too many ways for him to get back to Santa Ana. Unless...

"Grant offered to help, right?" Tino nodded, and I went on. "Ask Grant to take him sailing overnight. Then there's no way he can get away until after the sit-down."

"That might work. Ain't no pay phones in the middle of the ocean. The weather supposed to be okay?"

"I don't know, but we can find out."

"I'll call him, get him to meet us for dinner. He can act like it's his idea." Tino already had his phone out, punching the speed dial. I turned to see Gus walking back up the beach toward us. By the time he arrived, Tino had finished the conversation and was pocketing the phone.

"Was that Gordo? Or Joaquin?" Gus pretended not to be too interested as he brushed sand from his feet and then sat on the bench to pull on his shoes, but I could feel the tension in his arm as it brushed my own.

"No, it was Grant. I told you about him."

"The dude who's been helping you with the tests and shit?"

"Yeah, him. We're meeting him for dinner. Mercy, you wanna come?"

My instinct was to say no, but I knew there wasn't any food in my house, and I was too tired to go to the grocery store. "Where are you going?"

"Mutt's. It's pizza night."

Pizza and manipulation. What better way to spend an evening?

10

Mutt Lynch's occupied a corner spot along the board-walk near the Newport Pier, which was even more massive than the Balboa Pier two miles to the south. Mutt's was a popular hangout with the young residents who rented the rows of two-story beach houses in "Sin City," a section of the Newport Beach shoreline a few blocks to the north.

Those houses had been built in the fifties on land leased from the Southern Pacific Railroad, which ran a Red Car line down the peninsula in the early 1900s. Because the terms of the lease prevented the nearly identical duplexes from being torn down and replaced, the neighborhood had mostly escaped the influx of mul-timillion-dollar homes that had changed the character of the area farther south, at least until now. I'd read somewhere that the leases had finally expired, although it was unclear how everything had all been resolved.

After years of uncertainty, most of the houses were a little dilapidated, and many were rented by the week during the summer. Renters could get an off-season lease from Labor Day to Memorial Day for about the same amount per month as the summer weekly rate. Since this corresponded conveniently with the school year, students from the University of California campus in nearby Irvine flocked to Sin City in droves, with six or eight of them pooling funds to live within feet of the sand.

Mutt's was probably the only restaurant on the peninsula that was busy on a Monday night, relatively speaking. It had the biggest windows in town, so it was possible to see the boardwalk and the beach from virtually any seat in the split-level interior. On summer weekends college boys sat in counter seats along the front window and held up paper plates with numbers written on the back, rating bikini-clad pedestrians from one to ten. More than once woman had stomped inside to confront them or complain to the owner, and the police had even gotten involved a time or two. After each such incident, the practice would temporarily disappear. But old traditions die hard, and I had little doubt the ratings system would be resurrected the next time daytime temperatures reached the high seventies.

Gus was looking at the menu, puzzled. "What kind of pizza place is this, man? I never heard of this shit."

"You can get a regular cheese pizza if you're afraid to try something new," said Grant. "But why not broaden your horizons?" He scanned the menu. "I like goat cheese with caramelized onions and roasted red peppers. How does that sound?"

"Goat cheese?" Gus grimaced. "I ain't eating no goat cheese."

"No?" Grant's eyes seemed to sparkle. "How about barbecued shrimp with Thai spices? Or steak, gorgonzola and wild mushroom? I like the sound of that one."

"Ain't they got no pepperoni?"

"Yeah, they got pepperoni," said Tino, pointing to a section of the menu. "They got all the normal stuff. But more *sophisticated* customers like different things. You should try some, it ain't bad. I'm getting the—" he read carefully "—white pizza with artichoke hearts and pancetta."

I held my menu high, hiding my expression. I hadn't been at Mutt's for Tino's first visit, but Sukey had, and she'd told me all about it. His initial reaction had been almost identical to Gus's. I was sure he'd never used the word *sophisticated*, tasted an artichoke or known how to pronounce *pancetta* until pretty recently.

Other than the gourmet pizza, which Mutt's had served well before a couple of popular chains "invented" the idea, the place was beachfront casual. A waitress in cutoff shorts took our order, and Grant requested a pitcher of beer. Gus scowled when the waitress brought only three mugs. He consoled himself with a Coke as we waited for the food.

Grant turned to survey the sunset. "Another clear night. I've been meaning to take a sail over Catalina way, before it gets too cold to sleep aboard."

"You got a boat?" asked Gus.

"He's got a *yacht*," corrected Tino.

Gus perked up. "What's the difference?"

"A yacht," replied Grant, "is generally defined as any vessel being described to any person who is unlikely to ever see it."

Tino laughed, and I smiled at the well-worn joke. "Yeah, but I've seen Grant's boat," said Tino. "And his really *is* a yacht."

"Technically, the *Second Wind*'s a sloop," Grant said. "She's thirty-eight feet long."

"How many bedrooms are there?" asked Gus.

"Cabins. There's a captain's cabin, and the salon—the main living area—has two benches that convert to bunks. There's also a place just forward of the galley—the kitchen—where a smaller person can slide in."

"Is there a bathroom?"

"We call it a head, and yes, there is one, with a shower. Small, but quite adequate."

"Cool."

"I've always thought so," Grant agreed. "I've got a few days with no pressing business, so I'm thinking of heading out tomorrow. Tino, Mercy, either of you have any interest in coming along?"

I shook my head. "You know I love to sail, but I have a couple of busy days at the office. Maybe next time."

"Yeah, I got some business, too," said Tino, and Gus deflated.

"Too bad," said Grant. "I can handle her by myself, but it's a lot easier with a second pair of hands."

"Maybe," said Tino, "Gus could go with you. He ain't busy."

"Me?" Gus almost squeaked.

"Not a bad idea," said Grant. "Have you ever been on a sailboat?"

"I been on a boat, but it didn't have no sails."

"When were you ever on a boat?" Tino asked, but Gus gave him a look that plainly said, "Please don't say anything that will make him change his mind."

"Experience isn't a requirement, it just saves me a little time, explaining what everything's called. But as long as you can take orders—"

"I can take orders."

"—then I'm sure you'll work out fine. What do you say, Tino, can he go? I only plan to stay out the one night—we'd be back in the harbor by late morning."

"Fine by me. What time you want me to bring him by?"

"Nine or ten. The wind doesn't get up much before that."

"Can we bring Cupcake?" Gus nodded toward where the dog was tied to a parking meter near Mutt's front door.

I laughed. "Cupcake loves short sails, but I don't know how he'd be overnight."

"He's one of the best trained dogs I've ever been around. If Sukey says it's okay, I have no objection. But you," Grant said, pointing to Gus, "will have to be on pooper scooper patrol. Cupcake learned to pee over the side about five minutes into his first visit, but I'm afraid to have him try to balance with his rear hanging off the stern."

"No problem," said Gus. He looked almost happy.

* * *

"I need a tune-up," said Hilda. She was in my therapy room, relaxing in the easy chair. "I want you to hypnotize me again."

"You haven't gained back any of the weight," I protested. Hilda had been, ostensibly, my first weight-loss client, although her problem sticking to her diet was more about alcohol than food. Not that she was an alcoholic—she had just been bored, lonely and pining for her lost youth. When she got bored, she drank, and once she was a little buzzed, she completely forgot about her eating plan.

It hadn't been my original intention to turn her into a teetotaler, but, to my knowledge, she hadn't had so much as a sip of champagne since our first session. I'd been feeling a little guilty about that, but it was hardly worth a full session to suggest she might indulge in the occasional Bloody Mary.

In any case, I needed to find out what was really troubling her before I did any "tuning up." Besides, she had insisted on paying for the session, so she should get all the considerations of any other client.

"No, I'm still a size four." She patted her flat belly, which probably owed as much to cosmetic surgery as to diet and exercise. "I've just been kind of stressed lately, and not sleeping all that well."

"Perfectly understandable, with your lover's hoodlum baby brother occupying your house."

She shuddered. "You're right about that. But Gus is just the latest thing. This has been going on for weeks."

"With insomnia, there might be a medical reason. Have you talked to your doctor?"

"I have, and he prescribed pills. They knock me out, but then I'm groggy in the morning. Last time we had a session, I felt so *good* afterward, like nothing could ever bother me again. And I slept like a baby. Now…"

She trailed off, and I nodded. "Okay, let's get started."

I took her through the opening sequence I'd developed, based on my hypnotherapy curriculum at the West Coast Institute for Healing Arts and Sciences. While what I did was not strictly hypnosis, it was what my customers expected and, I'd found, a sound way to start a session.

"Close your eyes. Let yourself relax completely." I supplemented the familiar words with a light press. "It feels good to let all of the tension leave your muscles, doesn't it?"

"It feels *wonderful*." Like all my repeat clients, Hilda embraced the press-induced reverie like an old friend. I was especially careful with repeat customers, because they were, if anything, even more susceptible to my commands.

"Tell me what you want to change about your life."

"I want to be young again."

I sighed. This was exactly how Hilda had started her last session, and I'd never really addressed this issue. I'd given it some thought in the interim, but not so much that I felt prepared to simply tell her to accept her true age—whatever that was—and move on. Refusing to age gracefully was such a core part of her personality that I was reluctant to mess with it. Instead, I focused on the stated issue.

"Tell me what happens when you try to sleep."

"Thoughts keep me awake."

"Tell me about the thoughts."

"I worry about Tino. All the time."

This surprised me. At least on the surface, Hilda showed an amazing lack of concern about Tino's more nefarious activities.

"Are you worried that he will…get hurt?"

"Yes, sometimes."

"Is that the main worry?"

"No. I'm worried that he'll leave me because I'm old."

This made more sense. I understood—sort of—how the whole Hilda/Tino thing had gotten started. He was young, hot and, once you got to know him, basically a good guy. Hilda was his passport into a world of money and privilege. And she was undeniably beautiful, even if she had fattened her cosmetic surgeon's bank account to stay that way.

But, I had to admit, I'd thought the bloom would be off the rose by now, on both sides. Tino had a plan to make his own fortune and was constantly being approached by younger women. And Hilda needed… what? I guessed that was what I should be trying to find out.

"Tell me how you feel about your relationship with Tino, and where you see it going."

"I'm crazy about him," she said. "He's fun, and he's

gorgeous. I enjoy taking him places and showing him new things. He makes me laugh. And he's fabulous in bed."

Too much information was a common hazard of my work.

"I want him to stay with me," she went on. "I think he will—for a while. But, eventually, I'm not going to be able to keep it up anymore."

"Keep what up?"

"Hiding my age. And pretending that he's—that he's not..."

She trailed off, frowning. Under the press, she would be incapable of evasion or dishonesty. Therefore, her pause meant she hadn't thought this out for herself yet. I waited.

"I'm afraid I'll have to admit that he's never really going to be sophisticated enough for me," she finally said. "I'll get bored with him."

"Tell me," I asked, pressing cautiously—I didn't want to suggest anything, just get clarification. "Are you bored with him now?"

"No," she said without hesitation. "I'm having a great time. I'm just afraid it won't last."

I sighed. It hadn't been my intention to pry into the details of their relationship; I just wanted to know what was keeping Hilda up at night. If she'd been a stranger, my knowing that her love affair had a limited shelf life wouldn't matter to either of us. As it was, this had the potential to be uncomfortable. Unless I direct them otherwise, my clients remember everything that goes on in a session. Maybe it would be kinder if I induced some memory loss—then only one of us would feel awkward. But, no, that didn't seem honest. I'd only blocked out a client's memory of part of a session on one occasion, for a self-serving reason, and I still felt guilty every time I thought about it.

"Okay, Hilda, from now on, when you are ready to go to sleep at night, you will feel very relaxed. If you start to have worries about Tino and your relationship, you will find it easy to release them. Will you be able to relax when it's time to sleep, Hilda?"

"Yes," she replied, and I could already hear the relief in her voice.

I debated with myself over the next bit, but ultimately decided I owed it to Hilda to continue. "You no longer feel an aversion to alcohol. If you want to have a drink, you will feel comfortable doing so." She started to nod, and I hastily added, "You will drink alcohol only when it is appropriate, and in moderation. Do you understand?"

"Only when appropriate, and in moderation," she repeated, smiling. She was probably already planning her first martini.

"If you drink alcohol, you will not drive until after the effects have completely worn off," I added.

I finished the session with my usual mild presses to feel relaxed and renewed. When we were done, she got up, then turned to me, puzzled.

"What was that last bit all about?" she asked. "I didn't mention drinking, did I?"

"No," I admitted. "But in our last session, I gave you a—a post-hypnotic suggestion to avoid alcohol. I only did it to help you stay on your diet. I didn't think it was necessary anymore. The suggestion would eventually wear off on its own, but as long as you were hypnotized, I decided to go ahead and release it."

"I see," she said. She opened the door to the outer office, and I heard the sound of Sukey's laughter and caught a glimpse of Tino leaning against the wall opposite her desk.

"Tino was just telling me about Gus and Grant," she said, wiping her eyes. "Tell Mercy about the shorts."

"I just dropped Gus off at the marina," he said. "And he was wearing his leather jacket and his jeans—like he normally wears, you know?"

Hilda and I nodded.

"And Grant says the leather jacket is going to be too heavy, so he argues some, but he takes it off and gives it to me. Then Grant says—" Tino bent over and beetled his brows in a remarkably good imitation of Grant "'—sailors don't wear jeans because, if you fall in, they're too heavy. And you're going to slide all over the deck in those basketball shoes.'" He resumed his normal posture and went on. "So he goes down below and comes up with this pair of shorts—can't have been his, because they're way too small, and these old deck shoes, and tells Gus 'Here, put these on.' And Gus is like, 'No way, man. *Hombres Locos* don't wear no fucking shorts.'" His impression of Gus was even better than that of Grant.

"So I tell him, 'Ain't no *Hombres* gonna see you out

in the middle of the ocean, man, so change your damn pants, *niño*.' He's so mad, I swear he almost changed his mind about going. But he goes down into the cabin, and when he comes back up, he's got the shorts on. His legs are white as paper, and his face is all dark red 'cause he's embarrassed. He looks so funny, I get out my cell phone—" he lifted his phone, demonstrating "—and I take his picture. He was like, 'Aw, man, what you wanna do that for?' and I said, 'Tomorrow, when you get back, I'm gonna ask Grant how you acted, and if he says you messed up, I'm gonna send this picture to all the *Hombres*, starting with Joaquin.' I'm pretty sure he's gonna behave himself."

"Let me see the picture," said Hilda, and Tino punched a couple of buttons and then handed it over. She looked at the display, and laughed. "Oh, my, look at his face. He's furious."

"He'll be fine. He was already getting interested in the stuff on the boat by the time I left. But I'm gonna keep this picture just in case I need a little—what's it called? Oh, yeah, *leverage* later."

"Did you come by to give me a ride home?" asked Hilda, returning the phone to Tino. "Because I've got the Mercedes." She glanced toward me, and I could tell she was thinking about what she'd just admitted in the therapy room.

"Yeah, I saw it," he said. "I want to talk to Mercy for a minute." He turned to me. "You got time?"

"There's a half hour before my next appointment," I told him. "Let's go to Alta Coffee."

"I'm going to stay here. I have studying to do," said Sukey. "Quiz tonight."

Tino looked relieved. Whatever he wanted to say, he didn't want to do it in front of her.

"I'll see you later, then?" asked Hilda.

"Yeah, I'm going back to the house after this." He kissed her lightly, and we all headed out the door, Hilda toward the parking lot, and Tino and I diagonally across the street to talk.

11

It was cool on Alta's shady patio, but more private than indoors, and Tino headed there as soon as we both had our cups.

"I been thinking about the meeting tonight," he said. "I want you to come."

My stomach gave a sudden flip, and the excellent coffee took on a bitter taste. "Tino," I said, "even your mother thought it was weird for you to be talking *Hombres* business with a woman. What makes you think the people you're meeting with are even going to let me in?"

"They'll let you in if I tell them to," he said with bravado, but I shook my head.

"The *Hombres*, maybe. But aren't those other guys going to be there—the *Tiburónes* and…what's the group from Ghost Town called?"

"The *Hermandad.* Yeah, but just three of each. The leader and two *tenientes*—everyone else gotta stay outside. I was going to bring Gordo and Joaquin, but those two don't get along so well, and I can't trust Joaquin to hold his temper. So, instead, I'm gonna bring Gordo and you." He gave me what was probably supposed to be an appealing smile and took a sip of his coffee.

"First, isn't that going to piss off Joaquin? And second—" I looked around to see if anyone was paying attention, but we had the patio to ourselves and none of the staff was near the door "—how are you going to explain bringing a nonmember, a woman, to the sit-down?"

He grinned. "I thought about dressing you up as a dude, but—" He glanced appreciatively at my breasts. "*That* ain't gonna work."

"I'm serious, Tino. There's no way they're going to let me in."

"Yeah, they are. See, the *Hermandad* operates in L.A. County, right?" I nodded, and he went on. "Well, you know last year, when they had the big sit-down with the police and all that shit?"

I vaguely remembered. A couple of times in recent years, multiple branches of law enforcement, gang leadership and some church-based organizations had negotiated what amounted to peace treaties between the highest profile Los Angeles gangs. These had been, at least temporarily, effective, and the strategy had become a model in anti-gang violence initiatives all over the country.

"It was mainly the Crips, Bloods and the Latin Kings, right? But other gangs had representatives there, too. The *Hermandad* was one of them."

"Where are you going with this, Tino?"

"Just listen to what I'm saying here. It went pretty good for the *Hermandad*, who were having some trouble with the Kings over some territory north of Ghost Town. So they know about, like, working with outside negotiators."

"But if I come in with you, there's no way they're going to accept that I'm an impartial third party. They're not going to believe you."

"No, but they'll believe *you*. You just hypnotize them, and they'll do whatever you say."

"Tino, we've talked about this, and I told you, it doesn't work that way."

"It worked pretty fucking good on Marisol, back at the projects." His tone was losing some of its persuasiveness and starting to sound pissed. "And when you got Gus to stop, when I was chasing him. You gonna tell me that wasn't something you did?"

Careful, I warned myself.

He waited, and I thought. I didn't want to do this, not even a little. I could refuse and, if he kept arguing, press him to get off my case.

But how would pressing Tino, without his knowledge or consent, be any less wrong than pressing a bunch of gang members?

I pictured a room full of killers and sociopaths, all undoubtedly armed, and shuddered.

"You're scared, right?" Tino no longer sounded menacing.

"Fucking-A right, I'm scared. Tino, these guys are killers. Hypnosis isn't going to do me much good if they decide to start shooting each other."

"No way," he said. "They agree to a sit down, it's guaranteed no fighting. Everyone takes off their guns— one of the reasons the *tenientes* are there is so we can all search each other. It's at a neutral place, and no one is allowed to come within this, like, safe zone around the building, and the guards—we each get one at the door—can't fuck with anyone coming in or out. Long as I can remember, no one ever got killed at a sit-down."

"I notice you say, 'killed at,' not '*hurt* at,' or 'killed *after*.'"

"Mercy, if it was just for me, I would handle this by myself. But I promised Mami I'd make sure that when I left the gang, I'd set it up so Gus would be okay."

Yeah, hit me with the maternal guilt card. Good timing.

"If, hypothetically, I were to agree to come to this meeting…" Tino started to grin, and I went on. "And I'm not saying I'll agree, what would I be doing, exactly?"

He'd been ready for this, and took a piece of paper out of his pocket and unfolded it. I was surprised to see it was typewritten—probably done on Hilda's computer. I wondered if she'd helped him with it, or if Grant had, which was probably more likely.

"You read off my terms, one at a time. Then you hyp-notize them to say they agree." He handed me the paper, and I read aloud.

"One. All members of the *Tiburónes* and the *Her-mandad* will recognize Luis Vasquez Quintillo as the new *jefe* of the *Hombres Locos*."

"That's Gordo's real name. Maybe I should put that in—'known as Gordo,' something like that." He bit his lip, and I thought about how hard he must have worked on this list.

"Two. After *Señor* Quintillo becomes the *jefe*, the borders of the turf controlled by the *Hombres Locos* will remain at their current location." I looked at him. "Didn't you say the *Tiburónes* were trying to take over some of the territory?"

"Yeah, that's why that's in here."

"But they might not agree about where the 'current location' is. You probably want to put down the exact streets and blocks." I heard myself and winced—he might think that because I was offering suggestions, I was agreeing to attend the meeting. Which I wasn't.

"Okay," he said. "That's a good idea. Also, it gives us some…what does Grant call them? Some negotiating points, in case we gotta give something up to make it work for everybody. There's a couple of blocks there, not too much happens on them, I'd be willing to let go, maybe."

"Three. Javier Augustín Pelón—" I looked up, puzzled.

"I gotta put in 'known as Tino.'"

Nice name. "Will receive twenty percent of the revenues received by the *Hombres Locos* from the following lines of business. Neighborhood insurance payments collected from businesses in the territory described in item two."

I looked up. "The *Hombres* collect *protection* money?"

"Yeah, and we earn it, too. Someone breaks in to one of those places or causes trouble, we take care of it."

"Like Flaco did for your mother?"

"Sort of. That was our apartment, not a business."

"Are they going to agree to this? Sounds to me like they were collecting this money before you came along."

"Some of it," he admitted. "I expanded the territory, got it all organized."

"Maybe this should be one of those negotiating points you were talking about."

"Yeah, maybe. Keep reading."

"Car and parts sales to All Star Auto Body." A chop shop, I assumed.

"Sales of recreational materials inside the turf described in item two. Shit, Tino, is this about drug sales?"

He shrugged. "What do you think? Where'd you meet me, anyway?"

He had a point. He'd admitted distributing drugs during our very first conversation. I'd somehow managed to avoid thinking about it in the intervening months.

"You know, this money stuff, this seems like internal *Hombres* business. The *Tiburónes* and the *Hermandad* aren't going to have anything to say about it. In fact, the only thing on here—" I scanned the rest of the document, which listed a few more businesses "—that even concerns the *Tiburónes* is the one about the borders."

"That ain't true. First, it's important they see Gordo's the new boss. And they'll hear Gordo agree to the payment stuff, which is good—it reminds them that the

Hombres are strong, got a lot of respect in the *barrio*. But the most important thing is, once Gordo says he gonna do it, and the *Hermandad* kind of, you know, put their blessing on it, then guys like Joaquin and Nestor, they're more likely to go along."

Which will give them even more reason to resent being left out of the negotiations, I thought.

"Are you so sure the *Hermandad* is going to do it? Give you their blessing, I mean?"

"I told you, that's where you come in. You hypnotize them, they agree to all of it."

I shook my head. "There are going to be…how many people in the room besides you and me? Seven?"

"More than that, if the *Hermandad* invite someone from the Blood Brothers. Probably they won't."

"What about the Vietnamese gang?"

"No way. They stay in their neighborhood. They wouldn't recognize the agreement, anyway—they keep to themselves."

"Tino, I don't think I can pr—that I can hypnotize seven people at one time."

"You ever try?"

"No." Though I'd done a couple of two-fers a few months back, and it had worked out just fine.

"Maybe you could practice. We could go to the mall or something—"

"Tino…" He was starting to sound like Sukey.

"Okay, forget it. Just an idea. But you wouldn't have to hypnotize everyone. I already talked to Gordo, and he's gonna go along with everything. The *tenientes* gonna do whatever their *jefes* say. So, really, it's just two guys."

"Do they both speak good English?"

"Yeah, man, they're all Chicanos, like me. And they might agree to it all on their own. You might not have to do anything but read the paper."

I couldn't believe I was starting to consider the idea. I was, I had to admit, intrigued. I'd seen TV specials on gangs, which played up the violence and volatility of the members. But a lot of the guys they interviewed were surprisingly articulate. Certainly Tino was smart—he wouldn't have survived, never mind taken over the gang while still in his early twenties, if he wasn't. I wondered what the other *jefes* would be like.

"I been thinking about what you should wear. Gordo and me, we gotta be in our colors. You show up in *Hombres* colors, it's maybe the wrong message. But you gotta be careful you're not wearing one other gang's colors. So the best thing is you wear all black. Not a problem for you, I'll bet." He grinned—he'd heard Sukey call my closet "the black hole."

"Tino, I haven't said I'd do this." But, mentally, I was already picking out an outfit—black jeans, T-shirt and athletic shoes.

He ignored me. "Nothing sexy, no makeup and nothing low-cut. We don't want their minds on anything but the negotiations. And no shoes with a logo on them."

Scratch the athletic shoes. That brought me back to reality. Rose, my friend who ran a battered women and children's shelter, said that in some Southern California neighborhoods, you could die because you wore the wrong brand of basketball shoes.

I was shaking my head again, about to speak, when Tino's cell phone trilled. He looked at the readout and grimaced, but punched a button.

"Mami. What's up?"

I could hear Spanish coming through the receiver, and, even if I couldn't make out the words, the tone seemed agitated.

"Mami, Nestor ain't got no business on St. Gertrude. I already told Joaquin, Gus ain't there, and he knows it's neutral—we don't do no business on that block. You didn't let him in, did you?"

He listened for a while, then went on. "Nestor got something to say to me, he needs to go through Gordo. Gordo's got my cell number."

Teresa's voice seemed less strident, or maybe Tino was holding the phone at a different angle.

"Mami, I'll take care of it. It's all gonna be settled tonight, and no one should be messing with you after that. Gus? He's fine—nothing to worry about. I promise, Mami, I got it handled, okay?

"*Sí,* Mami, I love you, too. I'll come see you tomorrow, okay? Take you for a ride, get some dinner. Of course I like your cooking. I just thought…okay, Mami, I'll call you. *Hasta mañana.*"

He ended the call, glowering. "What the fuck does Joaquin think he's doing, sending Nestor over to Mami's? Nestor wouldn't go over there on his own."

"Maybe they didn't believe that Gus really isn't there," I suggested.

"I'm still the *jefe*—until tonight, anyway. I say Gus isn't there, then he ain't there. Even if he *is* there, you know what I mean?" There was a look in Tino's eye that would have made me step back if I'd been the reason for it.

"Does Joaquin know you're planning to make Gordo *jefe* tonight?"

"If he don't, he's stupid. Which he ain't."

"Do you think he might try to stop it from happening?"

He scowled. "No. Maybe." He put his head in his hands, a gesture so uncharacteristic as to be startling. "I don't think he's ready. He'd have to get most of the *Hombres* to go along with him, and, except for Nestor, nobody's going to go against me."

"Would they go against Gordo?"

"Not once the *Hermandad* recognizes him. Which is why—" He turned to me, his expression almost pleading. "I got to have an ace up my sleeve at this meeting tonight. You."

He put his hands flat on the table and stared at them. "Mercy, when Grant and me first started talking about starting a new life—a good life, one where I don't have to worry about getting arrested or killed, or something happening to my family…" He looked up, staring intensely, as if he were trying to drill his meaning into my head. "I thought it was just a dream, you know? But then I took my real estate exam, and we did this business model, talked to investors, and it…it all seems like it can really happen. Grant wants me to forget the *Hombres,* move Mami down here somewhere, put all that behind me."

He smiled, but it was a ghost of his normal pirate's expression. "Grant don't know Mami. It's gonna take a SWAT team to get her out of that house. When Flaco was the boss, then me, we kept everyone off that street. But when I'm gone, I can't be sure. There's people might mess with her, just because they had something to settle with Flaco."

"You're worried for her safety?"

"If I just walk away like Grant wants, yeah. Gus is too young to protect her, and he don't have no standing in the gang, not yet. What respect he's got, it's because he's Flaco's son and my brother. But with Flaco dead and me gone…" He shrugged.

"Do you really think you can get her to move out of the neighborhood?"

"It won't be easy but, if Gus comes, too, yeah. She ain't gonna leave as long as Gus is still in the *barrio,* though."

"And to keep Gus out of the gang—"

"I gotta make sure Gordo is *jefe.* And for that, I need the *Hermandad.*"

And for that, he needed me.

Life was so much simpler before I had friends.

The Rendezvous Ballroom was located upstairs over some Main Street shops that had, so far, managed to escape the renovation taking place just a few blocks away. According to Tino, it had been the venue for countless wedding receptions, anniversary parties and *quinceañera* celebrations—the Latino version of the coming-out party, given on or shortly after a girl's fifteenth birthday. For that reason, it was neutral.

An enormous disco ball hung from the ceiling, about a quarter of its mirror tiles missing. A few spotlights with red, blue and green lenses were mounted nearby. An empty bar ran along one wall, opposite a stage framed by dusty purple velvet curtains. Stark illumination from hanging fluorescent lights lent a dismal quality to the room. One, thankfully not over the table, flickered at about the same rate as the pounding of my heart. The windows that ran along the front were too high to reveal anything except the tops of streetlights.

Too high for someone to shoot through.

We'd met Gordo in the parking lot at Papi's, the drab Santa Ana bar where I'd first encountered Tino. It hadn't changed since I'd last been here—a concrete square in the middle of a parking lot strewn with broken glass. I saw that the graffiti I'd noticed on my first visit hadn't been painted over: *Gangsta Girls* and, more prominently, *Mad Tino*. Now that I recognized it, the *Hombres Locos* symbol was ubiquitous. We were too deep in *Hombres* territory for the *Tiburónes'* shark to be displayed.

Gordo turned out to be at least as big as his name implied, but, despite his enormous gut, he looked too solid to be properly called fat. He had more tattoos than Tino, a bullet-shaped shaved head, and a single eyebrow that stretched across his forehead like a wooly scar.

"Who's she?" Gordo's voice was surprisingly soft,

with a not-unpleasant hit of gravel. He didn't look at me after his initial sizing up.

"She's a negotiator. She's coming with us." Tino's tone implied that the matter was not open for discussion, and Gordo nodded. The other guys—I counted twelve of them leaning against the building and cars—shifted uncomfortably, cutting their eyes at me and away again. There was a quiet buzz of comment, which Tino ignored.

Inside the bar, I recognized Papi, his basset-hound eyes sadder than ever, carefully not watching as Tino, Gordo and a few of the other men gathered around a table and spoke in Spanish. I waited at the bar, and saw Tino point to me and use the word *negociador*. The other men didn't seem quite as sanguine about the idea as Gordo, but, from what I could make out, Tino wasn't opening the table for debate. They spoke for only a few minutes before Tino stood and called to me.

"We're ready to go. Come on, Gordo's riding with us." I followed him out of the bar, avoiding looking at the other *Hombres*. I hesitated, not sure which car door to open, and Gordo solved my dilemma by sliding into the front. Most of the other men resumed their casual poses, but four got into a club-cab truck with heavily tinted windows and too much chrome. As we pulled out of the parking lot, they trailed behind us.

"Tino, I wanted to ask—which of those guys are Joaquin and Nestor?"

"They didn't show up," said Tino, and Gordo punctuated the statement by muttering a couple of Spanish curses and spitting out the window. "I already told Joaquin he wasn't coming inside at the sit-down. But they still should have been at Papi's. I woulda had them in the backup car."

"Backup car?"

"They park on the street outside the Rendezvous. Make sure no one comes inside and interrupts the meeting. Also, they can, like, carry in a message if it's an emergency, but someone from the *Hermandad* gotta search them first."

I nodded and sat back in the seat, taking very deep breaths. I could press him to stop the car and let me out. I didn't have to do this. It wasn't too late.

But we were already pulling onto Main Street, and within a few blocks we pulled over and Tino stopped the engine. I looked at my watch. It was a couple of minutes before eleven, and there were only four other cars parked on the block. From what Tino had told me, there would be two cars from each gang. That meant the *Tiburónes* and the *Hermandad* were already here.

The truck's door opened, and one of the *Hombres* walked over to where two men stood on the sidewalk, next to a doorway with a set of stairs leading up. A sign above the doorway said *Rendezvous Ballroom* in fading neon. Without any discernible greeting, the *Hombre* got in line next to the other two men.

"Are we going in?" I asked. Not that I was in a hurry,

"Be patient. We go last, because I asked for the meeting." He pointed. "See, those guys are from the *Hermandad*. They're going first."

Three men got out of a black Escalade and approached the trio next to the doorway. One by one, they held up their arms and submitted to what looked like a very thorough pat-down by two of the waiting men, including the guy from the *Hombres Locos*. I shuddered—I would have to go through the same gauntlet before I could get in that door.

It wasn't too late, I repeated silently. I could still back out. I swallowed to keep from speaking, afraid anything I said would contain a press.

As soon as the three arrivals had finished being searched and filed up the stairs, a second car door opened. The three men who got out looked, to my untrained eyes, identical to the first group—leather jackets over bulky sweatshirts and black jeans—but I knew to look for the red bandanas.

"Hijos de putas." Gordo's shoulders had tensed as the men crossed the street. "Couple of them were trying to jack a car off Grand, right down the block from the auto body shop. I tell you that?"

"After tonight, they'll know to stay out of that neighborhood," said Tino. "Stay cool, Gordo, and it's all gonna come out like we talked about. You'll see. Trust me—Mercy can talk anyone into doing anything."

Gordo grunted, and I thought I discerned skepticism in the sound. I couldn't blame him. I hadn't spoken five sentences since we'd met.

The second trio were searched and disappeared up the steps. "Come on, we're up." Tino opened his door, and Gordo did the same. I put my hand on the door handle but couldn't seem to pull it. I looked up to find Gordo's expressionless face staring in at me. He opened the back door and stood back. I saw the three men, two of whom were waiting to search me, and wondered what they were thinking about my hesitation. Crap. It took me a second, but I managed to swing my legs out of the car and stand up.

When we walked over to the doorway, Gordo raised his arms and let the *Tiburónes* and *Hermandad* goons begin the search. Tino nodded for me to go ahead of him, and I took a step forward.

"You brought a *gringa?*" sneered the one with the red bandana, the shorter of the two.

"None of your business," said Tino without rancor. "Just do your job."

"Hey, man, just asking. I rather pat her down than you." He grinned at me, and I repressed a shudder. "Turn around, Mami, Paco's gonna feel you up."

I resisted the temptation to compel him to attempt a few anatomically impossible acts, took a deep breath, turned my back and raised my arms. I was trembling and knew Paco could feel it. He settled his hands on either side of my waist and leaned forward to speak into my ear.

"I'm going to enjoy this."

"Just check me for weapons like you would anyone else." The press was subtle enough that I didn't think the other men would notice. Paco patted me down thoroughly but without groping, and I managed not to gag. I stood back as the *Hermandad* representative finished with Tino. I half expected them to find something, even though I'd watched him remove his guns and knives, and turn off his cell phone. Everything was in the Malibu's trunk, and I had the feeling Tino was feeling pretty naked without his usual complement of fire-power.

"I need you to point out which men are the leaders so I know who to hypnotize first," I said as we filed up the stairs. I was pretty sure that the guys waiting at the top weren't going to be as accepting of my presence as Paco had been, and I would probably need to press quickly.

"The *Hermandad's jefe* is Chuco. He got a big scar on his cheek. The *Tiburónes* guy calls himself Gato. His real name is Felix." In other circumstances, I might have found someone named Felix referring to himself as a cat funny, but not today. "He'll be the one running his mouth."

Someone had pulled a large round folding table into the center of the room, and nine metal chairs were arranged around it. The rest of the men were standing, waiting for us. They stared, faces expressionless. A feeling of unreality gripped me. The deserted ballroom looked like the set of a Tarantino movie, its shabby theatricality too contrived to be real.

But this was real, all right. The sheer physical presence of the men waiting at the table was tangible, like the buzz you hear near big electrical transformers.

I think I would have known Chuco even without the description. He had an intensity that drew the eye. He glanced at me for only a second, but I had the feeling he'd taken in every detail. My skin prickled. I realized

I was looking at the top of the food chain, at least in this neighborhood.

"Tino. Gordo." Chuco gave an infinitesimal nod.

"Chuco," Tino responded, and Gordo nodded.

"I'm gonna assume you got a good reason for bringing an outsider."

"Fuckin' A." The new voice came from one side, and I checked out its source. A muscular man in a black undershirt glared at me. I had time to register a jeweled earring in the shape of a cat before I returned my attention to Chuco.

Showtime. I focused on Chuco and pressed.

"I'm a professional negotiator. It's okay for me to be here."

Chuco narrowed his eyes and looked directly into my face for the first time. For a second I thought the press hadn't worked. Then he nodded.

"A negotiator, huh? Okay."

"What's this shit?" Gato took a step toward me, and I felt, rather than saw, Tino move up on my left. "You just gonna take her word for it?"

I was about to direct the same statement at Gato when Chuco spoke up.

"I said it's okay. You got a problem with that?"

"Yeah, I got a problem with that. A woman? And what's this shit about her being a negotiator? We don't need no fucking outsider, tell us what to do."

"It's okay for me to be here," I cut in. I aimed my press at Gato, but I tried to let the influence spread to the two men who flanked him, too.

"But *you* say it's okay," Gato went on, still directing his comments at Chuco, "we're good with that."

"It's okay for me to be here," I repeated a third time, this time sending my press toward Chuco's two companions. If a little bit of authority flowed over onto Gordo, who was standing nearest to them, so much the better.

"We ready to sit down?" asked Tino, and at a nod from Chuco, we all approached the table. Chuco sat facing the door, his *tenientes* on either side. The *Tiburónes* clustered to his left and Gordo and Tino to his right, leaving me to sit with my back to the door. I wasn't too comfortable with the position but figured it was the least of my worries. Everyone looked at Chuco. I realized he was older than I'd first thought—in his fifties, maybe. His buzzed hair was peppered with gray.

He returned each person's gaze, one by one. "Tino, this is your party. Why don't you tell us why we're all here."

Tino cleared his throat, and, for the first time, I realized he was nervous, too. I didn't blame him. There was a look about the three *Hermandad* members, the *tenientes* as well as Chuco, that was, indefinably, more serious than any of the *Hombres Locos* or the *Tiburónes*. This was the major leagues.

"I want to thank Chuco for showing me the *respect*—" Tino's glance flicked briefly toward Gato "—to agree to this sit-down. It does the *Hombres Locos* honor, and I appreciate it."

Chuco nodded in acknowledgement. His two companions might have been carved from granite.

"I also want to thank Gato and the other members of the *Tiburónes* for setting differences aside and coming down here tonight." Gato and his *compadres* glanced at each other but remained silent. Tino went on. "I hope that we can all come to an agreement that will guarantee peace for the Santa Ana neighborhoods in the future."

I realized this was a rehearsed speech, and I thought he'd delivered it well.

"The reason I asked for the sit-down was because I'm planning to step down as the *jefe* of the *Hombres Locos*."

"What?" Gato's posture went rigid. "What's that mean, 'step down'? You quittin', man?"

"Explain what you mean," said Chuco.

"I mean I'm not going to be involved in the day-to-day operations no more. I'll be retired."

"Retired?" Gato snorted. "You don't retire from no gang, Tino. What, you think you gonna get social security or something?"

"Let him talk, Gato," said Chuco quietly, and the other man slumped back in his seat, arms folded. Chuco turned his attention back to Tino. "This ain't exactly normal, Tino. Usually, someone only leaves the gang when they got to."

"I know. They get sent up for a long time, or they get shot up so bad they can't get around no more."

"Or they're dead," Gato chimed in, sneering. "Like Flaco."

Gordo made as if to get to his feet, but Tino put a hand on his arm, and the larger man settled heavily into his chair.

"Like I said, I know it ain't normal. That's why I wanted this sit-down. I got…I got an opportunity. It's a hundred percent legit, and it ain't in Santa Ana. But to do it, I gotta, like, separate myself from all this." Tino's gesture encompassed the table, the room, the entire city.

"So it's like, 'I got some *opportunity*—'" Gato's scorn was tangible "'—so fuck the *barrio*, fuck everybody, I'm outta here.' That what you saying, Tino?"

Chuco held up his hand, and again Gato shut his mouth, but the look the *jefe* gave Tino was far from friendly.

"I said I'd let you talk, Tino, but it's like Gato said. Sounds like you're walking out on the *barrio*."

"It ain't like that," said Tino. "That's another reason I asked for the sit-down. I want to make sure the *barrio's* taken care of, and that nobody—" he glared at Gato "—thinks that just because I ain't *jefe* no more, they can take advantage, you know?"

"You can listen to his terms," I added, directing a press toward Chuco. "It can't do any harm to hear what they are."

Gato made a derisive noise and opened his mouth to speak. I turned to him. "You can listen to his terms, too," I added.

"We came all the way down here to hear what you got to say," said Chuco. "We may as well hear it."

Gordo shifted uncomfortably on my left. He was probably curious why everyone kept agreeing to everything I said. So far, I hadn't done anything to press him directly.

Tino nodded toward me. "Mercy, please read the terms."

I took out the printout that included Tino's latest revisions and unfolded it. I paused and looked around at the men, and tried to encompass all of them in my intent. This would be my first attempt at a true group press. I wished Chuco and Gato were sitting next to each other, so I could concentrate my efforts on the two of them, but there were two other men between them. So far I'd had to repeat everything, which, I supposed, I could just keep doing if necessary.

Here goes nothing, I thought.

Returning my focus to the printed page, I read aloud. "One. All members of the *Tiburónes* and the *Hermandad* will recognize Luis Vasquez Quintillo, known as Gordo, as the new *jefe* of the *Hombres Locos*."

Chuco nodded, immediately echoed by the other two *Hermandad* members. I looked at Gato to see if my press had worked on him.

He shrugged. "I got no problem with Gordo." I wasn't sure if that meant he'd been pressed or not. If it didn't, the next item on Tino's list would probably tell me. I continued.

"Two. After Gordo becomes the *jefe*, the borders of the territory controlled by the *Hombres Locos*—"

Raised voices erupted downstairs, and I stopped and turned my head just as all of the men at the table got to their feet in unison. A couple of metal folding chairs clattered to the floor.

The *Hermandad* member who'd searched Gordo

and Tino appeared at the top of the stairs and stepped into the room.

"What's this shit?" said Gato. "No one's supposed to come up here but us."

"I told you to stay downstairs," said Chuco.

"I'm sorry, *Jefe*, but one of the *Hombres*, guy named Jaime, says there's an emergency. Something to do with Tino's family."

"Let the fuck *go* of me," came a voice from the stairway. "I told you, it's a fucking emergency."

Tino started toward the stairs, but the man on Chuco's right shot out a hand to restrain him.

"It's okay, let him come up," said Chuco.

"What is it, Jaime?" asked Tino, shaking off the man's hand. "Is it Gustavo? I'll fucking kill him— how'd that little *pendejo* get away from Grant?"

Jaime appeared at the top of the stairs, panting. "It ain't Gus, Tino. It's Teresa. She's been shot."

12

The emergency room at the San Gabriel Hospital in Santa Ana didn't look much like the one at Hoag. There, one lost old man had warranted a newspaper reporter. Here, no one took any special notice of a gunshot wound. The waiting area was packed, the nurse behind the desk was harried, and the whole place smelled of antiseptic and fear.

"I'm sorry, I don't have any information for you," the nurse told Tino when we finally made our way to the front of the line.

"Listen, *mujer,* it's my Mami back there, and—"

I interrupted him before he could reach over the counter and strangle the poor woman. "Let me." I caught his eye, and he got my meaning and moved to let me stand in front of the desk.

"Tell us what you know about Teresa Pelón," I said, pressing.

The woman turned to her computer and tapped on the keyboard. "She came in at 11:08, by ambulance, with a gunshot wound to the abdomen." She looked up. "She went straight in. It doesn't say where she is now, or which doctor is seeing her. They don't usually update the computer file until the end of the shift, or if they get a break."

"Is there someone you can call who'll know something?"

"Maybe."

"Do it." She nodded and dialed. "Yolie? Hi, it's Maria. You got a gunshot wound back there, a woman?" There was a pause. "Yeah, that's her. What doctor? You know how she's doing? Was she...*sí, sí, gracias,* Yolie." She hung up and looked at us.

"She's with Doctor Rashad. Yolie doesn't know anything, but the doctor didn't call for a trauma team or a crash cart."

I considered pressing our way into the patient area, but thought about Tino, in his agitated state, pushing curtains aside and threatening staff, and decided against it. "If you don't hear anything, call again in a few minutes. Okay? Let us know what you find out."

"Okay."

I managed to steer Tino back to one of the chairs. Gordo, Jaime and the other guys from the backup car hovered near the entrance, making the people waiting nearby distinctly uneasy. Gordo threaded his way over to where Tino was slumped.

"*Jefe,* you want me to go over to the house, see if the neighbors know anything?"

"Yeah, but leave your guns off. You're gonna run in to cops, asking questions." Tino looked up. "Not that anyone's gonna tell them nothing."

Gordo nodded but didn't move.

"Why you still standing here?" Tino snapped.

Gordo didn't exactly shuffle his feet, but he looked uncomfortable. "I was wondering…" He stopped, and I saw him swallow.

"What the *fuck*, Gordo. You got something to say, say it."

The big man lowered his voice, so that only Tino and I could hear. "The *Hermandad* agreed on me being *jefe*, right?"

Tino blew out a frustrated breath. "You were there, Gordo. Yeah, they agreed. The *Tiburónes,* too. What's your point?"

"When do I take over? I mean, they already agreed."

"You take over when I *say* you take over." Tino was trying to keep his voice low, but he was agitated, and the statement drew a couple of quickly averted glances from other people in the waiting room. In this neighborhood, most of them probably knew who he was.

"Okay, *jefe*. I find out something, I'll call." He left, taking a couple of the men lurking at the door with him.

"It ain't no coincidence, this happening just before the sit-down," Tino said for about the twentieth time.

He fidgeted, unsure of what to do with his hands. "I tell you one thing, I'm glad Gus is with Grant. If I had to worry about him right now, I'd go crazy."

"Have you called Hilda?" I asked.

"No. She'd just get all hyper, want to come up here."

"She expecting you tonight?"

"No," he said, then shrugged. "Maybe. I told her I'd let her know how the sit-down went. Maybe I better…"

He pulled the phone out of his pocket. Tino and Gordo had gotten their phones and guns out of the Malibu's trunk as soon as they'd run out of the Rendez-vous. For a minute I'd thought the guys in the *Tiburón* and *Hermandad* backup cars would misinterpret the action and open fire, but Chuco had been right behind us on the stairs and had signaled everyone to let the *Hombres* vehicles go.

"I got a message," Tino said, punching a couple of buttons. "It must have come in while my phone was in the trunk."

I knew that very few people had Tino's cell number, and watched while he held the phone to his ear. His face went white, and he closed his eyes. I saw muscles work in his jaw. "*Fucking* Joaquin," he said. "That motherfucker is *dead*." He punched a button and handed me the phone.

"Tino, it's Mami." It was Teresa's voice, clear and tense, with no hint of panic. "I'm calling with a message from Joaquin." There was a pause, then muffled voices, as if someone was holding a hand over the receiver. Then Teresa resumed. "Joaquin says that if you name Gordo the new *jefe*, he's going to kill me. You need to call off the sit-down. Call him back after you do that and I won't be hurt." She drew an audible breath, then said, "He also says—"

She was interrupted by a loud male voice, which yelled, "Watch out, Nestor, the bitch got a knife." There was a clunk, as if the receiver had hit the ground, then more yelling. I could make out Teresa, screaming Spanish curses, then what was undoubtedly a gunshot.

"Fuck, Joaquin, you *shot* her," said a different male voice. "Let's get the fuck out of here." What sounded like a chair scraping on linoleum was followed by a silence. The message ended.

I looked up at Tino's grim smile. "She pulled a knife on them," he said, and his voice almost broke. "I can see it—there's this big fucking knife, stuck in the butcher block right by the phone. If she was standing the right way, she could hide it with her body." He swallowed, and I saw proud tears threatening to leak from his eyes. "She pretended to go along with what they wanted, then she eased over and got that big machete…." Finally he choked. "Ah, fuck, Mami, why you always got to be so stubborn? Why'nt you just go with them, man? I'd get you back. You know I'd get you back." He ran the back of his hand roughly under his nose, stifling a sob. I wanted to reach out and comfort him, but I was tangibly aware of all the carefully averted gazes.

"I gotta get out of here, man. I gotta find those *cabrónes* and fucking kill them." He got to his feet, and I reached for the sleeve of his jacket, ready to press him if I had to.

"Tino, I don't think—"

"Excuse me." We turned to see the nurse from the admitting desk. "You wanted to know if something was happening with Señora Pelón."

"Is she okay?" Tino and I said, simultaneously.

"They're taking her into surgery. There's a waiting

room on the fourth floor." She pointed toward the elevator, and, plans for revenge temporarily abandoned, Tino sprinted for it. I caught up before the doors closed.

The doors opened onto a foyer in front of a wide reception desk. "Teresa Pelón," said Tino, running up to it. "She's here for surgery."

The male nurse looked at a computer screen. "Yes, she's in operating room four-C. There's a waiting area across the hall, down there." We headed in the direction he pointed, and, as we walked, we heard a bell from another elevator at the opposite end of the hall. A gurney, pushed by an orderly and with another walking alongside, rolled into the hall and turned toward us.

"Mami?" Tino recognized the figure on the gurney before I did and dashed to her side. "Mami, you okay? I'm here, Mami. Tino's here."

I caught up with him in time to see that her eyes were open. The hand without the intravenous hookup groped for his.

"I'm okay, Tino. I'm gonna be okay. They just gotta get this bullet out of me."

"I'll get them, Mami. I'm gonna get the *cabrónes* that did this to you." All pretense of macho was gone— tears ran down Tino's face, and Teresa reached up to brush them away.

"Shhh, *hijo*. I want you to stay here, wait for me. Okay?"

"I'll be back before you wake up, but right now—"

"But right now I need you to stay *here*." Teresa's

weak voice still managed to carry authority. "Promise me, *hijo*, that you'll stay here until I wake up. *Promise!*"

"I promise, Mami."

Her eyes shifted to me. "You."

"Hello, Teresa," I said. Her gaze pierced me.

"We gonna have a talk, you and I, soon as I'm better." She nodded toward her son. "Keep an eye on him—make sure he don't get any ideas about going after those guys."

"He won't." I looked over to where Tino stood with his back partially turned to us, wiping his eyes. I was pretty sure I wouldn't have to press him. I'd felt the sincerity of his promise.

"We need to go in now," said the orderly on the other side of the gurney. We stepped back and watched as they pushed her through a set of double doors that swung silently back into place behind her.

We settled down to wait. Tino fidgeted, actually seeming to vibrate. He picked up a magazine—*Entrepreneur*, I noticed—and thumbed through the pages before tossing it down. He looked at his watch about fifty times.

He called Hilda a little after 1:00 a.m. and managed to convince her to stay at home until he called back, and then resumed fidgeting. He got up and paced, sat down, got up again.

Watching him exhausted me, but I wanted to know what was going on, too. I looked at my own watch. Teresa had been in surgery for over two hours. No wonder Tino was a mess. How long did it take to get a bullet out? If Sukey had been here, she might have been able to listen to the surgeon's thoughts.

Of course, maybe *I* could, too.

Tino walked over to the window to have conversation number three hundred with Gordo, who kept calling in with updates from St. Gertrude Place. After assuring myself he was occupied for the moment, I closed my eyes and tried to listen with my mind rather than my ears.

All I could hear was Tino's muffled phone conversation, definitely auditory. I settled myself more comfortably into my chair and called upon a breathing exercise from my long-abandoned yoga class. I counted as I inhaled and exhaled, willing my heart rate to lessen and my mind to empty. I'd never really gotten the hang of this but, at one time, I'd worked at it regularly.

Something…what was it?

It's that gang guy. José pointed him out to me when we were at the club that time. The surgical team better not mess anything up—I'd hate to be the one who made a mistake with Mad Tino's mother.

I opened my eyes and looked around. The voice had been male—or had it? Had I just assumed masculinity because the last person we'd talked to had been the male nurse? The reception desk was out of sight from where I was sitting, but whoever was there would have a clear view of Tino, who was still on the phone next to the window.

I got up and crossed the narrow space, and looked toward the desk. I saw a sign that said Vending and signaled to Tino, who nodded and returned to his conversation. An alcove on the other side of the reception area housed three machines, selling, respectively, soda, snacks and hot beverages. The nurse glanced at me and back at his computer screen as I passed the desk, and I watched him surreptitiously as I pretended to scan the snack selections.

She came in with him, but he doesn't act like she's his girlfriend. I jumped—he was thinking about me.

Okay, so I could hear him. Could he hear me? I hadn't spoken when we were at the desk, so he wouldn't ever have heard my voice. Would that make a difference?

I tried to focus my thoughts on him, the same way I did with Sukey. It felt awkward eavesdropping on a stranger. Sukey's mind was so familiar, it was like turning on a television that only had one channel. Now what I had to do was figure out how to use the remote control.

You dropped something, I said. Or tried to say. There was no reaction. I was starting to feel self-conscious— I'd probably been staring at the vending machine just a bit too long. I steadied my breathing but didn't close my eyes, as I had in the waiting area. I moved my eyes without turning my head and tried to zero in on the unfamiliar mind of the man at the desk.

You dropped something.

The man frowned, then pushed his rolling chair away from the desk and looked at the floor.

Oh, shit, it had worked. I hadn't actually expected it to. I looked away, digging in my pocket for change, which I stuck into the slot without counting. I made a random selection, and something fell into the compartment at the bottom of the machine. My pulse pounded in my ears as I bent over and picked up—what? Pretzels.

As I returned to the waiting area, I hazarded a glance at the nurse, who'd returned to his computer, a vague frown still creasing his forehead. I felt like I had when, at age nine or ten, I'd made a prank phone call on a dare.

I sank back into my seat and opened my pretzels. Too salty—I wished I'd had the foresight to get a soda, as well. I could have gone back to the machine, but I felt absurdly self-conscious. And I was no closer to my original goal of overhearing what was happening in the operating room. I was about to try again when Tino, having finished his call, flopped into the chair next to me.

"Gordo says the neighbors didn't see much. Just a couple of guys running out of there, which they probably didn't say to the police."

"Who called the ambulance?"

"Old guy next door. He knows I hang out at Papi's, so he called there and told Papi there were gunshots. Papi told him to get an ambulance, then *he* called Jaime."

I tried to picture the phlegmatic Papi taking decisive action in a crisis and failed. There must be more to the old guy than I'd guessed.

"Pelón family?" I looked up to see a woman in scrubs, a mask dangling around her neck. Tino and I both stood.

"Are you done? Is she okay?" asked Tino.

"She's in recovery. It took longer than we expected—we had to repair some intestine, and that takes time. But it went well, and I think we can expect a full recovery."

"Can I see her?"

"As soon as she wakes up, we'll move her to a regular room."

"How long will that be?" I asked. I was afraid if it was too long, Tino wouldn't wait, now that he knew Teresa was going to be okay.

"Not too long—a half hour, maybe."

"What floor?" asked Tino. "Or should we wait here?"

"She'll probably be down on three. Why don't you wait here, and someone will come for you when they're ready to move her."

Tino thanked the doctor, then took out his cell phone and punched in a number. "Hilda? Yeah, she's in recovery. Doctor said everything's gonna be fine. No, don't come down. I mean it, Hilda. I got enough to worry about without—" He looked at me and rolled his eyes, and used his fingers to mime talking. His grin was almost normal. "No, baby, I didn't mean *you* make me worry, I just rather you stay home, get a good night's sleep. I might need your help tomorrow."

He said goodbye, ended the call and immediately called Gordo with the same news. He was still on the phone when two uniformed police officers walked into the room.

One was Hispanic and proportioned about like Gordo,

without the tattoos and the gut. The other, a blond woman who, though shorter than I am, had the kind of neck muscles that made me suspect steroids. The man spoke.

"Mister Pelón?" he said.

"You know who I am." Tino's tone was matter-of-fact, not belligerent. "How's your *abuelo*, Frank?"

"Pretty good. Still works in his garden most days. He's going to be sorry to hear about your mother getting shot."

"Mister Pelón, we have a few questions for you," said the woman, putting her shoulder between the man and Tino, who continued to look at Frank.

"New partner?"

"Yeah. Officer Cynthia Nelson." Frank turned to the blonde. "This is Tino. Tino, Cindy."

"Nice to meet you, Cindy." Tino grinned but didn't offer his hand. He was probably smart enough to know she wouldn't shake it. I'd seen her give Frank a nasty look when he used her first name.

"Javier Augustín Pelón, aka 'Mad Tino.' *Jefe* of the *Hombres Locos*. Over twenty arrests, three convictions, currently on probation for—"

"The man knows his own sheet, Cin," said Frank.

"It's okay, Frank. Nice to know she's taken an interest in me."

Cindy went on doggedly. "Where were you between ten and eleven p.m. yesterday?"

This took the good humor out of Tino's expression. "Frank, you think I shot Mami?"

As if the question had been directed toward her,

Cindy answered. "It's pretty common for family members to assault one another. Or you could have been a witness."

"No one saw anything, right?" Tino's smile was back, but it had a mean edge to it. "Hate to tell you this, but I got about twenty witnesses, tell you I wasn't anywhere near Mami's house."

"And I bet all of them are known gang members and have felony records." Cindy didn't back down, and Tino again turned to Frank.

"Serious, ain't she?"

"As a heart attack," said Frank.

"Well, she's gonna lose that bet. Mercy——" He turned to me. I'd taken a step back but hadn't seen any practical way to flee. "Meet Frank and his new partner, Cindy." Both pairs of eyes cut toward me, and I saw the speculation in Cindy's.

"Mercy ain't got no affiliation with the *Hombres*, and she ain't got a felony record. Not that I know of, anyway. Mercy, you ain't got an arrest or two I don't know about, do you?"

"No." One of the few things I'd liked about the press, especially during my teen years, was that I was pretty good at getting policemen to stop asking questions and let me go.

Okay, so I'd even done it once in the past year. Hopefully I wouldn't have to tonight, but I didn't want my name in a Santa Ana police report if I could avoid it.

"I'll need to get a statement. What's your full name?" Cindy took out a notebook, but Frank interrupted her.

"Actually, we came down to see if we could talk to Teresa. If she tells us who shot her, how it went down, we may not need Mercy's statement." He glared at Cindy, who, to my surprise, put away her notebook.

Tino was shaking his head. "She's still in recovery. I ain't even seen her yet. She ain't gonna be in any condition to answer questions. Come on, Frank, cut me a break here."

It was on the tip of my tongue to mention the phone message, but I thought better of it. Tino would be furious if the police got to Joaquin before he did.

Frank looked apologetic. "Sorry, Tino, it's standard procedure for anyone admitted with a gunshot wound."

"She won't tell you anything."

"We still have to ask."

Tino obviously didn't like this answer, but, as a veteran of hundreds of conversations with the police, he knew the drill.

"Okay, Frank. But just you, okay? I don't want your partner all up in her face."

Frank looked uncomfortable. "It's her case, too. Don't worry, she's a professional. She's not going to act inappropriately with someone who just got out of surgery." He turned his head toward Cindy, and she frowned, but nodded.

We all stood around and looked at each other. Shit, were they going to stay here and wait with us? That ought to be comfy.

"Excuse me," I said, and headed toward the ladies room. I was afraid Cindy would follow me, but I made it around the corner and exhaled a breath I hadn't realized I'd been holding.

I took my time, washing my face and finger-combing my hair. When I returned, I was relieved to see only Tino in the waiting room.

"Where'd they go?"

"Frank managed to get Cindy to go to the cafeteria, get some coffee. He told the nurse to call them when Mami's out of recovery. Man, that Cindy is a piece of work."

"You obviously know Frank."

"Yeah, he grew up down the street from me. His grandfather brings Mami vegetables he grows in his own garden."

"Is he…friendly to the gang?"

"You mean is he bent?" Tino shook his head. "No, man, Franco's as straight as they come. He just knows how shit works in the *barrio*. He ain't Chicano, neither. He's Cuban. In our neighborhood, his family were, like, foreigners. We used to give him shit because he couldn't eat anything with hot peppers without choking." He smiled, probably remembering some prank involving jalapeños.

"Will Teresa tell him what happened?"

"Mami? No way. She knows this is *Hombres* business, not the police's, and that I'm gonna take care of it."

I thought about what that meant.

"Tino, if you're going to go after Joaquin, I won't have anything to do with it."

"What you mean, *if?* Of course I'm gonna kill Joaquin. Mami knows it, too."

* * *

"I want you to promise me you're not going to go after Joaquin," said Teresa. "I mean it, *hijo*. I want you to let the police handle it. I'm going to make a statement, tell them everything." Teresa was so pale she was almost gray, and it was costing visible effort for her to speak. Yet her voice, though quiet, carried a strength of will that was daunting to witness.

Tino was incredulous. "Mami, you know this is for the *Hombres* to take care of. Since when do you go to the police?"

"Since you're getting *out* of the *Hombres*. Since you're taking Gus with you."

"But, Mami—"

"*Don't argue with me!* I spent my whole life worrying about the men in my family. First my father and brothers, always in some kind of trouble. Then your father, when he got sick."

"Mami—"

"*Silencio.* I'm not done talking." She swallowed, and I could see she was sweating. How much pain was she in?

I shifted uncomfortably where I was leaning against the wall next to the door. I'd accompanied Tino into the room, figuring it would be the lesser of two evils— Frank and Cindy were waiting in the hall. Right now I was thinking I might prefer hanging out with Cindy.

"When you started working for Flaco, I was crazy all the time. I started going down there so I could see for myself you were okay. I—I thought if I was nice to Flaco, friendly, it would be easier to keep an eye on you.

And that, if he liked me, maybe he'd make sure you were safe."

Tino turned pale, but he didn't say anything.

Teresa took a shaky breath, marshalling her strength. I couldn't imagine what this argument was costing her. "Tino, I didn't know any other way to take care of you. I wasn't making enough money to get us a decent place to live. And, I knew I couldn't keep you out of the gang—the *Hombres* were everything in the *barrio*. I even thought it might be better for you, having them to watch your back. But when you started staying out later and later—" Her gaze was imploring, asking him to understand. "I thought that if Flaco and I were living together, you might come home nights. And it worked. But I never wanted another man in my life after your father. Never."

"Funny," said Tino. "I guess I thought you ended up loving Flaco."

She shrugged. "Sometimes I thought I did. He didn't hit me, he gave me respect. And he made sure everyone knew I was his woman. The people in the *barrio*, they treated me nice. He got me the house. My house. But I never married him, no matter how many times he asked. I am still Señora Pelón." Her tone was proud, and, even as she lay back against the pillow, I saw a little of that arched neck that had first made me think of a Thoroughbred horse.

She went on.

"Tino, when you started telling me about these new friends, how they were helping you, how you were going to leave the gang—I was afraid to believe it. You know how I knew it was all true?"

"How?"

"Joaquin. Last night, he said a lot of things. He said you were stepping down as *jefe*, going to some meeting to name Gordo to take your place. He said you made all the *Hombres* swear they wouldn't let Gus back into the gang."

"Mami, I told you about Gus."

"I know, you tried, and I should have believed you. But if you really named Gordo *jefe* at the sit-down—"

"I started to, but we got interrupted."

She looked at him sharply. "So you didn't do it yet?"

Tino blinked, then turned to me. "Well, yeah, I guess I did. Everyone agreed, right?"

I cleared my throat. "Yes, they all recognized Gordo."

"So he's *jefe* now?" Teresa struggled to sit up straighter against her pillows. Tino reached forward to help her, but she waved him away.

"Not exactly," said Tino. "He's still waiting for my say-so."

"So what's stopping you? Tell everyone he's in and you're out," said Teresa.

"But we didn't agree on my other terms," he protested. "We got interrupted before we got to them."

"What other terms?"

"Territory, payments, stuff like that."

Teresa shook her head. "None of that matters. *Hijo*,

as long as Gordo's the new *jefe*, no one's going to let Gus back in, right?"

"Joaquin never agreed," said Tino, looking mulish. "I gotta take care of him before—"

"Joaquin's gonna be too busy to mess with Gus," said Teresa, "once I give my statement to the police." She crossed her arms over her chest and lay back with an air of finality.

"*No fucking way!* Look, Mami—"

"*Ay, hijo,* are you trying to kill me? How am I supposed to get better if I have to worry about you?" Tino looked chastened and I suppressed a grin. Nice guilt trip, Teresa. Well done.

"Tino?" Frank was poking his head in the door. "We really need to talk to your mother now." He looked apologetically toward the bed. "Sorry, Mrs. Pelón, I already gave him more time than I should have."

"No, it's okay, Frankie, come in. I have a lot to tell you."

"Mami…" Tino protested.

"Tino, why don't you go get some sleep? They aren't going to let me out until tomorrow, at least. And after I'm done talking to the police, I'm going to need to sleep myself."

"Mami—"

"Go!"

"But—"

"Come on, Tino," I said. "I think your mother has made up her mind."

He made one last exasperated sound, but Cindy and

Frank were already moving toward the bed. "Call me when you wake up," Tino said weakly, as I followed him out of the room. I turned my head just in time to see Teresa holding out her hand to be introduced to Cindy.

13

"What on *earth* is going on here?" Sukey's voice echoed my own puzzlement. "Who do you think all these cars belong to?"

We were on the sidewalk in front of Hilda's house on Lido Island, our progress blocked by vehicles spilling from her driveway.

It wasn't so much the quantity of cars as the quality; these weren't the upscale sedans, sports cars and SUVs one expected to see in this neighborhood. A rust-pocked pickup truck crowded closely behind a violently green Dodge Charger. Parallel to them sat a white 1970s Oldsmobile sedan, clean but faded, and about the length of an aircraft carrier. A plastic Madonna, arms outstretched, festooned the dashboard. Several more vehicles were parked at the curb, some of which looked as if they were held together by baling wire and others that were low-rider works of art.

"Some of Teresa's relatives must have come by to visit," I said, squeezing between vehicles.

"And I'll bet Hilda's neighbors just *love* that." Sukey rang the doorbell.

The door was opened by a boy of about six. He held a ratty stuffed animal of indistinguishable breed and looked up at us with enormous eyes.

"Well, hello there!" said Sukey. "What's your name?"

The eyes got a little bigger, but otherwise there was no response.

"*Alejandro?* Alejandro, where—" Hilda came around the corner into the foyer. "There you are, you little dickens. Come on back and finish your breakfast." She hoisted the unresisting child onto one hip and turned to us. "Well, don't just stand there, you two, come in."

I followed her, mystified. She continued to talk to the child. "You didn't finish your cereal. Don't you like bananas? Your auntie said they were your favorite!" As we turned into the kitchen, Sukey stopped so suddenly I almost bumped into her.

The room, including the adjoining breakfast nook, was full of people. Hilda put the boy down on the bench that ran behind the table, and he climbed onto some pillows and started solemnly spooning cereal into his mouth. One of the two men seated at the breakfast nook reached over and tousled his hair.

"Everyone, I want you to meet Sukey and Mercy." Hilda raised her voice over the buzz of conversation, and I watched as several unfamiliar faces turned to look at us. The room was redolent of breakfast smells and, if I wasn't mistaken, cigar smoke.

"Let's see if I can get everyone's name right. Sukey, Mercy, this is Teresa's brother, Javier, and her cousin Jorge." The two men at the table nodded. "And this is

Lourdes—have I got that right, dear?" A young woman, who was pouring orange juice from a pitcher into a row of glasses on the counter, smiled and nodded. "She's Alejandro's mother. And this is Maria, *her* mother, and her father, Benny. And…where'd Gloria go?"

"She's outside, with the twins. They wanted to watch the boats," said Lourdes.

"Oh, dear, I should have told them to be careful on the dock. I have life preservers in the boathouse. Sukey, could you run outside and show Gloria where the life preservers are?"

"Sure," said Sukey. She looked over her shoulder at me as she headed out the door, eyebrows raised. *I don't even know what to think about this,* she said silently.

I could feel her amusement, even if I couldn't hear it. I looked away quickly, afraid I'd burst out laughing myself.

"Mercy, don't stand there like a statue. Wouldn't you like some breakfast? How about coffee?"

"Coffee will be fine," I said automatically.

"I'll get it," interjected Estela. She'd been unloading the dishwasher when I'd entered the kitchen, and when she turned to reach for the coffeepot, the expression on her face was thunderous. She pulled a mug from the top rack and filled it for me.

The phone rang, and Hilda crossed the room to pick it up. "Hello? Oh, Isabella, I'm glad you called back. Did you get the directions?"

"Are all these people here to visit Teresa?" I asked Estela, as she put down the pot and opened the refrig-

erator to get cream. Tino had brought his mother
directly to Hilda's house from the hospital as soon as
she was released, with the idea that it would be a safe
and quiet place to convalesce.

Estela snorted. "Visiting? They're *staying* here."

"You're kidding me." I took a sip of excellent coffee.
Lido Island, the new *barrio*. Next thing you know, Hilda
would be voting Democrat.

"No, it's true. Teresa told Hilda all about this man
who shot her, this Joaquin person, and Hilda, she
decides that maybe he'll go after someone else in Tino's
family. So she invites them all to stay here until the
police catch Joaquin."

"Chickens?" Hilda said, still on the phone. "I don't
know, Isabella, that may not be such a good idea.
There's no fence around my yard."

"*Ay, Dios mío.*" Estela looked heavenward. "Tino's
great-uncle wanted to bring a *goat.*" She turned to interrupt Maria, who had picked up a wooden spoon and was
about to stir whatever Estela had cooking on the
stovetop. "*Es mi trabajo.*"

The woman gave up the spoon with reluctance, and
I retreated to the other side of the kitchen. Estela obviously wasn't taking this incursion into her territory very
well.

Hilda hung up the phone. "Sorry," she told me. "That
was Tino's cousin. She wasn't sure what to bring with
her."

"Is she really planning to pack the chickens?"

Hilda laughed. "I hope not. My neighbors are upset

enough about the cars, but there isn't anything they can do about it, as long as everyone's parked legally. I'll re-arrange later, and put the real eyesores inside the garage."

I looked at her more carefully. Whereas Gus's arrival had made her a nervous wreck, I saw no sign of stress on her face at this new chaos. On the contrary, she looked exhilarated. "Did you come by to see Teresa?" she asked me. "She should be awake from her nap soon."

"Sukey and I came to pick up Cupcake."

"He's not here yet. Tino went to the marina to pick up Gus. They'll be back any minute."

"I thought they were coming back yesterday."

"Grant called, ship-to-shore, and said they were having a good time and wanted to stay out another night. Since Gus didn't know about Teresa being shot, the timing was perfect."

Depends on what you call perfect, I thought. "It's going to be interesting when he finds out you kept it from him."

Hilda grimaced. "We'll just have to burn that bridge when we get to it." I wondered whether the mixed metaphor was intentional.

"Señora Hilda, we're out of milk," said Estela. "We're going to run out of everything else, too."

"I suppose you'll have to make an extra grocery run. Jorge? The Oldsmobile is yours, right? Can you move it, so Estela can get the Suburban out of the garage? Just pull it in after she leaves—she can park on the street when she gets back."

Estela removed her apron. "How many more people are coming? I need to know what to buy."

"I'm really not sure. Lourdes, how many children does Isabella have?"

"Four," said Lourdes. "And her younger brother stays with her, too."

"So, six more people. That makes…oh, I'm sure you can figure it out, Estela. Do you have my credit card? And don't forget diapers—Gloria said the twins are running low, and I think two of Isabella's kids are still young enough to need them."

"*Sí*, Señora Hilda." Estela sighed theatrically and opened a kitchen cabinet door to remove her purse. She turned the heat off under the bubbling pan, then looked around the kitchen. *They better not break anything while I'm gone.*

I almost choked on my coffee as the door to the garage slammed behind her.

"I'm going to have to give her a *huge* bonus," said Hilda. "Come on outside and meet the twins. Wait until you see them—they're completely adorable."

On the patio, Sukey sat on one of the lounge chairs, her sweater buttoned high against the wind, chatting with a hugely pregnant young woman. A thin man about Tino's age stood on the dock, supervising a pair of identical toddlers encased in matching oversized lifejackets.

"That's Eddie, Gloria's husband." Hilda waved, and the young man waved back, then returned his attention to the children, who knelt near the edge of the dock and peered over the side.

"You seem to be enjoying yourself," I commented.

"You know, I am," she admitted. "I was an only child, and my cousins didn't live nearby, so I've never been around big families. I thought they'd drive me crazy, but they're really no trouble."

"I don't think Estela agrees."

"Oh, she'll get over it. And they'd help if she'd let them. She about had a fit when Tino's aunt started a load of laundry in *her* washer. They're all used to doing things for themselves."

"How's Teresa?"

"Tired, but okay. I haven't had an opportunity to speak with her alone yet." A furrow appeared between her brows, the first sign of discomfort I'd seen on this visit. She turned to face the water. "She's not what I expected."

You're probably not what she expected, either.

"No, I suppose not."

I almost dropped my cup. Hilda had answered exactly as if I'd spoken aloud. It was a good thing she'd been turned away from me when I had the unspoken thought. I was going to have to be more careful.

I looked at my watch. "Hilda, I need to go open the office. I'd like to see Teresa later, though. I'll come by at lunchtime, if that's all right."

"Do you mind if I stay here until Tino gets here with Cupcake?" Sukey asked. "I can walk over to the office with him. Your first appointment is Mrs. Needham."

I nodded. Sue Needham was a repeat client. My methods meant that a follow-up appointment was usually unnecessary, but I had a one-issue-per-session policy. If a client wanted to quit smoking, start exercise *and* improve their work habits, I tackled the items one at a time.

I almost made it to the front door when it was flung open violently.

"Where is she?" Gus asked, looking around wildly. "Mami! *Mami!*" I had no idea in which room Hilda had installed Teresa, but Gus wasn't waiting for an answer. He sprinted down the hall just as one of the women—Maria?—came out of the kitchen and into the foyer.

"*¡Gustavo! Espera, muchacho, su madre necesita dormir.*" She set off after Gus, followed by the rest of the people in the kitchen. If Teresa was, in fact, sleeping, she soon wouldn't be.

Tino appeared in the doorway with a leashed Cupcake, who barked joyously at the general chaos. Tino's expression was murderous.

"I swear, I should have told Grant to throw that *pendejo* overboard somewhere between here and Catalina Island."

"He's pretty upset."

"And blaming me. He said it's my fault Mami got shot." *Which maybe it is.* I heard the words as loud as thunder. He shut the door and unhooked Cupcake's leash, upon which the big mutt followed the gang down the hall.

"It's not your fault, Tino. You were trying to settle things peacefully."

He ignored me. "Then he said that I should have

told Grant about it when he called yesterday, not let him stay out sailing a second night. He said I was trying to make sure he didn't go after Joaquin."

"Well, he's right about that."

"Yeah." *And if Mami hadn't made me promise, I'd have gone after the fucker myself.*

I squirmed. This was the first time I'd heard Tino's thoughts, and it wasn't something I wanted to get used to. I hoped I heard them now only because his emotions were so strong. I knew how to block someone's thoughts—my experience with Dominic had taught me that—but it took an effort. I was afraid a consequence of my recent telepathic exercises was that I was going to have to be on guard all the time.

He sighed deeply. "I better go get him. He's gonna get all crazy with Mami."

"Whatever you think. But you're not going to be able to keep him away from her forever, and right now she's got all your relatives to protect her."

He gazed down the hall for a moment, shrugged, then turned into the kitchen. I followed and watched as he poured himself some coffee.

"Tino, I need to ask you to do something for me."

He looked surprised. "I'm a little busy right now."

I shook my head. "It's nothing like that. It's about the…hypnotism I've been doing for you lately."

"What about it?"

I'd planned this speech. Tino might not be educated, but he was smart. "My methods are a little different from the way most hypnotherapists work. I'd rather you didn't tell anyone that I hypnotized those men at the meeting. Or Marisol and Gus. Or the nurse at the emergency room."

"Why don't you want anyone to know? That shit is powerful, man. You could make a fortune. You could, like, walk into a jewelry store and tell them to give you a Rolex."

I sighed. I'd also planned the next part, just in case. "You will not tell anyone you have seen me compel someone to obey or agree," I pressed, twinges of guilt like bee stings in my mind. "If someone asks you about it, you will say that you saw nothing unusual. Will you do that?"

"Sure. I didn't see nothing unusual." He sipped his coffee.

Sukey came into the kitchen, followed by Hilda. "Did I hear Cupcake?"

"Yes. We need to go now, or I do."

"I'll come with you. Let me just go get—" Before she could head down the hall in Cupcake's direction, the dog heard his beloved's voice and bounded around a corner toward her.

"My *baby!*" she crooned. "Mama missed her best baby boy, didn't she? Yes she did!"

It was a mad dash, but we made it back to the office in time for Sue Needham's appointment, and my morning clients were comfortingly routine. I was glad none of them had come in for the purpose of dealing with family issues, at least not today. Between Sam and Tino, I was about done with families.

Or so I thought.

"I heard back from the adoption agency," Sukey said, seating herself next to me on our makeshift balcony during my morning break. The pages in her hand appeared to be faxes.

"The adoption agency?" I'd almost forgotten about my own family issues.

No, that wasn't true. I'd thought about Bobbie Hollings a thousand times in the last few days but firmly stifled the thought each time. I'd watch both Sam and Tino risk everything for the sake of their respective families.

The only thing I'd ever done for my own family was destroy it.

But they weren't my real family. Maybe that was why—

"Bobbie was right, you were abandoned. See? The orphanage listed you as a foundling. I didn't think anyone actually used that word, at least not on legal papers."

"They probably don't anymore," I said. "I guess it means they found me somewhere. Does it say where?"

"Yes, it does. I mean, not the exact place. But it was in a church."

The tendrils of a chill wrapped around my spine. Why?

"A church?" I repeated stupidly.

"Yeah, probably an Orthodox church. Because the orphanage was called—" She read from the page. "'St. Michael the Archangel Orthodox Orphanage.' I looked it up on the Internet. It's still there, but they don't call it an orphanage anymore. Now it's the 'Home for Children.' Political correctness has hit the church, too."

It's still there, I thought. The chill got stronger, and suddenly the day seemed too cold for sitting outside. An Orthodox church—for some reason that resonated.

"Orthodox? You mean like Greek Orthodox?"

"Not specifically, at least I don't think so. Anyway, I called them, to see if there's anyone around who remembers what church, or if they have some paperwork that's not in the file you got from your mother."

"Bobbie's not my mother," I said automatically. *But she was—once. And she still would be, if I hadn't decided to…cut myself off from her.*

"Sorry, I meant the file you got in Tucson. Anyway, I'll let you know what I find out."

"Thanks." *I think.*

She grinned. "I heard that."

I looked at her carefully. For a long time I'd assumed Sukey only heard my thoughts when it was my intention for her to do so. Now I wondered what percentage of my thoughts she regularly overheard. I hadn't told her what I'd learned in Tucson, at least not the part about having pressed the Hollingses to let me go. I intended to tell her everything. But…not yet.

If she were picking up on this mental debate, her expression didn't show it. I didn't think she was even capable of deception—her face was like a child's, showing every emotion.

The phone inside the office rang, and she got up to answer it. "Hollings Hypnotherapy, how may I—" She stopped in midsentence. "Oh my God, when? Just a second. Mercy, it's Hilda." I'd already gotten to my feet. She extended the receiver to me.

"Hilda, what is it?"

"It's Gus," she replied. "He stole the Suburban. Estela left the keys in it when she got back from the grocery store, thinking we needed to rearrange cars, and he sneaked out while Tino was in with Teresa. Tino thinks—"

"He's gone after Joaquin," I finished. "Where's Tino now?"

"He went looking for him. But Teresa's afraid he's going to be too late, and that Gus may know somewhere to look for Joaquin that Tino and the police haven't thought about. Some of the uncles and cousins are talking about going after him, too, and Teresa's got herself all worked up." She paused for a breath, and I jumped in.

"Maybe the cops will stop him," I said. "A fourteen-year-old kid behind the wheel should stick out, and he's got to drive practically in front of city hall to get off the peninsula—there are always a lot of police coming in and out of there."

"We'd have heard by now if that happened," she said. "I'm not sure when he left, but he's had plenty of time to get to Santa Ana, or wherever he thinks Joaquin is. Please, Mercy, can you come over here? Teresa wants to talk to you."

Aw, crap. I'd thought that with my instructions to keep my special hypnosis techniques confidential, I'd put Tino's family issues behind me this morning. "Yeah, okay. I'll be right there." I hung up. "Sukey—"

"I'll reschedule your late morning appointments," she said. "There're only two. Will you be back after lunch?"

"I don't know yet. I'll call you when I do."

She was already dialing the phone. "I'll come over to Hilda's once I've reached the clients."

That wasn't necessary, but Sukey wasn't the "sit and wait" type.

On my way to Hilda's, I dialed Tino's cell, but my call went straight to voice mail. I left my Honda at the curb and found Hilda's front door slightly ajar. Tino's relatives were back in the kitchen, and Estela was at her place in front of the stove. She turned toward me, and I could see the strain on her face. *I shouldn't have left the keys in the car. If something happens, it'll be my fault.*

I closed the door in my mind that I used when I didn't want any telepathic interruptions. In this emotionally charged house, I would be overwhelmed by the babble.

"Hilda called me. Where is she?"

"In Teresa's room," Estela replied. "Down the hall on the left—the one facing the water." I nodded and found my way to a room that mirrored the master suite situated on the other side of the U-shaped house. Teresa was sitting up in bed, supported by a mound of pillows, facing the door. Hilda sat in an armchair that had been pulled up near the bed.

"Ah, you have come," said Teresa, holding out her hand. Her color was vastly better than it had been in the hospital. I took the extended hand awkwardly.

"Hilda said you wanted to talk to me. I'm not sure what I can do to help."

She stared at me intently, then squeezed and released my hand. Some kind of look passed between her and Hilda, who stood up.

"I'll leave you two to talk." As she left the room, I noticed that a large flower arrangement, dominated by three enormous sunflowers, sat on a pedestal next to the door.

"Sit." Teresa indicated the chair Hilda had vacated, and I sat down but didn't relax against the cushions. "I want to talk to you about my son. Both of my sons."

I nodded, feeling the coil of unease tighten in my chest. "Tino is my friend. I don't really know Gus." I heard the defensiveness in my own tone and suppressed a wince.

"So Tino has told me. But there is something he has *not* told me about you—something more."

Her gaze was relentless, and I resisted the urge to squirm.

"First, he brings you to my house, which is strange enough. Then, he takes you to a very important meeting of the gang leaders. I want to know why."

I cleared my throat. "He thought my hypnotism skills might be useful." It sounded like the lame excuse it was, but it was also, technically, the truth. Tino *did* think what I did was simple hypnosis, or at least he had before I'd suggested otherwise.

Teresa made a disparaging noise, waving one of those graceful hands. "Tino sees what he wants to see.

He told me he took you along because you are persuasive. But Gus told me something else—something I have been thinking about."

Hairs stood on the back of my neck. Was Gus aware he'd been pressed? "What's that?"

"He said you made him obey you."

I couldn't think of a response, so I remained silent. Teresa continued to watch me.

"A little close to home, I think," she commented after a pause. She nodded, then smiled at me. Her smile was more triumphant than warm, but she didn't seem hostile. "To be honest, Mercy, he didn't use those exact words. He said Tino was chasing him, and you told him to stop, and all of a sudden he didn't feel like running anymore."

"Maybe he was just out of breath." I didn't sound convincing, even to myself.

"Maybe, but I don't think so." She glanced over at the sunflowers, and her expression softened. She took a deep breath and exhaled audibly, then leaned back against her pillows, relaxing. "Tino and Gus were born in this country, and so were both of their fathers. Not me."

"No?" I was surprised. Her English was excellent—better than either of her sons'.

She shook her head. "No, my family is from Sinaloa. You know Mazatlán?"

I nodded, and she went on.

"Well, that's on the coast. Most of the state of Sinaloa is in the interior—desert, even. But near the mountains, the Sierra Madres, there are *ranchos*, some of them very large. I grew up on one—not one of the really big ones, but my father was the *dueño*, the owner."

I was surprised. Tino and Gus were so urban, and nothing Tino had said about his childhood pointed toward his mother being the daughter of a landowner. It explained her educated ways and proud, aristocratic bearing.

"How did you end up here?"

She shrugged. "Times changed. Farming changed. It had been getting more difficult, year by year. Then, a few seasons of drought in a row, and my father couldn't pay he taxes. He had to sell. Some of the bigger *ranchos* survived, but the smaller ones could not. My father came to California, to start a new life for us."

"How old were you?"

"Fifteen. I had my *quinceañera* in Culiacán, just before we left the country." She smiled, remembering. "There was music and dancing, and we pretended, my father and I, that the young men who came were suitors, there to win the hand of the *dueño's* daughter, as he had with my mother when she had her *quince*." The smile faded. "But my mother was dead, and the *rancho* was gone. Papa was not a *dueño* anymore."

I wondered why she was telling me this, but I was caught in the rhythm of her voice and could imagine a courtyard lit with twinkling lights, and a fifteen-year-old Teresa, holding out her hand to be led in a dance by a smiling young man.

"My father was an educated man, and not superstitious. But Xoatchil, the woman who cared for me after my mother died, she was Maya. Papa could not afford to bring her with us to America, and she was very worried about me going to live among *gringos*. So before we left Culiacán, she took me to see a *bruja*."

I knew the word. "A witch?"

"More of a wise woman. Someone with the power to see the unseen, and to make amulets to protect against evil. Xotchi wanted to buy me such an object—a *talismán*."

The power to see the unseen. I had a flash of Madame Minéshti, the woman who had recognized me for what I was. Remembering her face as she turned the Tarot cards, I shivered.

Teresa must have seen my reaction. "This makes you uncomfortable?"

"No," I replied. "I just—I met someone like that once. I was remembering."

She nodded. "Yes, well, I remember, too. We went to this little shop on a narrow street, and I was so exited, sneaking away with Xotchi, because my father would have disapproved. I thought it was an adventure."

"I imagine it was."

"Yes. And the inside of the shop was right out of my storybooks—dusty and full of boxes, baskets and bowls, herbs and roots hanging from the ceiling to dry. Cool, even though the sun was blazing outside. Spiderwebs everywhere. I could tell Xotchi was nervous, but I laughed at her. She was always so superstitious, and I thought she was old-fashioned and a little silly." Her lips quirked ruefully. "I was young, and I knew everything. It is common at that age."

I thought of Gus.

"Then the *bruja* came out and asked us what we wanted. Xocthi told her we had come for a *talismán* for me, and the *bruja* said that, in order to know what to put into the *talismán,* she needed to hold my hand."

I was suddenly there in that room, with the smell of dusty herbs and the cool, damp air.

"I was starting to get nervous myself, but I was showing off a little, wanting to seem mature, sophisticated, you understand? Then the woman, she was called Tsuritsa, took my hand."

"Is that a Mayan name?"

Teresa shook her head. "No, she wasn't Mayan. Xotchi tried to speak to her in *Yucatec,* but she didn't understand. She spoke Spanish with a strange accent. She looked at my hand for a long time, and I began to feel strange. Not afraid, exactly. It was just that she was so…still."

I wasn't sure I understood. "What do you mean?"

Before continuing, she gave me a look I couldn't quite interpret. "Most people, they are always in motion. Even when sitting still, their hands move, or their feet."

Teresa gestured as she spoke, illustrating the point. "When they try to be still on purpose, they move anyway. Their eyes move, and they blink. Even breathing causes movement. But not Tsuritsa, not once she took my hand. She was staring into my eyes, and it was if she had turned into stone. It went on for a long time."

I could imagine the contrast between Teresa, always so animated, and the woman she described.

"Just before she finally spoke, I saw the life flow

back into her face. The statue was gone and the *bruja* was back. She told me…" For the first time in her narrative, Teresa faltered, then continued. "She told me things she could not possibly have known. She refused to say anything about my future, but I could see the sadness on her face, and it frightened me. When she finally let go of my hand and started preparing the *talismán,* I couldn't wait to get out of there. The only reason I stayed was because of Xotchi."

Teresa looked at her hands, turning them over to see the palms, as if remembering what the *bruja* had told her. "From that day, I never saw that stillness in a person, not even in my sleeping children. Until—" She looked up at me, her expression sharpening. "Until a few days ago, when Tino brought you to my house. When you stood on the walk in front of my steps, watching and waiting for Tino to introduce you. For a moment I saw the *bruja*. Just for a moment, but long enough."

"Me?" I blurted. "I was just—I don't know. Waiting. I'm not…" I stopped, unsure how to defend myself. Or why I felt that I had to.

As a child of foster care, I'd learned how to be unobtrusive—to sit still and avoid unwanted attention. But surely not *still* in the way she meant. I mean, I blinked. Didn't I?

"Just for a moment," Teresa repeated. "I thought I had imagined it, but once I was watching for it, I saw the stillness again. Later, in the kitchen, when Tino was telling me about what was going on with Gus. As soon as I started asking you questions, you came out of it. But there was no mistake. You did it just now, while you listened to my story."

"I don't know what to say." If this really was something I did, no one had commented on it before. Not even Sukey.

"You don't have to say anything," said Teresa. "Just know that I see something in you that Tino is too...too busy to notice. There is power in you. I came to understand that the *bruja's* stillness had something to do with going inside to access the source of that power. Tino thinks you hypnotize people because that is easier to believe."

"Well, I *am* a hypnotherapist—" I protested, but she cut me off.

"Yes, a very good one, I have no doubt. But I believe there is more to it than you say. You don't have to talk about it if you don't want to. But if you have power—" Her voice took on a different, rawer tone. "If you have power, please, *please,* will you use it to help my sons?"

14

"He's still not answering his cell phone," said Hilda. "I think it's turned off. Why would he do that?"

"He's got to be in Santa Ana. If he's looking for Gus, the first thing he'll do is get some of the *Hombres* on it. Gordo or Jaime—one of those guys," Jorge said. Or was it Javier? I'd been introduced to Teresa's brother and cousin, but I didn't remember which was which. Wasn't Tino's real first name Javier?

"I think we should go to Papi's bar," said a younger man, the twins' father. Eddie, I remembered.

"You're not going anywhere," objected Gloria, his wife. "You promised me—"

"I'll go," I said. "Papi may know something, or some of the *Hombres* may be there. And if not, it's a good place to wait, in case Tino decides to answer his phone."

"I'll come with you," said Javier/Jorge.

"No!" said a voice from the hallway, and we turned. Teresa stood there, her face white.

"What are you doing out of bed?" Hilda hurried to her side. "The doctor said two more days, at least."

"I'll go back to bed in a minute," Teresa said, shaking off Hilda's hand. "I heard you arguing. I don't want you all running around Santa Ana, putting yourself in danger."

"But—"

"*No*, Javier." She held her head higher. The younger man—her little brother, I realized now—backed down. "You don't know anything about guns or gangs or fighting. I know you want to help, but I'd just be worrying about you, too."

"I'll go," said Eddie.

"You have twin babies," Teresa said. "No, Mercy can go by herself."

A cacophony of voices rose in protest, and Teresa raised her hand for silence. Everyone backed off except Eddie, who said, "A woman? You say we don't know about guns and fighting—what does *she* know?"

"Mercy has other talents," Teresa replied. "She's helped Tino out before, and Gus. They'll listen to her. She's the right one to go." She looked around at each face, her expression imperious, and I saw the daughter of the *dueño,* commanding the denizens of the *rancho.* I wasn't surprised when everyone backed down.

"I think I got it working." I turned to see Jorge, Teresa's cousin, standing in the doorway that led to the garage. "There's nothing going on right now."

"Jorge found Stan's old police band radio in the garage," explained Hilda. "He liked to sit out there sometimes and listen to the emergency calls."

"If Gus goes after Joaquin and there's a fight, gun-shots or something, maybe someone would call 9-1-1,"

Jorge said. "It's a long shot, but I don't mind listening for a while."

"*Ay, Dios.*" I turned to see Teresa clutching the wall. Apparently, Gus's name and the word *gunshots* in the same sentence was too much for her. Several relatives hurried to prop her up.

"Take her back to bed," Hilda fussed. "And don't worry, Teresa, no one's going to follow Mercy to that place—what did you call it?"

"Papi's," I said. "Look, my cell is on, and I'm going to try to keep reaching Tino." I had a thought. "Teresa?"

The procession leading her back down the hall paused, and she turned to look at me. "Yes?"

"Do you think Gus could have gotten hold of a gun?"

She bit her lip. "I don't think anyone in the *Hombres* is going to give him one right now, with Gordo in charge. Except Joaquin, and that's who he's going after."

"Do you think he already has one? Hidden in the house?"

She shrugged, then winced, pain visible on her face. "It would have to be hidden pretty well, otherwise I'd have found it when I was cleaning."

I thought about that spotless kitchen and nodded. "Even so, it might be worth stopping by, to see if he's hiding out there. Do you have a key?"

"In my purse, in the bedroom."

I followed the group down the hall to get the key. Once Teresa was reinstalled in the bed, she reached for my hand. I gave it to her.

"Remember what we talked about. Whatever you can do."

You have no idea.

She quirked an eyebrow, and I wondered if she'd heard the thought. She released my hand, and I left.

"My cell will be on," I called back to Hilda and crew from the front door. "Call me if you hear anything."

I'd gotten an entire ring of keys from Teresa, including one that bypassed the security code on the front gate. Yellow police tape crossed the front and side doors, but I doubted there was an active crime scene investigation going on, since Teresa had identified her attackers.

I let myself in through the mud room, passed the laundry area and headed into the kitchen. "Gus?" I called. "Are you here?" Then, pressing, I added, "Answer if you can hear me." I'd never pressed someone out of my line of sight, but it was worth a shot. The house remained silent.

A chair still lay on its side, and there was blood on the floor, a puddle near the counter, and then footprints and wheel marks, probably from policemen and ambulance personnel, and the gurney that had carried Teresa out. A sugar bowl was broken on the floor, its contents mixed with the congealed blood. It gave me a queasy feeling, and I turned toward the sink.

A glass and plate were sitting there, milky water half filling the glass. I couldn't imagine Teresa leaving dishes to soak, even for five minutes, so they probably hadn't been there at the time of the shooting. Gus must have been here. And, being a teenager, he'd taken time for a snack.

"Gus?" I pushed through a swinging door, finding myself in the small dining room I'd come through on my way from the front door on my previous visit. The living room was on the opposite side of the staircase leading to the second floor, and I only glanced around it before heading up the stairs. "Are you up here?"

The sunny front bedroom leading to the balcony was obviously Teresa's. The bed was made, the inevitable sunflower bedspread immaculate, and everything looked undisturbed. Gus wouldn't hide something in here—Teresa probably dusted it, including the back corners of the closets, twice a week.

There were smaller rooms on the opposite side of the hall. I opened the first door and found myself in a time capsule. Not one from a different century, but perhaps twenty years ago. Movie posters dominated the walls: *Goodfellas, Pulp Fiction* and *Terminator 2.* There was a bookcase with few books, and a stack of magazines sat in one corner—*Low Rider* and *Classic Car.* Some martial arts gear was on display as well—Chinese throwing stars and a ceremonial dagger.

Tino's room, probably decorated when he was Gus's age or a little older. I backed out.

Gus's room was a more current version of Tino's, with posters tending toward horror and military titles, most featuring lots of gore and half-naked women. The one commemorating *Memento* felt out of place.

There were still some carryovers from little-boy days, a lampshade depicting Spider-Man, and an action figure—one of those that's either a robot or a heavily armored alien or both—on his bedside shelf. The bedspread looked slightly rumpled, as if someone had been sitting on the bed. I would lay odds Teresa demanded hospital corners on sheets and smoothed any wrinkles out of the bedspread the moment she spotted them.

I opened the closet, which was far too neat for a teenager's. Hell, it was far too neat for me, my own closet being relatively tidy only because it was less than half-full. I closed the door and turned around, embarrassed at this glimpse into someone's private domain. I'm not a voyeur by nature, and, in any case, this was pointless. If there had been a gun hidden somewhere here, Gus had already retrieved it, snarfed down a sandwich and headed off.

As I turned to leave the bedroom, I noticed another poster next to the door. It was for a movie called *City of God*. The picture showed a dark-skinned boy of eleven or twelve, his body covered with sweat and his teeth bared, face contorted in ecstatic rage. He was pointing an enormous revolver at someone off camera, its muzzle glowing as a shot exited the barrel. I shivered.

Papi's was almost empty, except for a couple of grizzled patrons who might have been carved into the furniture. Although it was not yet noon, half-filled beers and shot glasses sat in front of them. They would, I knew, nurse the drinks to make them last as long as possible, keeping enough alcohol in their systems so their hands didn't shake, but never quite achieving the oblivion of a full-on drunk.

Men like this, with different accents but similar stories, had taught me to play pool in the barrooms of a city on another coast. Back then I skipped school, then used the press to convince bartenders and patrons that I was old enough to stay. The dimly lit, dusty environs were better than the noisy video arcades and malls, where I'd have to dodge truant officers and older kids. Libraries and bookstores had offered sanctuary, but well-meaning clerks and librarians asked questions, so I'd fled to pool halls and dingy, sour-smelling bars, where daytime patrons had little to say.

"Has Tino been here?" I asked Papi.

He stared at me, then shook his head, bulldog jowls quivering.

I sighed, wishing he would just tell me the truth without my having to force him, but no. I pressed. "Papi—" I started, then changed my mind about what I was going to ask. "Tell me your name. Your real name."

"Eduardo."

"So Papi's just a nickname."

He shrugged. "It came with the cantina. I bought it, people started to call me Papi. I don't see no reason to stop them." His English was heavily accented, but good. He'd just spoken more words that I'd heard from him in all my previous visits combined.

"Eduardo, tell me if you've seen Tino or any of the *Hombres Locos* this morning."

"Tino was here about an hour ago. Gordo was with him, and some of the other *Hombres.*"

"Did you overhear what they were saying?"

He shook his head again. Annoyed, I realized I'd forgotten to press. "Tell me what you overheard," I said, and he winced. I'd pushed harder than I'd intended.

"They were talking about Joaquin and Nestor. Who their relatives are, stuff like that. Places they might hide out."

"Were they going to look for them?"

"Yes."

"Do you know where? Tell me."

He grimaced, and I forcibly calmed myself. I was pushing way too hard.

"Gordo went with Jaime to a restaurant in Anaheim—Joaquin's *tío*, his uncle, runs it. And Tino was going to some junkyard."

Tino would have chosen the most likely lead for himself. As I recalled, there were a lot of salvage yards in the area, many of them in a neighborhood not far from the train station. Tino and I had passed by one when we'd gone to pick up Gus. I remembered the sign warning trespassers about a vicious dog and wished I'd brought Cupcake with me.

"Do you know the name of the junkyard?"

"No."

Damn. I picked up a bar napkin and pulled a pen from a cup next to the cash register.

"I'm writing down my cell phone number. If Tino comes back in here today, or Gordo, I want you to call me. Will you do that?"

"I'll call you if Tino or Gordo comes in."

"If they come in *today*." I didn't want to still be getting phone calls from Papi—Eduardo—six weeks, much less six months, from now. With luck, I would never have a reason to set foot inside this place again.

Back in my Honda, I called Hilda. "Can you look something up on the Internet for me?"

"I can try. Or maybe Lourdes can do it—she's been on the computer a lot since she got here. Did you find out where they went?"

"Maybe."

"I'll get Lourdes to pick up the phone in my office. *Lourdes!*"

I listened to the indistinct buzz of voices for a moment—Hilda must be in the kitchen—then there was a click, presumably the office extension being picked up.

"Hello?" said an unfamiliar voice.

"Lourdes?" I asked.

"Yes. Hilda, I got it. You can hang up now." There was a clunk, and the muffled voices were silent. "Hilda said you wanted me to find something on the Internet." Lourdes had virtually no accent, and I could hear the click of fingernails on the keyboard.

"Yes, I'm looking for junkyards in Santa Ana, and maybe Orange or Tustin—something near the Santa Ana border."

More clicking. "There's a lot of them," she said. "You didn't get a name?"

"No, but I seem to remember there are a bunch of them all on one street. Tino's in the Malibu, right?"

"I think so, yes."

"Well, it wasn't parked at Papi's, and it's pretty easy to spot. So I figured I'd head over to that street—"

"I got you. There's Buzzy's and Part Heaven on First Street, and then there's a whole bunch over on Washington. You know where that is? Sort of behind the train station."

"I remember seeing the area from the freeway, but I wasn't sure how to get to it."

"You near Papi's? You know how to get to Main Street?"

"I'm almost there."

"Turn left when you get there, go up to Santa Ana Boulevard, and you'll see the signs for the station. Go on past it, and turn left on Lincoln, toward the freeway. There's a tire place on the corner, I think."

"Thanks, Lourdes. If I don't see Tino's car around there somewhere, I'll call you back, and we'll figure out where I should try next."

"Okay."

I was stopped at a light, so I punched in Tino's number again, but it was still going straight to voice mail.

The Santa Ana Regional Transportation Center was an attractive building, built in the 1930s and restored in the 1980s, when it was expanded to become a hub for buses as well as trains. The blocks immediately adjoining it were respectable enough, but a couple of turns and I was on junkyard row. High walls topped with razor wire mostly hid the blocks of derelict cars from passing traffic.

The walls were occasionally punctuated by chain-link gates that exposed rows and rows of automobiles in various states of salvage. Squat buildings operated as storefronts, dotted with signs offering discounts for customers and threats to trespassers.

Perro Feroz signs appeared on nearly every business, many showing the outline of an angry looking canine with huge fangs. Signs advertising *Pick Your Own* confused me, until I remembered that many of these places simply directed visitors to a car of the desired make and model, and let them remove whatever parts they wanted. There were plenty of cars parked along the street, but I didn't see any baby blue convertibles. I drove slowly, peering into alleys and side streets, with no luck.

I was circling back, trying to figure out if I'd missed anything, when my cell phone rang. I looked for a place to pull over but didn't see anything convenient. "Hello?"

"It's Lourdes. Jorge heard something on the radio."

"On the radio?" I was momentarily confused. "You mean the police band radio?"

"Yeah. A report of shots fired on First Street somewhere." She paused, and it sounded as if she had put her hand over the receiver, as she shouted. "*Tío* Jorge, did you get the address?" Then, to me, "He didn't get it, but I thought—"

"Hold on," I told her. "I think I hear sirens."

"Are they close?"

"I can't tell where they're coming from. But I'm only a few blocks from First Street, so I'll go that way. I should be able to see where the police cars are headed."

I was back on Santa Ana Avenue, heading toward Main, when a couple of cruisers, lights flashing and sirens blaring, flew by on Main Street, still several blocks ahead of me. Before I made it to the intersection, they were followed by a paramedic unit. My heart rate increased. What the hell did they need paramedics for? I stamped down on the accelerator. No one was going to bother to pull me over for speeding with gunfire reported only a few blocks away.

I made the turn onto Main in time to see which direction the paramedic truck turned, but a red light and crossing traffic prevented me from catching up.

The enforced pause also gave me time to think. I couldn't pull up into the middle of a police situation and start asking questions. Well, I could, but I wasn't sure I wanted to. It probably has nothing to do with Tino and Gus, I told myself. This hopeful thought was shattered when I turned the corner and saw a huge sign in the shape of a tow truck pulling a wrecked car into a fluffy cloud bearing the words *Part Heaven*, maybe two and a half blocks down on my right. Gunshots at a junkyard—that couldn't be a coincidence. Two police cruisers blocked the street, and I slowed down, uncertain what to do next.

I pulled into a tiny parking lot in front of an unoccupied building that used to be a motorcycle repair shop. It connected to a driveway that ran along the side of the building. Wondering if it led to the alley in the back, I pulled in, but found myself in a smaller lot behind the building, access to the alley blocked by a concrete wall. I pulled forward at an angle, preparing to make a multiple point turn, when something caught my eye through a narrow gap in the wall. Something baby blue.

I put the car in reverse and backed up until I was even with the gap. I could just make out about ten inches of shining blue car body and a chrome logo. *Malibu.* The rest of the car was hidden by two Dumpsters, but it had to be the Tino-mobile. It made sense that he wouldn't park it in the street—the Santa Ana police would recognize a gang leader's car.

I put the Honda into a space next to the building and got out. It was a tight squeeze through the gap in the wall, but I eased into the alley, then across and between the Dumpsters. Tino's car was parked at the back of a building that must have faced Second Street, next to a door that said Manny's Auto Audio—Employees Only. There were no other cars in the tiny parking area, and I stepped back to the edge of the alley and looked in the direction of the buildings where the police cruisers had blocked the street.

The alley continued for a couple of blocks, then deadended at a wall that was about ten feet tall, completely covered with layer upon layer of gang tags and topped with razor wire. While I looked, a police cruiser crossed the alley, coming from Second Street and heading toward First. I waited to see if any more vehicles followed—I could still hear sirens, but couldn't tell the direction—then stepped into the alley, staying close to the backs of the buildings and their attendant Dumpsters.

I came up to the back of a two-story building on the First Street side, and saw that metal doors had been rolled up to reveal the bays of an auto shop. I could see through to the street and, although I still hadn't come parallel to the barricade, I could make out the reflection of the flashing lights in the windshields and paint of the cars parked inside. Men in mechanics' jumpsuits were clustered near the front of the building, their heads turned in the direction of the action. Another cruiser crossed the alley, and I stepped quickly into the shelter of a bay. At the sound of the siren, one of the men turned his head toward me, making eye contact.

I'm none of your concern. I sent the thought toward him, feeling foolish. I had no idea if it reached him. Or if he spoke English. Or if that mattered. *Pay no attention.*

It might have worked, or it might not, but he turned his head back toward the street, resuming his conversation with the others, none of whom looked toward me.

I stepped back into the alley and continued toward the end, moving quickly as I passed an intersecting alley. I glanced back over my shoulder, just in case, but I didn't see anyone. Undoubtedly all the commotion on the street drew more interest than an empty alley.

There was less cover on the next block, where the backs of the buildings featured back doors that didn't look as if they got frequent use. I reached the dead end and found that a narrow walkway ran parallel to the wall in both directions, although the First Street exit was blocked by a chain-link gate with a padlock. Through it, I could see the cruiser barricade. The other way led through to Second Street.

I was trying to decide whether to go back in the direction of my car or down the walkway when my cell phone rang and I jumped, switching it quickly to vibrate. The caller ID displayed Hilda's home number.

"Did you find them?" It was Hilda this time.

"Not yet." Looking up at the wall, I got an idea. "Is Lourdes still on the computer?"

"Yes, she's right here. Sukey's with her. Do you want to talk to one of them?"

"Give Sukey the phone."

After a short pause, Sukey came on. "What's happening?"

"I'm in an alley between First and Second Streets, and the police have First Street barricaded. There's a big wall between me and the junkyard. Or junkyards—I think Lourdes said there's more than one down here."

"What do you want me to do?"

"You know that aerial view thing you showed me on the computer?"

"Google Earth?"

"Yeah, that. Do you think you could look at it and

see if there's a way past this wall without going down First Street?"

"I'll have to load it onto Hilda's computer. And it will help if you can give me an exact address."

"How long will it take to download it?" I was beginning to wonder if it would save me any time, or if I should just keep exploring on my own.

"Not long. A few minutes, maybe."

"Okay, call me back when you're ready, and I'll try to get a street number. Oh, wait—can you look up Part Heaven? That's the name of one of the junkyards—there's a big sign. Use that address on the Google thing and call me back."

I hung up and walked back to the wall. The walkway leading to Second Street was strewn with trash but looked navigable. I stepped carefully around cardboard boxes and empty bottles, and came out on Second Street. I looked for police cars but didn't see any. Normal traffic moved up and down the street uninterrupted. The wall that had blocked the alley made a right-angle turn and continued along the block.

My phone vibrated. "That was quick."

"Yeah, Hilda's computer is really fast. I think I found what you were talking about. I can see where an alley dead ends. There are two auto salvage places, side by side, and they both have big walls around them. And both junkyards are huge. Together, they cover the whole block."

"Wow."

"Of course, there's no way to know how recent this picture is. It could be from two days or two years ago."

I looked up at the wall and its crazy quilt of spray painted gang art. Grass sprouted between some of the cracks, and chunks of concrete were missing from a few spots along the top. "This wall wasn't built any time recently. Hopefully they haven't made any major renovations since the picture you're looking at."

"Let's hope not." I could hear the tension in her voice.

"What I need to know is, where are there openings in the walls?"

"On First Street," she answered. "The walls are thick around the back, like they're made of concrete blocks or something. But in the front, they're thin, like wooden fences, maybe, or chain link. And there are driveways to get the cars in and out, of course, although there must be gates across them."

"The police have First Street blocked off," I told her. "I don't want to go that way."

"You could pr—er, sweet-talk them to let you in," she said.

"Too many of them," I said. "And they'll be on radios, and someone would probably say something about a pedestrian, and—"

A volley of popping sounds interrupted me. Not too close, but within a couple of blocks.

"Was that gunfire?" asked Sukey, and I heard Hilda's voice in the background.

"Gunfire?" she shrieked. "Sukey, what the hell is going on? Give me the phone."

"Shush, Hilda, I can't hear Mercy. Go pick up on the

extension if you want to listen in, but for heaven's sake, don't interrupt us."

Despite the involuntary tightening of my bowels that the noise of gunshots had instantly elicited, I may have grinned. Sukey's tone had brooked no argument.

"Yeah, those were definitely gunshots," I told her. I knew the sound from my foster care years—some of the homes where I'd been placed hadn't been in the best of neighborhoods. "They came from farther down the block, I think."

"Mercy, you need to stay where you are. You can't stop stray bullets."

"I know," I told her. "But, like you saw, this is a pretty thick wall, and they weren't that close." I heard a click that must have been Hilda picking up an extension.

"What are you going to do?" Sukey asked.

I hesitated. I did *not* want to walk in the direction of the gunfire, but, if Tino and Gus were here, that was probably where I would find them.

I remembered Teresa's voice in my head. *If you have power, please, please, please, will you use it to help my sons?*

I sighed. "Aren't there any gaps in the back side of the wall?"

Sukey hesitated; then I heard her sigh, too. "Let me zoom in. There's a shadow here…can you see any trees over the top of the wall?"

"Let me look." I made sure no cars were coming, then crossed to the other side of the street, feeling naked as I stepped away from the thick wall. In Balboa, it was easy to forget that Southern California is a desert. No such problem here, far from the land of irrigation. I scanned the wall, looking for treetops. A wispy eucalyptus tree languished in a square gap of soil in the sidewalk, near the other end of the block. "No trees inside the wall that I can see," I told her. "There's a tree on this side of it, though."

"Okay. With the shadows in the picture, I couldn't tell which side of the wall it was on. It looks like… there's something behind it. I can't make it out."

"Let me look." Staying on the opposite side of the road, I moved cautiously down the sidewalk. The dusty lot behind me was mostly empty, with only a small building in the front. The *For Lease* sign inside the ubiquitous chain-link fence was faded, as if it had been there for a while.

As I drew even with the tree, it was easier to see what lay behind it. "There *is* a gap," I told her. "There's a wooden fence across it, or a gate or something. Just let me—" I was about to cross the street when a police cruiser pulled around the corner and up to the curb next to the tree. Two uniformed officers got out, and moved to the gate and pushed against it. It didn't open, and one of the officers, a woman, spoke into her radio. The other glanced across the street and seemed to notice me. I turned away, continuing toward the corner. From the corner of my eye, I saw him return his attention to the other officer.

"What are you doing now? Is it a gate or not?" Sukey's voice in my ear startled me.

"The police got to it first," I told her. "I need to find a place—I can't just stand here staring at them."

"Why not? The police always draw a crowd."

She had a point, but I still didn't feel comfortable. "Not in the middle of a block, in front of a vacant lot, with no cars parked nearby and no houses I could have come out of," I said, but I stopped and turned my head to see what they were doing anyway.

The cruiser's trunk was open, and the woman was removing something that looked like a short log with handles. I'd seen something similar on *Cops* and said to Sukey, "I think they're going to break the gate open."

Sure enough, the female cop handed the log to her partner, then slammed the trunk shut. The man held the mini battering ram—I couldn't remember what it was called—parallel to the ground. The woman put her back to the wall and drew her weapon, then nodded. He gave the log a hearty swing, and the gate popped open with a bang. He dropped the battering ram and drew his own gun, then followed the woman through the gap in the wall.

"They went in," I told Sukey. Trepidation had been replaced by frustration. "Are there any other openings in the wall?"

"Not on Second Street. But I think there's something around the next corner."

This is taking too long, I thought in frustration. I looked toward the end of the wall. "What corner? The block dead-ends at the railroad tracks." Which was one reason there was so little traffic here.

"Yes, I see that, and there's some kind of fence that runs along the tracks, right?"

"Yeah, chain link, with barbed wire on the top." The railroad fence looked newer and in considerably better repair than the others in the neighborhood, though a fair amount of litter had blown up against its base.

"I can't tell for sure, but I think there's a gap between where the junkyard wall ends—the second junkyard, not the one the police just went into—and the railroad fence. I don't know if it's big enough for you to walk through, though."

"I'm headed that way." I crossed the now-empty street and walked along the wall. "Are there any gates on that side? It doesn't seem likely, with the fence right there."

"The wall may have been built before the fence went up. It looks like there's at least one gate—maybe two. It's hard to tell—there are a lot of shadows in the picture."

I reached the corner of the wall. "Shit, it's blocked off. The gap's big enough to walk through—barely— but there's this little extension thing, running between the fence and the wall." I grabbed the chain link and rattled it in frustration.

Then I noticed something. "Wait—it has hinges. It's technically a gate, I guess, but it's bolted to the wall."

"Can you climb over it?" Sukey asked.

I looked up. The barbed wire that ran along the fence hadn't been extended to the narrow gate, but the way it was bent forward, there was still no way for me to get past it. "I don't think so." I examined the bolts. They looked too substantial for me to pull out of the wall, but they were rusty. Maybe… "What I need is one of those things like the cops used to knock the gate down."

"You mean a breaching tool?"

"I guess so. How did you know that's what they call it?"

"It's in my P.I. textbook."

"Oh, right. In any case, the only way to get past this gate is to knock it down or cut through it."

"And I don't suppose you have a pair of wire cutters in your back pocket."

"No, but—" I got an idea. "Sukey, I'm going to hang up. I'm going to try something, but I'll need both hands. I'll call you back if I need more information."

"Okay."

I switched the phone off and headed back toward the eucalyptus tree. At its base, I could just make out the item the policeman had dropped before heading though the gate. I sprinted, scanning the street, certain a second police cruiser would appear at any moment. None did and, with one final look around, I grabbed the breaching tool, spun and headed back the way I'd come.

It weighed a lot more than I'd expected, and there was no way to carry it casually. I held it in front of my body with both hands, moving as fast as I could with the added weight. I was panting by the time I got to the corner.

I tried to remember the policeman's stance and the way he'd held the tool before swinging it at the gate. I looked at it more carefully. It looked more like a pipe than a log and was close to three feet long. *Thunderbolt*, said a label on the side. One end was narrower than the other, with a hard plastic shell, probably to prevent sparks. That had to be the business end, which told me which way to hold it. I planted my feet, got a good grip on the two handles, took aim at one of the rusty bolts and swung.

A shock wave ran through my body and rattled my teeth. The breaching tool bounced back, and I staggered, almost landing on my ass, and dropped it.

The gate sat stubbornly in place, and, as I rubbed my shoulder, I looked at the bolt. It looked as if I'd made an impression on it. Surely one more swing…

Who was I kidding? There were probably a couple of days' worth of training on how to use this thing at the police academy.

Still, I'd done enough damage with my first attempt to warrant another. I looked around, but the street was still empty. I picked up the tool, which seemed to have increased in weight since I dropped it, planted my feet and swung a second time.

The bolt flew off and the top half of the gate was forced back, crashing against the fence with a noise loud enough to draw attention from the entire neighborhood. Luckily no one was around, at least on this side of the wall. If someone was anywhere near this corner on the other side, they would surely have heard it.

I'd managed not to drop the breaching tool this time, and as I turned my body sideways to ease into the narrow gap, it caught against the chain link of the railroad fence. It was longer than the space was wide, and way too heavy to carry comfortably with one hand.

I hated to put it down—I might need it for whatever gate I found—but it was impeding my progress. I rested it carefully against the concrete wall and moved toward First Street as quickly as I could, considering I had to turn both my shoulders and hips sideways.

There was a rumble, and the ground seemed to vibrate. Oh, crap, not an earthquake. Not now! I'd barely had time to form the thought when a thunderous noise overtook me, along with a rush of warm, dry wind that first pushed me toward the wall and then sucked me back against the chain-link fence.

Not an earthquake. A train. I'd been so focused on finding an opening in the concrete wall that I hadn't seen or heard it coming. It had passed within less than ten feet of me. The train—it couldn't have been more than four cars long—was gone in seconds, but the sound of blood rushing in my ears went on even after the deafening noise subsided. I slumped against the concrete and forced myself to take shallow breaths. I tasted grit from the trail of dust the train had left swirling in its wake.

Focus, Mercy, I told myself. You have to find the gap in the wall. I straightened and kept going.

The door Sukey had seen on the camera was about forty feet from the corner, and recessed. At least I assumed it was a door. It was wooden, but any hinges were invisible, and there was no handle. I pushed against it and thought I could feel some give, but it was pretty solid. I would need the tool, but even with the door being recessed, I wasn't sure there would be enough space to swing it. I kept going toward First Street. I came to a place where the concrete blocks were newer and less discolored—there had been another opening here in the past, but someone had bricked it up.

Resigned, I made my way back to where I'd left the battering tool. As I'd thought, it was a bitch getting it back to the doorway, and I alternately snagged the blazer I'd worn to the office that morning on the chain link to my left and scraped it on the concrete wall to my right. Oh, well, Sukey had been nagging me to get rid of the shapeless jacket for months. She'd given me crap about my shoes, too, but I was glad I had on sensible footwear instead of the heeled pumps she was always trying to get me to wear.

The recess did give me enough room to swing the breaching tool, but just barely. Also, I couldn't be sure whether the hinges were to the left or the right, and I assumed it would be more effective to aim the tool at the opposite side of the door.

What the fuck, I thought. I have a fifty-fifty chance of guessing right.

I aimed at the left side of the door and swung as hard as I could in the limited space. It didn't have much effect, other than making a few splinters, but the door made a reassuringly hollow sound, and the recoil from the wood was much less than it had been from the metal bolt.

My second swing had a better result, with more splintering wood and a gap about an inch wide appearing between the wall and the door. Apparently I'd guessed correctly about the position of the hinges. I set the battering tool down and leaned my face against the door, trying to peek through the gap. I could make out some kind of metal band, which was probably part of the latch, or maybe a dead bolt.

I picked up the tool again—I would have sworn it got heavier with every swing—and braced myself for a third try. Concentrating all my effort on a spot a few inches to the right of the gap, I swung as hard as I could.

Wood splintered, and there was the sound of metal rasping against metal. The door flew back, but something big kept it from swinging all the way open. The gap was substantially bigger, though, and when I again pressed my face against the door, I saw another wall, this one composed of twisted metal. It looked as if flattened cars, stacked one on top of the other, had been piled in front of the door.

There was just enough room for me to squeeze through, although I knew I'd have to write off my jacket as a total loss. I eased along parallel to the concrete wall, looking for a gap in the stacks of cars. I found one almost immediately and passed quickly through it, only to find myself looking down a long pathway flanked by walls composed of the remains of hundreds, if not thousands, of cars. The stacks were surprisingly symmetrical, the corridors they formed obviously meant to be wide enough to walk through.

My scalp prickled and my skin crawled. It was a maze. I was in a fucking maze.

15

I never cried much as a kid. My response to fear or anger had been, instead, to freeze and go silent, like a deer caught in the headlights of an oncoming car.

It was this very response that had led to one of my earliest memories, back from when Tom and Bobbie Hollings were still Mommy and Daddy, and our suburban life had been almost happy.

The fair was on—the state fair, big enough to be the primary topic of conversation at the elementary school for weeks prior to its opening—and the three of us joined the throngs of families walking along the midway and through exhibits. I remember being somewhere between dizzy and ecstatic, enthralled by the flashing lights, raucous music and too-pungent aromas of animals, fried food and, near some of the more adventurous rides, vomit.

Tom, bored with the kiddie rides and rubber duckie games, had quickly abandoned Bobbie and me in favor of the shooting range and stock exhibits, and as the evening wore on toward closing time, Bobbie, too, had tired of the merry-go-round, the pony ride and the other amusements considered suitable for a six-year-old.

I remember thinking the entrance to the fun house, in the shape of an openmouthed clown, looked more frightening than fun, but Bobbie had said, "You go ahead with the other kids. There's nothing scary in there. That's why they call it the fun house." She then sank gratefully onto a bench next to a couple of other tired-looking parents, and I followed the line of children through the garish red lips and around a turn into a revolving barrel.

A group of other kids were having a great time playing on the moving floor, falling theatrically and pretending to be unable to get up, or seeing how high they could cling to the moving walls before sliding back down toward the floor.

Though most children of six have not yet reached the stage where they worry about looking foolish, I realize now I was more self-aware than the other kids in my first-grade class. Afraid of embarrassing myself, I moved quickly through the tunnel, placing my feet carefully so I wouldn't fall and avoiding the sliding, shrieking children.

I found the strange, undulating mirrors mildly amusing, moving from one to another in order to see myself growing impossibly tall or improbably fat. I made faces, turning bared teeth into foot-long fangs, and turned sidewise and extended my arms in order to look like a leaping saber-toothed tiger.

When a group of children abandoned the barrel roll

to join me, I became self-conscious and moved to the entrance to the next room.

The *A-Maze*, the sign read. Another, which I had to sound out carefully, said, *Enter at Your Own Risk*. Another clown face, painted with a lurid wink, showed that the warning was a joke, but this subtlety was beyond my six-year-old understanding.

The room was composed of corridors made of panels, some with mirrors and some painted with bright geometric shapes and the ubiquitous clowns. A few of the panels pivoted, creating new gaps and routes through the labyrinth, and others were stationary. After I'd made a few turns, I realized I had no idea how to get back to the door.

I tried to retrace my steps, but some other kids had come through—I'd heard their voices but not seen them—and either they'd moved some of the pivoting panels and blocked my escape, or I'd made a wrong turn. I started out in a new direction, only to find a sea of panels that looked so similar to the last that I wasn't sure whether I was going in circles.

That was when I panicked.

Whereas another child might have screamed or sobbed, running randomly, I pushed myself into a nook made by three of the stationary panels and sat down facing a pivoting panel painted with clowns. I pulled up my knees and wrapped my arms around them, then laid my head against them.

I sat there until the cold from the concrete floor seeped into my bones and made me shiver, but I didn't move or cry out. Even when the voices of passing children had faded, to be replaced by those of adults, I stayed where I was, frozen and silent.

The first adult voice must have been an employee, making sure the room was empty before shutting it down for the evening. The second was Bobbie's. I wanted to cry out, but I just couldn't. It was as if the blood in my veins had thickened, then gradually turned to stone.

I don't know how long it was before the clown panel in front of me turned and a flashlight beam shone into my space. I looked up, squinting into the light. Blinded, I could make out two silhouettes, but not their features.

"For crying out loud, Mercy," said Bobbie. "We've been looking for you forever. Why in heaven's name didn't you answer me when I called?"

I tried to respond, but my voice wouldn't seem to work. When she grabbed my arms and hauled me to my feet, it took all my concentration to make my stiff limbs work well enough to stumble along behind her as she followed the attendant back through the maze, past the mirrors and through the now-still barrel.

I still hate clowns.

And I still hate mazes.

Now, as I stood between the walls of automobile corpses, I tasted the familiar tinge of nausea and the metallic flavor of panic. And I froze.

Come on, Mercy, I ordered myself. It's not a real maze. And there are definitely no clowns here.

Just then two shots thundered somewhere ahead of

me. There was a pinging sound, as if one of the shots had ricocheted off metal, and then a shout from somewhere to my right.

"Fucking bastard, I'll kill you!"

It was Tino's voice, and it galvanized me in a way Bobbie's had failed to do all those years ago. I ran in the direction of the voice, quickly reaching another wall of cars blocking my forward progress and forcing me to turn left or right.

Another shot, this time closer, and not from the same direction as the first. This sound was sharper than the first—a different shooter, a different gun.

"*Cuidado, hombre*," called a voice I didn't recognize. "You don't want to hit your brother."

"Fucking *cabrón*." Tino's voice was closer now, and I guessed that last gunshot had come from him.

"Tino!" I called. "Tino, where are you?"

"Mercy? What the fuck are you doing here?" It sounded as if he was on the other side of the row of cars. Or rows—I had no idea how many there were between us.

"Teresa sent me. Where are you? I can't figure out how to get through."

"Stay where you are!" he shouted back. "That motherfucker is shooting at me."

That sounded like a good idea. I should just head back the way I'd come and—

My escape was blocked by an image of Teresa's face as she pleaded with me to help her sons. *Please, if you have any kind of power...*

And I did. If I could just get to where Joaquin could see and hear me, I could make him stop shooting. And I could make Tino leave with me. And…

"Where's Gus? Is he okay?"

"I told you to get out of here. Go."

Sorry, Tino, I apologized silently. As afraid as I am of getting shot, I think I'd rather take a bullet than face your mother without either of her sons.

I headed down the row, back toward the wall, hoping to find an opening to wherever Tino was positioned. I found one at last, but it was too tight to wiggle through, so I headed back the other way. In the direction of the first set of shots.

"Let him go, Joaquin." Tino's voice was still in the same general area, and I moved past it as quickly as I could. He had to be talking about Gus, but why didn't Gus say something?

I found a hole that led to the right and darted through it. The path made an elbow turn to the left, which was away from Tino's voice and closer to Joaquin's, just the way I was looking to go.

"This is the police," said an amplified voice, ahead and to my left. "Put down your guns and come out."

"I have a hostage—*a kid!*" screamed Joaquin. "You cocksuckers better stay back or I'll kill him."

The corridor made another elbow turn, this time to the right, and I took it, then stopped when I saw sunlight glinting off metal just beyond the row of cars to my right. I'd found the exit from the maze.

"Let the kid go. We just want to talk to you. There

are only two exits, and we have them both blocked," said the voice from what had to be a bullhorn.

The police must not have known about the track-side exit, or else they'd assumed it was closed off. I inched forward, trying to peek out without being seen.

More derelict cars, uncrushed and arranged more or less by model, sat in rows, but they weren't jammed as closely together as the flattened ones, and I could see between some of them.

"Let him go, Joaquin. The police aren't going to let you out." Tino's voice was almost behind me now.

"Fuck you," Joaquin responded succinctly.

I tried to follow the sound of Joaquin's voice and caught a bit of movement through the window of a pickup truck, the rear of which had been twisted and crushed in what had clearly been a horrendous accident. Bending low, I moved across the narrow open space to the side of the truck, crouching to keep it between me and where I'd seen the motion.

I was afraid to rise high enough to see through the window—afraid that Joaquin would see me and shoot before I had time to press him. Instead, I crawled toward the front of the truck, which looked to be squeezed up against another, larger pickup. Maybe I could see between the two vehicles. I had to keep my head low—the tires had been removed from both trucks, considerably shortening the distance from the ground to the top of the door. I lay flat on my stomach—my trousers would probably be ruined, too—and eased forward until I could peek between the juxtaposed bumpers.

The shock of what I saw almost made me pull back. A man I didn't recognize lay on the oily dirt, face up, eyes staring, no more than twenty feet away from me. A sizeable piece of his skull was missing, and I could see the grayish cottage cheese of his brain. My stomach lurched, but I willed it back down, forcing my gaze away from the corpse and to the movement behind it. At the back of an unpainted concrete building, an Hispanic man stood, his back pressed into the recess behind a Dumpster. His arm was around the neck of a shorter figure facing the same way, the muzzle of an enormous pistol pressed against his head. Gus's head.

Gus's eyes were closed, and his face looked gray and chalky in the shadows. His leather jacket hung open, revealing a white T-shirt with a red stain seeping from shoulder to hemline.

Shit. Was he dead?

No, Gus's eyes flickered open, and his head moved slightly, as if he were trying to pull away from Joaquin's gun.

Alive. Good. I remembered the paramedics' truck I'd seen screaming this way and hoped that meant they could get to him in time.

But it meant I had no time to lose. I pulled myself into a kneeling position and put my mouth as close as I could to the opening between the trucks.

"Joaquin!" I shouted. "Let the boy go and drop your gun." I watched for a reaction, but there wasn't one.

Suddenly Joaquin pulled the gun away from Gus's head and fired at something off to my right. I spun around just in time to see Tino somersault like a cinematic action hero, then dive behind the row of trucks to end up ten feet away from me, a row of sandy explosions following at his heels as Joaquin took three more shots.

"Put the gun down," I screamed again, as Tino crawled closer to me.

"What the fuck do you think you're doing?" he said, panting.

"I'm trying to press him—I mean, hypnotize him," I said. "I don't know why it's not working."

"He probably can't hear you," said Tino. "Joaquin's got that big fucking cannon of a gun. He's gotta be deaf by now, all the shots he's fired."

"Put down your weapons and come out," repeated the amplified voice. "This is your last warning before we come in."

The voice through the bullhorn must have been loud enough to overcome his deafness, because Joaquin shouted back, "I said I got a *hostage*, you motherfuckers."

Tino shook with frustration. "I gotta get him to let Gus go. He's bleeding bad."

"There are paramedics right out front," I told him. "If I can just get Joaquin's attention, I can make him surrender, and then they'll be able to get Gus to the hospital, stop the bleeding."

"Try again," Tino urged, and I shouted loud enough to hurt my lungs.

"Put the gun down!" Again I peered at Joaquin,

whose head turned as if he could hear something, but his stance didn't change.

"Shit. He can't hear me, or at least not well enough to make out what I'm saying. How many bullets does he have left?"

"I don't know. Depends on what kind of clip he's using. He's had time to reload." Tino started to get to his feet. "This ain't working. I gotta go after him."

"No!" I grabbed him by the jacket and pulled him back down. "There's—there's something else I can try."

"What?" Tino tried to get up again. "The police come in, they could hit Gus easy as Joaquin, and—"

"Be quiet and sit still!"

I hadn't meant to press as hard as I did, and Tino's head snapped back as if I'd slapped him. But he shut up and slumped back into a sitting position, staring at me with huge, angry eyes.

Whatever. I didn't have time to worry about that now.

I positioned myself to stare straight through the gap, then closed my eyes and tried to concentrate. It was hard to do with my heart hammering in my ears and my nerves jumping like bacon sizzling on a griddle, but I tried. I held a mental picture of the man holding the gun and tried to…*aim* at the image.

Joaquin, put down the gun. Put. Down. The. Gun.

I opened my eyes, but Joaquin hadn't moved. Damn.

Forcing my breath to slow, I closed my eyes and tried again.

Joaquin, listen to me. Put down the gun. Just put it down.

I took another quick look. Nothing.

This wasn't working. When I'd made the nurse look for something he'd dropped the other day, it had only been a message, not a press. I wasn't sure I *could* press telepathically—the idea had been wild-ass conjecture on Sukey's part.

I saw Tino out of the corner of my eye, still staring at me furiously and silently. I tuned him out and took another look at Joaquin. One more try. This time I would keep my eyes open—it had worked with the nurse.

Just as I reached for the press, Gus moaned and stirred, and Joaquin pulled back the big gun and cuffed him with it. Gus went totally limp, but the bigger man easily caught his weight.

Rage surged through me like a tidal wave forced through a narrow opening.

Joaquin, you motherfucker. I wish you'd just put that cannon to your head and pull the trigger.

Instantly Joaquin turned the gun toward his own temple and fired. Half of his face disappeared in a spray of blood and brains, and Gus slid to the ground, followed immediately by Joaquin.

I stared, frozen. *No, I didn't mean it. I was just going to have you drop the gun. But I got mad, and—*

My shock was interrupted by a loud metallic crash ahead and to my left. I rose up higher on my knees and looked through the empty frame of the truck's back window. Police, in full riot gear, were streaming in past the crumpled remains of a roll-up door.

I looked at Tino. "Come on," I said, somehow remembering to press. "We have to get out of here."

I turned and sprinted across the open space and into the corridor between the cars. Tino followed silently, and I remembered I'd pressed him to be quiet.

"You can talk now," I called over my shoulder, navigating a turn.

"I gotta go back for Gus," he gasped.

"The paramedics will help him," I said. I could hear shouts from the policemen, but couldn't tell if they were getting closer. "You aren't going to be able to do anything. The cops will grab you as soon as they see you, if they don't shoot you first."

"They're gonna find us back here anyway," he said, right behind me.

"No, there's a way out. Just follow me." He gave me a wary look—there was no way he'd missed the press this time—but he followed.

This time I didn't panic—didn't forget any of the turns. In moments I was back at the ruined door, squeezing through with Tino on my heels. "This way." I shuffled toward Second Street.

I was relieved to see only the lone empty police car on the street. I'd been afraid other units would have joined it by now. Even so, I didn't think it was a good idea to head back down this side of the street, so I darted across, toward the vacant lot. I wondered if they would ever find their battering ram.

I made myself walk casually, in case more police cars pulled up, and Tino was soon panting next to me.

"They see me, they're gonna recognize me."

"As soon as we get past the next building, we should be able to get over to Third, or the alley, or whatever's there."

"They'll find my car," he said.

I winced. Mine, too, but they might not take notice, since it was a couple of blocks away and not as recognizable as Tino's. "Do you know the people at the stereo place? Will they cover for you?"

"Yeah, they put in my sound system. I can call them. Shit, my phone's in the trunk."

"As soon as we get out of sight, you can use mine."

We made it to the alley that snaked off toward Third without being spotted, and I breathed easier.

"Man, I hate leaving Gus back there with Joaquin," said Tino. "What if Joaquin gets into it with the police and Gus gets shot?"

"He won't," I said.

"How do you know?" His tone was truculent, and I slowed, blowing out a breath as we came around the corner onto Third. Not a cop in sight, although I heard a helicopter approaching. Tino moved under an awning, and I followed him.

I might as well tell him—it would be all over the news before long.

"Joaquin's dead."

"What? The police didn't fire any shots. I thought—"

"He shot himself." With a little help from yours truly.

"*What?* What the fuck are you talking about?"

"I saw him do it." I wanted to say more, to offer a possible explanation, but a sudden vivid picture of Joaquin's head exploding like a rotten, blood-filled pumpkin filled my head. I just made it to the curb before vomiting.

"Shit, Mercy, we gotta get you outta here. Where's your car?"

I stood with my hands on my knees, my head swimming. When I was sure I wasn't going to vomit again, I looked up. Curious faces peeked from a window in a building across the way, under a sign saying *Cafe Sonora*. When they saw me looking, they moved back.

"My car's back near yours. Too close to the action. We'll have to figure out another way to get out of here."

Tino looked across the street in the direction of the cafe. "Come on, these guys know me."

We waited to make sure the chopper had passed before crossing the street and ducking into the tiny working class restaurant. A man behind the counter looked up, apprehensive.

Tino had a brief conversation in Spanish—I was too shell-shocked to concentrate on the words—then turned to me.

"Come on. There's a room upstairs. We can stay there for a while, let the police stuff die down a little. We'll get Hilda or one of my uncles to come get us later."

I followed him up the stairs and sank onto a bench opposite a cluttered desk.

"Can I use your phone?" Tino asked.

I handed it to him, listening distractedly as he called the stereo store, where the guys agreed to say they were installing a new subwoofer. Then he called Hilda.

"You better let me talk to Mami," he said, after briefly reassuring her that he was okay. He walked around the desk and sat heavily in the chair. The set of his shoulders showed exhaustion, along with his apprehension at conveying bad news to Teresa.

"Mami? Yeah, I'm okay. Gus is alive, Mami, but— he's been shot."

I could hear her shrieks as Tino pulled the phone away from his ear. "Mami, listen to me. He's with the paramedics. They'll take him to San Gabriel's probably. No, you can't go down there—the police will want to know how you found out so quick, and you're supposed to be in bed." Again he winced and moved the phone away from his ear.

I listened for a while as he tried to calm Teresa, then tuned him out when he switched to Spanish.

I'd killed a man. Again. And this time it was so much worse.

When I'd compelled Dominic to drive his Jaguar into Newport Harbor, I'd been defending both myself and Sukey. I hadn't seen any way to let him live and still save her, and I'd made a measured decision. While I'd never truly felt good about it, I'd managed to reconcile my guilt enough to sleep at night. Most nights, anyway.

All I'd had to do was tell him to put down the gun.

Which had been my intention as I'd stared at Joaquin, gathering the press and pushing it forward with my mind. But, just like so many times before, my anger had taken control. When I saw Joaquin hit a vulnerable, injured kid—a kid I was just starting to like—my telepathy and my press had risen on the wave of anger like a boat caught in a storm and flowed out before I had a chance to stop them.

It might not have been premeditated, but it was still murder. And what scared me the most was that, just for a moment, it had felt *good*.

"Here."

I opened my eyes—I hadn't even been aware of closing them—to see Tino holding out my phone. I took it and put in back in my pocket.

"Sukey thinks she can figure out a way to find out how Gus is doing. And *Tío* Javier is coming to get us right now—they'll all give us an alibi, but we need to get back there before the police show up asking questions."

"Why would the cops show up at Hilda's?" I was having a hard time thinking, as if my brain was encased in gelatin.

"Because of her car. Gus stole it, remember? It's parked right in front of the fucking junkyard, on the street. I saw it before I parked at Manny's."

I tried to picture it. "How did you get into the back of the junkyard?"

"From the one next door. There's an old gate between the two yards. It's locked up, but the guys there let me through. They won't tell the cops I was there."

I changed the subject. "How's Sukey going to find out about Gus?"

"She calls her detective friend, tells him about the stolen car. Then she'll say she heard about a shooting on First Street on the police band radio, say Gus said something about heading over that way and ask him to check on it. He'll find out someone was shot and call Sukey back. Then Mami can call the hospital."

That would work. I had another thought. "Who was the dead guy?"

"Nestor."

Made sense.

"Will the police be looking for you?" I asked next. "I mean, are there fingerprints or something?"

He shook his head. "They ain't gonna print the whole junkyard, not for a couple of dead *Hombres*. And I know better than to touch the bullets with my bare fingers when I load them into the clip. There ain't gonna be no prints on the shell casings."

There are some prints on that battering ram, though, I thought. I ignored that little loose end and asked, "You still have the gun?"

He nodded, lifting his shirt to show where the gun was tucked into his belt. "I'll drop it into the bay or something, or have *Tío* Javier do it. The police ain't gonna be looking too hard, not when they got the shooter in custody."

I was confused. "Didn't you kill Nestor?"

Tino slumped into the chair, suddenly looking exhausted and about ten years older.

"No, man. Gus did."

16

"You've got no reason to go back, Tino. None whatsoever." Grant leaned back against the cushions of Hilda's sofa and took a sip of his scotch.

"You listen to him, *hijo*." Teresa, no longer confined to bed, sat opposite Grant in a high-backed armchair. She looked like a queen on her throne, despite the circles under her dark eyes. She'd stayed up most of the night, sitting next to Gus in the hospital. He had been moved out of intensive care and into a regular room. He'd almost died from blood loss, and the surgeons had removed part of one lung, but he would recover. Technically, he was under arrest, but it would be a while before he was in any condition to appear in court. Still, his room was guarded.

Tino was still arguing, although not as vehemently. "I never got to the part about the territory, or my cut."

"The territory is Gordo's problem now, not yours," Grant said. "And you don't need your cut. You're going to be making plenty of money as soon as we get your business plan rolling."

"I'll need it, if I'm gonna pay you and Hilda back for those lawyers."

When Gus was well enough to appear for his indictment, he would be standing next to one of the best criminal defense teams in the state of California. Grant, who sailed regularly with the head of a famous firm, had secured their services, and Hilda had insisted on paying the half of the retainer Grant wasn't covering, as well as any fees moving forward.

"*I'll* be paying them back," said Teresa. "As soon as I sell the house on St. Gertrude."

"Aw, Mami, I was gonna wait until my real estate license comes through to do that."

"There's absolutely no hurry, Teresa," Hilda insisted. "You just worry about getting yourself well, and taking care of Gus."

"And we're gonna need the money from the house to get you and Gus a new place, closer to here, maybe. Costa Mesa, or maybe Huntington Beach. There's some real nice condos just went up near Huntington Harbor," Tino said.

"Teresa doesn't need to worry about that right now, either," said Grant. "She's moving into my guest house. I never use it."

Grant has a guest house? Damn, if I'd known, I'd have asked him to rent it to me.

I glanced at Sukey, glad she hadn't spoken aloud.

Teresa needs it more right now, I replied silently. *Especially if the lawyer can get bail for Gus.*

"Excuse me. Dinner will be ready in ten minutes."

Estela stood in the doorway, drying her hands on a dishtowel. She looked pleased to have her kitchen back. Teresa's relatives had returned to their homes now that Joaquin was no longer a threat. Various aunts, uncles and cousins were doing round-the-clock shifts at Gus's bedside.

"I'll help you put everything on the table," said Sukey, getting up to follow Estela into the kitchen. I followed, too, even though Estela would probably refuse our help.

She did, so, instead of going back into the living room and listening to round thirty-seven of the argument about Tino leaving the gang, I settled into the breakfast nook. Sukey sat down opposite and spoke quietly, so as not to be overheard by Estela, who, in any case, was humming along with a *corrido* playing on the radio as she moved back and forth from the dining room, carrying laden platters and steaming bowls. The smell made my stomach grumble.

"Are you okay?" Sukey asked me.

"I'm getting there." I'd told her about what had happened with Joaquin. Even Tino didn't know that part of it. He'd only seen me close my eyes and open them a few times, and, if he'd guessed anything about what I was trying to do, he hadn't mentioned it. Teresa had asked a couple of shrewd questions but hadn't pressed too hard for answers.

"You know that guy deserved it," she said. Again.

"That doesn't mean I had the right to make it happen."

The death had been ruled a suicide. Joaquin's gun was the only one at the scene big enough to make such a wound, and his were the only prints on it. Gus had been unconscious by the time the police got to him, clearly having lost too much blood to have hefted a gun. His pistol—which, Teresa had confided to me, had been hidden under the floorboards in his closet—had been matched to the bullet that had killed Nestor. Gus had been initially charged as an adult, but the attorneys were confident the prosecutor would back down on that count. It wasn't, after all, an election year.

I was relieved when Sukey changed the subject. "There was something else I wanted to tell you," she said. "I've been going over your adoption papers, and I found something funny."

"Funny how?"

"Funny odd. It's your name. It's on the original papers."

"Of course it is. My parents—the Hollingses, I mean—would have given it to the clerk when they applied for the birth certificate."

"I don't mean the birth certificate, I mean the original ledger page, when the orphanage recorded receiving you from the church. It says, 'Mercy, last name unknown.'"

"That makes no sense. My legal name is Mercedes."

"That's another reason it's odd."

I thought about it. "I'll call Bobbie tomorrow and ask her. Maybe she can clear it up."

"And there's another thing. I got a call back from the

orphanage, and they were able to tell me the name of the church where you were found," Sukey said.

"They were? What is it?"

"It's a Romanian Orthodox church. In New York City, right near Central Park. It's been there forever. I found pictures on the Internet—it's incredibly beautiful."

Romanian Orthodox. Why does that feel...familiar?

"When did you do all this?" I asked her.

"Yesterday, after you went home. I didn't want to bother you—you looked like you really needed some sleep."

Not that I got much. Had Sukey heard me think that? It didn't appear so.

"Anyway, I called them, and spoke to a priest. He wasn't assigned there when it happened, but he said the old priest, who's retired now, is still alive in some retirement home for the clergy. He promised to see if he could get in touch with him and call me back."

"Thanks, Sukey." I wasn't sure if I could deal with this right now, but she was so obviously pleased at her own detective work that I forced a smile onto my face. "I appreciate you keeping after this."

"Hey, no problem. It's actually pretty interesting."

"Dinner is ready," said Estela, returning to the kitchen. "I already called everyone else in—you two need to go to the table."

We rose obediently and went into Hilda's airy dining room, taking the two empty seats. I'd secretly always considered the enormous table—ten more people could easily have been seated with us, and that was before she added leaves—under the ornate chandelier to be a bit pretentious, but it looked pretty tonight, with its bright candles and flower arrangements.

Estela came in carrying a tureen, and, as she set it down, Teresa touched her arm. "Estela, you were so good to my family these past few days. Won't you join us for dinner?"

"My husband is expecting me," Estela replied, flustered.

She looked at Hilda, who shrugged.

"Call him," she said. "He can do without you for one evening." Then, when Estela still looked hesitant, she said, "Seriously, Estela, it's okay. You did all the cooking—you should enjoy it."

"Okay, I'll stay," Estela said, turning toward the kitchen. "Just let me get another place setting and turn off the radio."

"Leave it on," said Teresa. "It's nice."

"You like *corridos?*" Estela sounded surprised.

"I'm from Sinaloa. Of course I like *corridos*. We always played them, especially for holidays and birthdays. You can't celebrate a birthday without dancing to some *corridos*."

"Mercy's birthday is tomorrow," Sukey said.

So it was. I'd forgotten.

"It is? Then we must celebrate!" Teresa unfolded her napkin. "Have you planned a party?"

"We tried to," Sukey replied. "Mercy made us cancel it."

Teresa gave me a stern look. "Why don't you want to celebrate your birthday? You should enjoy it—any birthday could be your last." Somehow, coming from Teresa's lips, this didn't sound like an omen of doom.

"I just didn't want a big party," I protested. "I'm not crazy about crowds."

"How about dinner at a nice restaurant?" asked Grant. "We could go to the Villa Nova. No—what do you call them? *Corridos?* But we could sing along at the piano bar."

"Oh, I *love* the piano bar at the Villa Nova," said Hilda. "Richie knows all my favorite songs."

"And you have a nice voice, Señora Hilda," said Estela, returning with her plates. "You should sing there, at this piano bar."

Tino laughed. "Yeah, I'd like to hear that. I'll bet you're a real superstar. Why don't you ever sing for me?"

"So, then," Teresa said, nodding at me, "is this settled? Will you let us celebrate with you?"

"Well, if you're all going to gang up on me, I guess I'll have to."

"Excellent," said Grant, and Sukey clapped her hands like a child. "I'll call as soon as we finish dinner and reserve a table in the bar, near the piano."

"And you should call Sam," said Tino.

"But—" I stopped. Sam and I were supposed to be friends now, after all. What harm would it do, inviting him to join us? I realized everyone was still looking at me, waiting for me to finish the sentence. "But be sure to ask if his father is feeling well enough to come, too," I said, a bit lamely.

Maybe you should be the one to make the call. I looked at Sukey, who raised her eyebrows before reaching for a basket of bread and selecting a roll.

Maybe I should.

"They told me the name was stitched into your clothes when they found you. I wanted to name you Margaret, after my grandmother. She was always called 'Peggy.'" Bobbie Hollings paused, far away in Tucson, and I heard the soft sound as she inhaled on her cigarette.

"But it just didn't fit," she went on. "Once I'd gotten the name 'Mercy' in my head, it sort of stuck. I'd always liked that actress, Mercedes what's-her-name."

"McCambridge," I supplied. "Mercedes McCambridge."

"Yeah, her. And Tom didn't care what we called you, so when I filled out the paperwork, I just wrote in 'Mercedes,' and that was that."

"Stitched into my clothing? That has to mean…" I trailed off.

"It means that either your birth mother named you 'Mercy,' or else it was some kind of prayer. Like 'God have mercy on my baby.' I thought about it some, at the time, but I guess I forgot about it by the time you were old enough to ask."

My birth mother…

"Anyway, I'm sorry I acted so weird when I first

answered the phone, but I'd just been thinking about you, and then the phone rang."

"Thinking about me?" Why had Bobbie been thinking about me?

"Is that really so strange? I mean, after all, it *is* your birthday. I still think about it every year, you know, whenever it starts getting close."

"My real one? I mean, if I was abandoned, how do you know?"

"I don't, not for sure. But the doctor who examined you at the orphanage said you seemed to be about forty-eight hours old—I guess they can tell by the umbilical cord—so we just used the date two days before you were found. It's got to be within a day, one way or the other."

I guess they can tell by the umbilical cord. I reached under my untucked blouse and touched my navel. Where I'd been attached to my birth mother.

"Well, um, anyway, thank you for answering my question. I appreciate it."

"No problem. And, Mercy?"

"Yes?"

"Happy thirtieth birthday."

"Thanks," I whispered, just as a click on the line told me she'd hung up the phone.

"Hey, Mercy," called Sukey through the open door to the reception room. "Are you off the phone?"

"Yes," I replied. "Why?"

"I've got that priest on the line. The one who was at the church when they found you. Do you want to talk to him?"

Sure, why not? Why settle for one emotionally traumatic conversation in five minutes when you can have two? Actually, make that three, although the first call had been several hours earlier, when I'd called Sam and invited him and his father to the Villa Nova.

I closed my cell phone and put in back in my pocket.

"Sure, Sukey, I'll talk to him."

She stuck her head in the doorway. "He's on hold. Just pick up the phone and push the button."

Sukey labored under the impression that I was incapable of operating any of the office equipment. She was wrong—I felt I had completely mastered the coffee machine and the fax/printer. Well, the coffee machine, anyway.

"Hello, this is Mercedes Hollings. To whom am I speaking?" I sounded formal, stilted. Oh well, probably not inappropriate for speaking with an elderly priest. Still, I wasn't sure why I'd used my full name.

"This is Father Constantyn." The accent was Eastern European, the voice deep and resonant. "Your charming assistant told me you wanted to talk about the baby that was found in the church all those years ago. Is this correct?"

"Yes," I said, uncertain how to begin. "The other priest said that you were there at that time."

"Yes, it was Father Michael who gave me your number." I expected him to go on, but he remained silent.

"Do you remember the, er, incident?"

"Of course." He chuckled, the rumbling of bass notes

on a church organ. "Despite what you see in movies or read in novels, it is actually a rare occurrence to find a baby in a basket on the church steps."

"A baby in a basket?"

"A metaphor. The truth is much less dramatic. The baby was strapped into a plastic carrier and left in a pew. But it was exciting, nevertheless. She created quite a stir at the time."

I could imagine.

"It is curious that I received your message today," he went on. "I was thinking about it only recently. The anniversary is very close. Just a few days, in fact."

"I was wondering if you remember anything that might be some kind of clue about who left the baby there. Did anyone see someone, anything like that?"

"We considered the matter with great care at the time. It is a very serious thing to abandon a child, even in a place where it is sure to be found and cared for." He paused, and I thought I heard ice clinking in a glass. "Several people thought they had seen someone sitting in that pew shortly before the baby was found, but the descriptions did not match one another. Although more than one person said it was a woman, and she was too old to be the child's mother. There was a police report, of course, but nothing ever came of it."

Just the same, I was going to ask Sukey to see if she could get a copy.

"What about the baby carrier, or the clothing? Was there anything special about them?"

He paused for a long time, and I thought the connection might have been lost. Then he said, "When you answered the call, you said your name was Mercedes. An unusual name."

My throat was suddenly dry, but I resisted the urge to clear it. "My mother liked it."

"Your mother?"

Now it was my turn to pause. "My adoptive mother."

"Ah." Another of those resonant chuckles. "Tell me, Mercedes, would today happen to be your birthday?"

The telephone receiver felt heavy in my hand, as if it would slip from my grip. I managed to answer, "Yes, today's my birthday. At least that's what it says on my birth certificate."

"The same birth certificate on which your…mother put the name 'Mercedes'?"

"That's right."

"In that case, Mercedes, I will tell you what was unusual about the clothing. It had a word stitched into the collar. The name was 'Mercy.' But I think you already know this, perhaps."

"Yes," I breathed. "My adoptive mother told me. Today."

"Quite a day you're having."

You could say that.

"So," he said. "You are—you were—the baby. I cannot tell you what pleasure it gives me to speak to you. I've often wondered what became of you."

"You could have found out through the adoption agency."

"Oh, I did, back at the time. I found that you'd been

adopted by a couple in New Jersey. I must admit, I did not give the matter much thought after that. Until five years ago."

What?

"What happened five years ago?"

Again I heard the tinkle of ice cubes against the side of a glass. "A young woman came to see me at the church. It was just a few days before my retirement, you see. She claimed that *she* was the baby found in the church."

"She—*what?*"

"She was quite convincing—she knew the dates and had copies of the newspaper story, printed out from one of those machines at the library."

"A microfiche machine?" I asked.

"Yes, I think that is what they are called. We spoke for a long time, and she asked questions."

"The same questions I've asked?"

"Those and many more."

"And did you answer them? I mean, did you tell her about the name stitched into the clothes."

He sighed. "No. No, I did not."

"Why not?" My voice sounded foreign in my ears, as if someone else was speaking. What was this all about?

"Because I did not believe her. First, she seemed to be a little too young, although she had tried to make herself look older. Also, in fifty years as a priest, a person develops a pretty good sense of when he is being told a falsehood."

"And I don't give you that sense."

"No. And then there is your name. 'Mercedes.'"

"I'm actually called 'Mercy.'"

"I suspected as much."

We were both silent for a moment; then I asked, "The woman who came to see you—do you know who she is?"

"Yes," he said, to my great surprise. "I mean, I have the name she gave me. And a telephone number. She wanted me to call her back if I remembered anything else. Although I never intended to honor her wishes, for some reason I cannot explain, I have kept that information. Would you like to have it?"

"Yes," I said, scrambling for something to write on. My notepad was on top of my desk, but I grabbed it so quickly that the pen rolled off and landed on the floor. "Just let me get—" I groped under the desk, and finally the pen was in my hand. "Go ahead."

"The name is 'Charity.' No last name, I'm afraid. And the phone number is—" He read out a number with an unfamiliar area code.

"Thank you," I told him. "Thank you so much for calling me back."

"There is one other thing," he said, surprising me again. "Something else I did not mention to Charity."

"What?" The room seemed off-kilter, as if I'd had too much to drink.

"When the sisters from the orphanage came to take the baby, they brought a carrier with them. They didn't need the one the child had been found in, so I said I would have it cleaned up and given to the church's thrift store. It was late in the day, so I took it to my office. And later, when I moved it aside, something fell out of it."

"What was it? A note?" I could hear the rush of my pulse. Or was that static on the line?

"Nothing so revealing. It was a piece of jewelry. A necklace with a pendant or…I suppose you might call it an amulet."

An amulet?

"I intended to pass it along to the orphanage or give it to the thrift store, but I was curious about the inscription. I did not recognize the language, you see. So I put it in my desk drawer. But, I'm sad to say, I forgot about it. By the time I found it, weeks later, I knew you had already been adopted. It did not seem valuable—made of brass rather than gold or silver—and I still hadn't found out about the inscription. So I put it back in the drawer, where it became, I'm afraid, one of those things you get so used to seeing that you never think about it anymore."

"Do you still have it?" It seemed too unlikely to be possible.

"Yes, I do. After Charity's visit, I remembered it. I found it in a box of things I had already packed in preparation for my retirement. And I finally figured out the inscription." There was a note of triumph in his voice.

"How did you do that?"

"The Internet! My assistant had been trying to get me to learn to use the computer for years, but, I must admit, I resisted. Until I found out how easy it was to research things. Biblical things, for example. I fear I became quite 'hooked,' as they say."

"What did you find out about the inscription?"

"It was a single word. *Thagár.*"

"Thagár?" I repeated. My scalp tingled.

"Yes. It means 'king.'"

King? The tingling spread to my chest. "In what language?"

"Romanes. The language of the Gypsies."

17

Although it has occupied its prime Newport Harbor spot for forty years, the Villa Nova was originally located on the Sunset Strip in Hollywood. Opened in 1933, the place was a hangout for such celebrities as Charlie Chaplain, Bing Crosby and even Marilyn Monroe. In 1969, after the Strip had descended into seediness, the restaurant moved to the Pacific Coast Highway, just off the base of the Balboa Peninsula. With its *trompe-l'oeil* exterior depicting an Italian fishing village, the Villa Nova was famous for its authentic cuisine, extensive wine list and old-world service.

Hilda, who'd been a regular there for years, often spoke about the original building, with its rabbit-warren floor plan—a series of narrow, crowded rooms leading through to a spectacular bay view. In 1995 the place burned, and she'd been afraid that yet another Southern California landmark had been lost. Happily, it had been rebuilt and the splendor of its *trompe-l'oeil* murals restored. Although she claimed to miss the cramped, dark rooms of the original, even she had to admit that the spacious floor plan of the new building was more comfortable and quite beautiful.

Certainly there was plenty of room in the piano bar, where we sat at a long table. I sat at one end, with a view of both the bay and Lido Island, and the piano. Richie was massaging the ivories while a white-haired gentleman gave a surprisingly good rendition of an Italian aria. Richie was a Villa Nova fixture and had been playing everything from old show tunes to contemporary rock for more than twenty-five years.

"I see we have a guest singer in the audience," he said into his microphone, over enthusiastic applause. "Hilda, won't you come up here and do a song with me?"

"Oh, really, I couldn't," said Hilda with transparent insincerity. Sukey rolled her eyes, and I ducked my head.

"Get up there, baby," said Tino. "You promised Mami."

"And me," I surprised myself by saying. "It's my birthday, and I command you to sing." I was definitely feeling that second martini. And the champagne Sam had bought.

"Oh, well, if you all *insist*."

"We do," said Roger Falls. He was back on cranberry juice, I noticed—no beer after the incident at the pier— but he was enjoying himself, flirting equally with Hilda and Teresa, and ignoring Tino's occasional glares.

"I'm glad you liked your presents," said Sukey, as Hilda began the opening strains of "Someone to Watch Over Me." Her voice was lovely—deep and theatrical.

"I'm overwhelmed." The bounty was spread on the table in front of me. There was a lush red sweater from Hilda, who was in league with Sukey to get more color into my wardrobe, a pair of deck shoes from Grant, and a photo album from Teresa, with the inevitable sunflower on the hand-crafted cover. I'd been shocked when Sam handed me a box, which turned out to contain an elaborately carved figure of a man in old-fashioned sailor's garb, about four inches tall.

"Dad carved it," he said. "When I told him we were going to your birthday party, he insisted that I wrap it up for you."

"Do you think he knew—"

"Who you are?" he finished for me. "I'd like to think so."

I looked at his wistful expression and wondered what it would be like to have a father you loved and respected, and then see him slowly lose himself.

Sukey's gift had been surprising, too. The gilt gift bag had contained a box of cards and a corresponding book. *The Orthodox Tarot.* The cellophane-wrapped box lay unopened in front of me, and Sukey reached out and picked it up.

"I'd open them for you," she said, "but I read online that you shouldn't let other people handle them too much. You need to, like, *bond* with your cards."

"What made you think of Tarot cards?" Sukey always bought birthday and holiday gifts for me, usually articles of clothing outside my comfort zone.

"Well, remember when Madame Minéshti did that

Tarot reading for you? When you told me about it, it sounded like you were really intrigued."

"I was," I admitted. "But I didn't think about taking it up myself. I'm just not very metaphysical."

"That's rich, considering—" She stopped at a sharp glance from me.

"Actually, what I meant was, what made you choose this particular Tarot deck?"

"Well, after I saw the pictures of the Romanian church on the Internet, I kept thinking about all that gorgeous art. I read about it a little bit. Those paintings, of the saints and stuff, are called icons, and they're a really big deal." She took a sip of her champagne. "I knew I wanted to get you Tarot cards, so I went to that store that sells the crystals and stuff, and they had about a zillion decks to choose from. I had no idea which one to pick. Then I saw the picture on the box."

She turned the box over, revealing a picture of a beautiful robed woman with a golden halo, a cross emblazoned on her chest. The caption read 2—The High Priestess.

"It looked just like those icons. So I read the description on the back of the book. See? The cards are all based on religious images from the Orthodox Church. During the Dark Ages, Tarot readers changed the pictures on their cards to correspond with saints and things, so that Christian people wouldn't think they were practicing witchcraft. Some stories say the priests even used them." She shrugged. "They just felt right. Aren't you going to open them?"

"Tomorrow," I said. "When there isn't so much distraction." And I was one hundred percent sober. I was probably imagining the thrumming vibration whenever I handled the box, but I still wasn't comfortable opening them here.

Hilda finished her song to enthusiastic applause, and I looked up just in time to see Teresa start, as if coming out of a trance. She hadn't been paying attention to the song, I realized, and only Tino's loud applause had brought her back to the present.

"Do you think Teresa is getting too tired to be here?" I asked Sukey. "She's only been out of bed a few days."

"I think she's just worried about Gus. I'll go sit next to her."

"No, let me," I said. "I want to thank her again for the album. With everything that's been going on in her life lately, it's amazing she took the time to make something by hand." I got up and walked to the seat vacated by Hilda, who was starting a second song.

"Teresa, the album is beautiful. I wanted to thank you again."

"I'm glad you like it. I enjoy making them—it's important to have someplace special for pictures of your family."

I didn't stop my grimace in time—too much vodka—and she looked puzzled.

"Did I say something wrong?"

"Oh, no. It's just that—" No. Even after too much to drink, I wasn't going to indulge in self-pity. Not tonight.

"You were about to say that you don't really have a family," said Teresa.

"Yeah."

She shook her head, then made a sweeping gesture that encompassed all the people at the table. "What do you call this?"

"They're my friends," I said. She had no way of knowing how new that concept still felt for me.

"They're more than that. They're your family of choice."

"My what?"

"I saw this on television. They were talking to people who, for whatever reason, were not able to be with their natural families. Everyone from gay people whose parents had disowned them to holocaust survivors whose entire families had been killed in concentration camps."

Or, I thought, little girls growing up in group houses and foster homes, because they destroyed their own chances for a real family.

"Anyway, the people they interviewed had all built new families, with members of their own choosing. In the story, they concluded that the bonds in these 'families of choice' were every bit as strong as those in biological families. Stronger, sometimes."

Something was stinging my eyes, and I reached up to rub them, surprised when my fingers came away wet.

Teresa's hand was on my arm. "Mercy, are you all right? I didn't mean to make you feel bad."

I put my hand over hers and squeezed.

"You didn't. It's just—thank you, Teresa."

Another round of applause signaled the end of Hilda's song, and I joined in.

"Everybody, we have a birthday in the house," Richie said into the microphone. I felt my face redden and looked toward Sukey, who shrugged and grinned. A blaze of light appeared over her shoulder, and I focused on a waitress carrying a cake through the doorway that led from the main dining room into the piano bar. As Richie started to pound out the notes to "Happy Birthday," everyone at my table and, it seemed, in the entire restaurant, began to sing.

I'm going to punish you for this, I said silently to Sukey.

No you're not. You love me too much.

As the blazing cake was placed in front of me, the song ended. Everyone yelled, "Make a wish!"

I thought about what Teresa had said.

A family of choice, huh?

I'd made some bad choices in my life. Making myself an orphan, ditching school, killing— No, I wouldn't go there right now.

I looked at the faces surrounding me. It was good to know that, in one area of my life at least, my choices had been just fine.

nocturne™

New York Times **Bestselling Author**

REBECCA BRANDEWYNE

FROM THE MISTS OF WOLF CREEK

Hallie Muldoon suspects that her grandmother
has special abilities, but her sudden death
forces Hallie to return to Wolf Creek, where
details emerge of a spell cast. Local farmer
Trace Coltrane and the wolf that prowls around
the farmhouse both appear out of nowhere, and
a killer has Hallie in his sights. With no other
choice, Hallie relies on Trace for help,
not knowing if the mysterious Trace is a
mesmerizing friend or a deadly foe....

Available June wherever books are sold.

REQUEST YOUR FREE BOOKS!

2 FREE NOVELS
FROM THE ROMANCE/SUSPENSE
COLLECTION PLUS 2 FREE GIFTS!

YES! Please send me 2 FREE novels from the Romance/Suspense Collection and my 2 FREE gifts (gifts are worth about $10). After receiving them, if I don't wish to receive any more books, I can return the shipping statement marked "cancel." If I don't cancel, I will receive 4 brand-new novels every month and be billed just $5.74 per book in the U.S. or $6.24 per book in Canada. That's a savings of at least 28% off the cover price. It's quite a bargain! Shipping and handling is just 50¢ per book.* I understand that accepting the 2 free books and gifts places me under no obligation to buy anything. I can always return a shipment and cancel at any time. Even if I never buy another book from the Reader Service, the two free books and gifts are mine to keep forever.

185 MDN EYNQ   385 MDN EYN2

Name	(PLEASE PRINT)	
Address		Apt. #
City	State/Prov.	Zip/Postal Code

Signature (if under 18, a parent or guardian must sign)

Mail to **The Reader Service:**
IN U.S.A.: P.O. Box 1867, Buffalo, NY 14240-1867
IN CANADA: P.O. Box 609, Fort Erie, Ontario L2A 5X3

Not valid to current subscribers of the Romance Collection,
the Suspense Collection or the Romance/Suspense Collection.

Want to try two free books from another line?
Call 1-800-873-8635 or visit www.morefreebooks.com.

* Terms and prices subject to change without notice. Prices do not include applicable taxes. Sales tax applicable in N.Y. Canadian residents will be charged applicable provincial taxes and GST. Offer not valid in Quebec. This offer is limited to one order per household. All orders subject to approval. Credit or debit balances in a customer's account(s) may be offset by any other outstanding balance owed by or to the customer. Please allow 4 to 6 weeks for delivery. Offer available while quantities last.

Your Privacy: Harlequin is committed to protecting your privacy. Our Privacy Policy is available onlirie at www.eHarlequin.com or upon request from the Reader Service. From time to time we make our lists of customers available to reputable third parties who may have a product or service of interest to you. If you would prefer we not share your name and address, please check here.

BOB09